ALSO BY DEON ASHLEIGH

Collection

Well Wishes from a Prompt

Anthology

When All That's Left Are Stories

THE PRICE

OF A

BEATING

HEART

Book One of The Price of a Heart Series

DEON ASHLEIGH

Paperback ISBN: 9798324371425
Hardcover ISBN: 9798324378219
Large Print ISBN: 9798344543291

Imprint: Independently published

First Edition

Dev edited by Ellie Nalle | Book cover by Keylin Rivers

—+—

Errors. Most likely, they've stowed away in these pages.

If you spot any of those sneaky rascals, send them to
deonashleigh.com/feedback

THE PRICE OF A

BEATING HEART

BOOK ONE OF THE PRICE OF A HEART SERIES

DEON ASHLEIGH

To the empty futures
we must create

ONE

THE BELL DINGS, and I become a murderer.

I hold the knife with my thumb and middle finger and cut the wight into small cubes. Place each piece— marinated in thrice-boiled synthHoney and pureed tomatoes—gently in my mouth and chew silently. Slowly. Counting each movement of my jaw.

Twenty-five—that is the correct number of chews for each piece.

The magnificent blend of sweet and sour massages my senses. This is the best wight I have ever tasted. The best place I have ever been. I always want to dine in such comfort. Sit across from my husband, James of the Pillars. Be embraced by a floor-length dress with many shades of blue, a short train, and glittering gold words. Enjoy the light blue cuffs with black dots at my wrists, matte white pearls around my neck, V3454 Scarlet on my lips. And on my feet, glossy, black, one-inch heels.

My seat is luxurious. High-backed and made of real oak and leather. The air smells of fresh, spicy lavender and sweet cream.

After five years of planning, we are here: Ancient Dreams.

The finest restaurant in Urban. I cannot believe it. Oh, I cannot believe I am actually here, in all this beauty.

I match myself to the quiet energy of them. To the red glow all around me. To the Anomalies. They are everywhere, sat at circular tables, and it is grander than I could have ever hoped for.

A spherical chandelier made of twigs hovers over each table; tiny crystals create a soft glow from their branches' centers. Each sphere rotates above us, its lights bouncing off the cream-colored walls and gold trim.

Red slats cross the towering ceilings and are matched by lattices that follow the curve of the arched doorways. They are stunning. Thick tufts of dyed-black shrubs peppered with slender gold-painted leopard orchids grow along their openings.

It is a near-perfect replica of our world 470 years ago. Different only because there is no green anywhere.

"Delicious." I massage my fork's smooth metal once more and set it on my left.

James of the Pillars glances around. Four black dots trail down each of his temples. He is thin and wearing a matching blue suit with a train that grazes the ground. Unlike my dress, it glows a faint red.

He eats little and drinks much. Tiny waves of his nerves ripple in my cup as his leg bounces under the table. Rustles the gold stripe on our black tablecloth.

I reach for his hand. Slowly slide my thumb between his index and ring fingers. The healed-over skin of his missing middle finger is soft and smooth.

"Relax, my husband." He sighs and smiles at me.

Here, our life is perfect. Here.

Three hundred eighty years ago, The Dome was built. But one headquarters was not enough to govern our Earth and keep you wild humans in line, so we erected another. Virtual visits available daily. Your favored show, Today in the Past!

Much of the other patrons' talk is of James of the Pillars. Some loathe him, but most are excited to see him after these eight years. Next to a few is a black tray holding red bottles painted with drizzling gold accents—symbols of their immense status.

They glance at him, but none will be so impolite to approach him while dining.

A soft blue light comes from the floor-to-ceiling windows to my right. The clouds drift sleepily as the sky fades under the setting sun, still touching the Grand Anomalies' glowing statues. Magnificent. They are made from red marble and positioned next to each other over softly lapping water.

Each statue's arm reaches to the next. They touch their fingertips together, holding a tiny piece of our world between their palms.

One day, after he has been old and gray, a statue will be erected for my husband. In his likeness. It will be beautiful like him, but I hope to never see it.

"More Manoir de Sang?" He drinks the last drop of the blood wine before raising my hand to his lips and kissing the tips of my fingers. A spot of red remains on the middle one.

"Of course, but I'll pay. Husband, I urge ya tuh not drink this bottle as if you've been choking and it's air." Three empty bottles, different shapes decorated with ornate windows, sit on a black tray next to us. "Hoarding. It's a word." I suck the sweet red from my finger loudly.

He laughs. "Hoarding? Me? My love, you have withheld your units all night. My ledger is near negative, yet you scold me when you *finally* decide to pay."

"Don't tell me 'finally.' I've tolerated ya excessive thirst our entire dinner."

"True. I love this wine more than you."

I laugh and motion to the bottles. "Clearly."

He snaps his fingers and signals a happy-maker, who pours other patrons' beverages even quicker and rushes to our table.

To wait.

Ding. 60,000 units.

Like the others darting to and fro, the man wears a tailored gold suit jacket and cream-colored pants and shoes. Thick makeup covers his face, and red permapaint coats his fingertips. He does not write anything down; a happy-maker's memory is their greatest pride.

The man stands still. His eyes never leave James of the Pillars's back as he searches for something he dropped. I tap my foot. Rub small circles in our tablecloth's fabric. Soft like infant skin.

Tap, tap, tap…

Tap, tap, tap…

The wall moves. My tapping stops.

A woman, draped in cream-colored clothing and gold shoes, steps forward. Her smile widens as she walks to one of the tables and blows out seventeen candles on a boy's birth day cake.

The woman is not looking at the cake. She is staring at the glass next to it, her eyes glued to the water's condensation sliding down it.

"My candles're out, Keeper. Get away from me."

She blinks and nods. Goes back to the wall. The room is painted in those like her. They stand next to one another. Arms at their sides, palms out.

Silent. Attentive. Smiling. Waiting.

Ding. 90,000 units. All like her are near the same worth.

Tap, tap, tap…

A minute later, my husband pops up from under the table, holding a small gold doorknob. It is a key part of the beautiful mansion the four wine bottles will become after he assembles them.

He pockets the tiny ball and looks from me to the waiting man, who is grinning harder than I thought possible.

"Take her order."

The happy-maker turns to me.

"I'd like the final bottle of Manoir de Sang. Non-alcoholic." I slur the words together and smile because of it.

Arch an eyebrow at James of the Pillars. He said the final bottle is the best flavor. I do not know how the other three can be improved upon, but I will be the judge of that.

"That'll be five thousand units, marm." I put my left arm out, palm up, and the man places The Charge to my elbow.

The vial-like device beeps. A beam of green light shoots from it and makes a small green dot on the ceiling. Twelve feet high, it does not feel like a gentle grin doting on me anymore but a hard, judgmental sneer stabbing into me. Tiny compared to it.

Worthless.

Some of the patrons giggle. There should be no light. No beep. No green. The happy-maker's smile falls.

So does mine.

He assumed I would not have enough for the wine before reading my ledger. Programmed The Charge to react too quickly. I thought this practice had gone out of favor long ago.

I hold my arm straighter, my chin tighter. No one will see it tremble. I stare into his eyes.

You are Common like me. How could you do this?

He drops his gaze to the small machine and presses the button. The Charge reads my barcode, branded into my skin, and a small pinch tells me when the large needle pierces through. Six seconds later, my blood fills the container to the fifth line, and The Charge squirts a clear liquid on my skin.

Lights red to indicate success. He pulls it away. The invisiband's wetness dries quickly and stops my blood from running.

The man hurries to get our final bottle.

"My love—" James of the Pillars reaches out to me, but I pull my hand away to stop what he will say next.

His words will not bring the wight's sweetness or the eve's lightness back. It is sour now. Heavy. It was supposed to be *perfect*.

Stupid man.

I wait. Again. Irritated. Both by the growing pain under my belly and the spreading sickness bubbling within it. I know it well. A suffocating wave overtaking my thoughts.

I stare at the soft inner skin of my elbow.

I am as valuable as any other person. I am worthy.

I am worthy?

I study my clothing. The Anomalies'. I matched myself to them perfectly. Spent hours checking, adjusting, twisting, checking again. I made sure none of me was left.

How did the happy-maker know I did not belong? What did I do wrong to make him use The Green Charge? I peek at James of the Pillars. His face is scrunched up. Sour. Angry. Sad.

We are thinking the same thought, he and I: Will anyone else be suspected of inferiority? Illegality. Inability to pay.

Our moods worsen as we scan the room, watching other patrons.

*Ding*s. Many billions of units. The zeroes clog in my mind. How are these numbers truly possible?

A woman a few tables over purchases imported First Africa Northlake wight—and is not subjected to The Green Charge. Neither is the couple behind James of the Pillars, who purchase real, organic lettuce for their salad. And the man to my right with a large slab of uncontaminated cow? Nothing. It is only we who are forced into humiliation.

James of the Pillars huffs. "I will get a refund."

"It's not allowed." I only want to go home.

"Well, I will force it. This is a most heinous discrimination."

He marches to The Charge counter a few feet from us. The attendant mumbles "manager, manager" in a device. Glances around the room. Steels himself for the onslaught.

Ding. 520,000 units.

Every happy-maker adds The Charge counter to their circuit. They bow deeply, ask if they can do anything, get him anything. My husband declines each one, and they apologize before rushing to their next table.

When his grievances rise far above the restaurant's din—only a few whispers now—I grab our jackets, the bottles, my purse, and walk as fast as I can to him. Heavy with pregnancy, my belly is five times its original size, and the band under it rubs against my skin.

I lean close to his ear. "It is not worth it. You waste our savings." I revert to my birth accent, enunciating my words as the low-class must.

James of the Pillars's mid-brown neck has gone bright red. At my words, he quiets and looks around, close to tears. All stare. Politely, if that were possible. He looks away from me, whispers, "You deserve more, my love."

A woman smooths her hair as she strides toward us. Her multicolored suit is as bright as her smile. Neither hide the slight sheen on her face or that more sweat is gathering on the lone dot at each of her temples.

Ding. Oh my. 3,400,000,000 units.

The happy-maker trails behind her, bent low. A perfect position for the miserable weeping willow he is. When she reaches us, he drops to his knees, forehead touching the floor, palms up.

She does not look at me, only shoves the final bottle into my hands a moment before I bow to her. I strain my eyes upward to watch what is happening.

"James of the Pillars, I'm very, very sorry." She greets and bows to my husband. His four dots far outrank her one. "I'm the manager, and I take full responsibility fuh this man. What can I do tuh improve ya experience, sirn?"

She hands him a lifetime dining card. No refund.

He glances at me, holding the expensive, thick-glassed bottles and everything else. Narrows in on my purse swinging from my wrist. Less than. Common.

"You may unbow, my love." At his words, I unbend.

A muscle spasms in his neck as he gathers the items from me. It twitches harder when the manager looks back and forth from me to him, her thought clear:

Your donkey should be carrying these.

Her look pierces through me. My eyes lower to the pristine black marble as I fill with the urge to grab our belongings from him. Make things right.

A second passes, and I lift them. James of the Pillars squeezes the neck of the final bottle, and the woman steps back. He is about to explode bigger than a hundred uncorked wines. I cannot let that happen. Am I not embarrassed enough?

I pull at him gently, my hand shaking on his arm. Nod toward the other patrons. The massive room has been silent for a long time.

He takes a few calming breaths. "You can do nothing, marm. You and this man have disrespected my wife. I am immensely dissatisfied." He hands her the three bottles. "Expect a notice of closure. Enough time to replace you and those you have trained. This establishment is—" He shakes his head.

We leave the dining area after he drops the card to the floor. I stare at it. A lifetime of dining at Ancient Dreams. Left here.

Soon, I lean on him more. Slow more. My back aches, and the pain under my stomach worsens. The manager trails him, apologizing profusely. Only stopping when he tells her to not follow.

I look back when she turns on the happy-maker, loud now. "Why're ya still here? Ya unemployed. Get away from me."

The happy-maker grabs none of his possessions, as is custom. Tomorrow, he will receive a new life position with far lower pay in a rural shack of a restaurant—rather than in the fanciest establishment in Urban. Also custom.

Good. He deserves it. Wretched man. This night would have been perfect if not for him.

I have waited so long for this night.

How could this have happened?

My thoughts loop this question as we continue down the long, red carpet. Walk past large, gold-rimmed pictures of Grand Anomalies. I studied each when we arrived, watched their speeches, but now I avoid their eyes. They should not have to see me sniffling and wiping snot from my nose.

"I apologize, habibi."

He has no reason to apologize. He is why I was able to come here. Commons cannot enter Ancient Dreams without an Anomaly.

"It is okay. Relax, my husband." The building is large, and the exit is far away. He holds my hand, rubbing my fingers with his thumb.

The happy-maker bows to him and speeds past us.

Too fast for me to think of a most unpleasant thing to say. It is there. I can feel it on the tip of my tongue...

Nothing.

After a few minutes, I stop to catch my breath. The band under my belly has tightened, and the arch of my foot throbs. Neither hurts enough to dull the misery inside me. Hide the truth.

I am not worthy; I cannot even pretend to be.

Antoine of the Glades walks up to us with a large, ripe tomato in one hand and a greasy piece of fried wight in the other. His lips are oily, and a tomato seed sits in his neatly trimmed mustache.

Ding. Zeroes bunch in my mind. It stutters, trying to fathom them. Calculates. 21,200,000,000 units. What. Wow. I am still unused to Anomalies' numbers.

I stare at him. He has added gold flecks to his light gray eyes. Many in Urban add small changes; you cannot even see the alterations with subtler mods. His change should make his concerts even more popular.

I have listened to all of his compositions, and I want to pepper him with questions. But now is not the right time. I hold myself still.

Antoine of the Glades stands in front of my husband. He is older but looks younger. Taller. A line of five black dots is on each side of his temples.

James of the Pillars bows deeply to him; I bow as far as I can. He straightens. I do not.

Tap, tap, tap…

It echoes in my head.

"You may unbow," the other man says. I hold in a groan as I unbend.

"We are going home." My husband sidesteps him, but I motion for us to stay.

It has been many months since he casually spoke with another Anomaly, and he would welcome the conversation. This night cannot get any worse, so why not spend a few minutes more?

There is so much beauty here, and I have waited all my years to enjoy it.

James of the Pillars points to the dining area. "Are you sure?"

"Yes, I need to rest anyway."

He and I move to the benches lining the hallway's walls. I lean back and rub my fingers on the cushion's down. Magnificently soft.

"Speak freely, my love." My husband permits me to join their discussion.

As Antoine of the Glades comes to the bench, he puts the tomato in the crook of his elbow. Wipes his hand on his pants. Like the other Anomalies, his barcodes glow red. Bright against the tomato's smooth skin.

They stand in front of me. Hold their fingers together and touch their palms in greeting. The man hums a tune

12

I have never heard in his deep, resonant, perfect pitch. It is more stunning in person.

The layered notes soothe the turmoil inside me. Fade away as if I had not heard them at all. My husband's shoulders lower, and he closes his eyes. Our belongings fall to the floor. His throat works a moment, eager to reply with a more exquisite sound—but instead, he presses his lips together and opens his eyes.

One by one, he picks up our belongings. Drops a few once more. Antoine of the Glades looks vaguely in my direction and holds his hand up near his body. I scoot forward and reach my palm out, stopping an inch from touching his. I feel better. Most, like him, do not offer me any greeting. To them, I do not exist.

James of the Pillars stands, his arms full again. He makes every effort to elicit my opinion, but I give none.

They talk while I sit back and meld into the cushions. Smell the fresh paint on the walls—J5900 Cream. This is the third version Urban has made. Lacquer and hints of sweet cream scent waft from the paint.

Soon enough, I cannot hear them. Near-transparent films cover their mouths so that they can speak of new ideas and inventions. James of the Pillars makes large gestures, his entire body animated as he takes up much of the conversational space.

Almost as quickly as their private conversation began, the films flatten into their cheeks, and their words fill the air. They talk of old Common laws.

No large gestures. No smiles. No passion-lit eyes. My husband has gone dull once more.

When their discussion finishes, Antoine of the Glades leans forward and taps him on the forehead. Scans him from head to toe. "Ya speak... differently, and ya look awful. Ashen. Sickly. You've grown thin."

James of the Pillars pokes the other man's belly; it jiggles. "And you've just grown."

They laugh. My husband speaks quickly in his relaxed, natural, high-class accent.

Antoine of the Glades glances away. "We need ya. Our world needs ya—fully."

"Never. Never, but I very much wish that was possible."

"It's possible." He motions to the dots on my husband's temples. "I know it must be exhaustin' livin' as a lowly four-dot and havin' tuh travel when called to duty." An empty circle surrounding an upside-down triangle broken into pieces glows on the man's neck. Fades. "Returning tuh Urban would be easier, James—"

"I said never."

Antoine of the Glades sighs as he puts his arm out. "A grand eve to ya." They press their palms together again. The man shoots me a glare. "Both."

Another machete slices through my heart. I look down. It is not my fault James of the Pillars left Urban; that was his choice.

I pull him back when he steps toward the man.

"He is not worth it. Let us go home, my husband. I cannot take anymore." I take his offered hand, stand, and pull my jacket tighter.

We continue to the exit. This night could not have turned more horrid. I cannot sift through my feelings fast enough. They are hardening into an unreadable boulder in the bottom of my stomach, so I stare at the man's neck as he walks off.

I have seen that triangle many times before.

It is dangerous.

When we reach the outdoors, I look up, once again entranced by the magnificence of Urban. Skyscrapers covered in fluorescent graffita murals, the freshest of air, lush grass, 200-foot redwood trees, small, living animals scurrying around, hundreds of bikes and bike racks. HoverCars. Invisible and silent, the sky looks clear as citizens move here and there, traveling through the dark blues and fading oranges.

Much life and laughter bustle in the late eve of this small city.

And comfort.

And excess.

I will have this. One day, I will have this for myself.

I bring my gaze down. The happy-maker is bowed with his forehead touching the concrete. James of the Pillars chastises him with quiet words, but I stop him from this.

A few moments pass before my husband forces out, "You may unbow."

The man unbends and stands. He is the same height as my husband but does not meet his gaze.

I ball my fist, about to do him harm, but decide against it. He has given himself the worst punishment—he will never see Ancient Dreams again. Has lost Urban forever.

Plus, I do not want to get blood on the dress.

"How did you know I did not belong?" This is the only answer I must learn from the happy-maker.

Three hundred eighty-five years ago, the Distribution War split all continents into multiple regions. Be kind. Share. Your favored show, Today in the Past!

"Full-gloss black shoes with a blue dress were in style this morn; they went out of style this aft." Oh. "I am remorseful, miss."

He no longer calls me "marm" but "miss." A demotion. It cuts deeper than all else because he did not mean it to cut at all.

I stare at him. He has no jacket, and his complexion has already begun to lose its color. Thick tear streaks have cleared a path through his makeup. Under it, cavernous bags hang from his eyes, and a bruise sits on his green-tinged cheek. His head hangs like mine did.

He has less than we do. A lot less.

James of the Pillars watches us silently, his lip curled.

I move closer to the happy-maker. "Do you have enough for a taxi?"

He shakes his head. "I was to be paid today."

Each of his words is clipped, painfully enunciated. Unlikely, but, "Do you live in Valley?"

"No, Abyss." Oh, poor thing.

James of the Pillars touches my elbow as I reach into my purse. Leans near my ear. "You do not know what he will purchase with it. You know how these… people are."

I pull away; he turns around. Walks far from us.

I dig around, pull fifteen thousand units from my purse, and place the large vials in the man's hand. Urban taxis are expensive, and Abyss is two hundred miles away. Much too far to walk or risk asking for a share ride. Many are more desperate than him, and they will violently take their desperation out on him.

"Here. This should be enough to get you home. Be safe, my dear."

He smiles at me, holding the three vials tightly. "Many thanks, miss."

I pat his shoulder and give him 500 units more to purchase a filtering in Abyss. They cost so much there.

"I am truly remorseful," he says. "I will never do such a thing again. I should not have. I thought you were his..."

He looks away.

Shame. That suffocating wave. It is all that is left in me. He thought many things about me—wife was never one of them.

James of the Pillars walks around us, pulls out his access card, and swipes it in front of the streetlight near the bike road. The scanner beeps.

His card's metal is red. Its gold words and border glow brightly.

Under his image—*Legal,* under mine—*Illegal.* Like all Urban citizens, he is legal in every city of our world, but when traveling with me, his card details his restrictions:

Two citizens, three-hour stay, Urban to Valley, 160 miles. Late departs will not be tolerated.

Our hoverCar lands and the door of an antique Noire Droptail opens. Altered, well restored. The top is down, and the dark rose-red paint gleams on the sleek design. I do not have to bend low; this is a tiny reprieve from this night.

I crash into the seat and call a taxi. Push a button to put the top up. Urban disappears behind the tinted windows, and we are surrounded by darkness.

"Husband." My voice cracks at the end.

He holds me close as I squeeze my eyes closed, my chin shaking uncontrollably. I cslench the dress in my fists. Rub my palm on the fabric. Sear its magnificence in my mind.

It is a rental, and tomorrow, I must return it.

This night was supposed to be perfect. Perfect. It has been anything but.

After a long while, I lift the dress, and he helps me adjust the prosthetic leg that chafes as my belly grows larger. Its withering top will leave a deep, bloody bruise above my pelvis bone.

TWO

MY BRACELET JANGLES in the wind; the handsomely designed letters glisten silver in the morn sunlight.

"How many inscriptions… have you purchased?" Marguerite, a seven-aged neighbor, asks in broken words. Broken because her breaths are long gasps. She sits across from me on my porch and glides her finger along the charms on my bracelet.

"How many letters have I?" I hold my arm aloft, letting the charms dangle. She counts.

My breath pauses at the whirring. The wind fades. The chirping dies. All disappear as my ears focus only on the light whine of the engine. Listen for any stutter. Any sign it will stop.

The white groundVan circles our block of fifteen homes. I put my hand to my chest, wishing to quiet my heartbeat as I watch it crawl by.

Lurk along the smooth concrete.

Red eyes scanning us from the driver's seat.

Neon red coating the groundVan's underbody, so it glows in the night. My neighbors and their children pause too.

If we do not move, the driver may not question us or take us away.

Marguerite shivers. "I am scared of The BloodBid." Her voice is near silent as she taps her thigh quickly, her eyes following the groundVan's slow movement.

I set my hand on her panicked finger. Too loud. A giant sprinting for its life.

Shh. They will hear.

The whirring stutters and she grabs my hand. Squeezes it hard until all is quiet again. Only then does she stop humming lightly—and relax.

In Valley, we are unrelaxed a great many times each day. Far less than those in Abyss, but more than other cities.

Three hundred ten years ago, Kuru Acid was discovered. Much needed to protect our brains. Do not forget to take yours. Your favored show, Today in the Past!

She wrinkles her nose before saying, "James of the Pillars enjoys Kuru Acid, but not me. I think it tastes funny."

World news, reminders, and Urban commercials pop up from the device implanted in the front of our brains— every hour, on the hour. Each feels like a tugging in my

20

head, as if the information is a memory I have been trying to grasp. A moment later, it settles into an epiphany.

We will not forget the past.

She frowns. "What was I doing?"

"You were counting, my dear."

She nods and tilts her head, counting my charms by twos again. Her maternal has taught her well. Though she smells of sewage and rotten lemons at all times, she is clever. If she continues this way, she may qualify for courses next year. Maybe.

Ding. 90,000 units.

Her hair is lackluster, like mine. Black braids frame her ears, their parts intricately designed in triangles. One hangs from each side of her face, dry like straw. She is an odd child with a washed-out complexion and slight wrinkles around her eyes. A lack of blood leads to that. I want her toffee color to bloom, but her paternal has gone ill—so this will not happen.

"My maternal has only one charm; you have eight. If you had one more, you would have… as many charms as I have fingers. That is wight." She giggles. "Not wight! I meant—" She gasps and goes silent. Watches a girl a bit older than her. The same girl she has watched before.

A few homes down, the girl cranks the clothing line down to her height and holds up dingy, gray, patch-filled garments. The hooks close, and the line slides to the next open set.

I watch the girl a moment, too. A bell dings. It is from a memory long ago.

The girl's numbers pop up along her body. Considerations. Calculations. Criteria. Even without her

21

smell or touch, I sum the amounts and make an assessment: 129,000 units. A decent number. With that, we could pay our housing's rent for four months.

Stop. No more.

Sourness twists my stomach. A creeping sludge of guilt. I shake my head to see the girl, not her numbers, but it has been so long since I began my position that I tally worth automatically.

Marguerite continues staring as the girl hangs clothing. When she finishes hanging, she turns, smiles, and holds her palm out. Not to me, but to this daring child next to me, who meekly holds up her palm in return.

The girl stands still, balancing the small basket on her head, and walks over. She is of a healthier weight than Marguerite but still thin. Agile with two above-the-knee prostheses. And yet, she hesitates with each step.

Halfway to us, the girl pauses again and peeks at Marguerite through her fingers. Seconds pass before she turns away and runs behind the home.

"I will marry her when I grow up." Marguerite's hand is still raised. "She will be my beloved." I touch her wrist, and she lowers it to her lap.

"First, you must be bold enough to ask if she has interest in you."

She taps her thigh, glances at me. "What if she says no?"

"Then you must be bold enough to leave, rejected, with confidence intact."

She nods and taps her thigh once, hard. "Okay, I will ask her."

I do not tell Marguerite her chances with the girl are favorable. I do not tell her the clothes, blowing in the wind, were dry when hung.

Instead, I rest a moment in Lower Valley 7. Squat, sagging, brightly-colored homes sit side by side, resting with me. Each batch of homes is separated by numbered streets. None worth enough to be given a name.

Each of our homes has a triangular front, rectangular back, six windows, and three stairs leading to the porches. They are identical except for the meticulous, varied paint and large numbers stretching from roof to floor.

1, 2, 3, 4, 5, 6, 7, 8, 9, 10, 11, 12, 13, 14, 15.

My voice, young, echoes in my head. I enjoyed strolling along the streets, counting our blocks of 15 x 15 homes to see if the builders had made any mistakes. Made something other than a square. They had not, and I adored them for that. It was pleasant to know someone in our world kept their promises.

I glance at my neighbors again. Rickety porch chairs trembling under the weight of ragged gray-clothed people resting from repairing their homes. Only a few are out here. Most are at their positions.

After many hours, they will return to unbroken concrete and no grass. As our past with dirt is unpleasant, we have access to little. Many years ago, The Dome planted small, inedible bushes on the side of the walkways. Each is under a clear, porous cage ten feet apart from the next. Even *we* need fresh oxygen.

It is all so... less.

I will not accept less. Why should I when there is more?

A shaking on my thigh.

"Did you know my brother hates pickles?"

"No, Marguerite, I did not know your brother hates pickles. Do you too? What is your favorite? Did you know pickles are infant cucumbers?"

"They are?!"

I laugh. "Yes."

This child.

"The community garden only has infant cucumbers, but they do not taste like pickles. Is it because they are old?"

"Little one, they are not pickles immed—"

"I love pickles coated with breadcrumbs, baked, and injected with red sauce." She launches into her full history with pickles. I adore them as well, but I tune out the rest of her dissertation on the pros of pickles and why her brother is a fool for hating them.

Each home has a tiny patch of dirt in its side yard, surrounded by an invisible fence to prevent theft. Some citizens do not want to walk to the community garden, where we are rationed vegetables and fruit—the stale, soft, unwanted runts unfit for Urban.

"When he is older, he will... love pickles like me. I will teach him how."

I shrug, still looking out.

Every home nearly overlaps the next. One citizen blends into the next. There is barely enough room to breathe. I think on this until a clatter from our kitchen draws my attention. James of the Pillars. I hope he did not drop the ClearJuice; he can be clumsy.

Marguerite slouches on the soft seat of her leaning board, which she has propped up like a metallic pyramid behind her. Humming as she holds a hand to her chest. Resting a moment. It must take immense energy to talk from the sun's awakening to its sleep.

I stare at the board for a moment. Small, light to carry, strong. Helpful. But Lower Valley 7 is no place for sickliness, and requiring a leaning board is not a good sign.

I fear for her. The Dome severely cut her family's quota when her paternal fell ill. Though James of the Pillars has shared what little extra he has through the Donation Facility, it is not enough. She is in pain.

I am in pain. It is pulsating from my wrist. I lift my arm from my lap and adjust my bracelet. The ache from the thick scars surrounding my wrist lessens.

"What have you heard of your maternal's pay?"

She shrugs. "Not much. They discuss when I am in bed, but"—she cups her hands around her mouth and whispers loudly—"I heard my maternal and paternal talking. The Dome denied her… a stable rate."

Oh. A stable rate would have been grand for her family.

I smile at her, thinking. Like most of us, she combines The Dome and its thousands of facilities into one. They are not the same, but there is little need to separate them. The Dome dictates; the facilities enforce and collect. All belong to The Dome.

Marguerite absentmindedly rubs the smooth area where her pinkie once was. She taps the skin—thinking, worrying. "If they lower her pay more… I will submit my arm as wight."

She launches herself into my face and whispers, "Want to smell? I am O negative."

Sweat gathers at my palms, and a panicked flush sweeps through my body after she says my name. I take deep breaths.

"Do not say my name. I have told you this." I lean away from her. She stinks, and the universal blood donor type is not quite to my liking. Tolerable but overrated.

"The Dome will give much to my family."

Yes, this may be true. Some markets adore sour blood.

"But it is my maternal's wish… to keep me as whole as possible. I do not understand why." She prattles on, talking much on each breath. "My paternal painted my pinkie nail as a farewell… and the Wight-Harvester laughed. She laughed so hard. Did you know my maternal… did not allow me to be bled until I was aged a month? A month!"

Hmm. I stare off into the southern distance. Abyss. Turn to its opposite direction. Urban. I smell the oak seat beneath me. Feel the silky wine on my taste buds.

My better life. It will be grand.

"You should not be so keen to send yourself away, little Marguerite, lest someone else become just as keen, and you find yourself parted with only a torso and head to spare."

I fall into deep contemplation until she giggles and hums softly. Her gasps for air fade as I sing the words in my head:

Tiny child, loud mouth, and not a care
Broken toys, scraped knees, scolded when fair
Maternal signs and sends you there
Paternal signs, sends you where
To The Dome, To The Dome, for parts to snare

One of each paired organs to spare
A torso, a head, tiny child, a tiny pear

I smile. My paternal sang this when I misbehaved. He always kissed my forehead before the last word, so I knew he would keep me.

All of me? I would ask him.

All of you, my angel.

"Do they take these as well?"

I open my eyes, grab her hand a moment before she pokes my left breast, and nod.

"In a half-bid, everything not life-sustaining is halved and auctioned."

I remove the barrette hanging slightly askew from one of her braids and clip it back on straight.

Perfect.

The wind blows. Fresh today. I breathe in deeply but pull back when she shoves her arm to my nose.

Sewage and—

I tense my stomach against the loud growling, but it rumbles anyway, and I turn from her. My assessment is wrong; her true scent is hidden.

Ding.

I—my brain—*I* recalculate her numbers. Her blood is immensely sweet; it is decadent like Diane Candies, the best in all our world. I had a few as a child. Just five units for each back then. My mouth hangs open as her numbers sum. Bids for her wight would be astronomical.

On smell alone, millions of units. On age, so tender, tens of thousands more. City of origin, thousands less. Complexion—

2,100,000 units.

I shake my head as she smiles.

"I know. Two years ago, the Wight-Harvester told my paternal… I would make very, very sweet wight." Her tone is boastful.

Clearly, she has forgotten her wistfulness. Though, if she were bid, there would be nothing left of her to be wistful for.

Distracted, my hand rests on my prosthetic knee. The metal is cold even though I wear thin black shorts under my dress. I press a finger against the unnaturally thin leg. Nothing. Press harder. Lifeless.

I promise this. His voice. Soft. Reassuring.

My paternal was wrong. This leg is not mine. It will never be mine. I put my hand on my birth leg. The warmth is comforting.

Marguerite sniffs her arm, and her stomach rumbles hard. Louder than mine, though she is unable to smell her blood's sweetness.

She sticks out her tongue. I slap her cheek lightly.

"No. Autodevouring is not allowed." Perhaps her intellect is not as promising as it seems.

She drops her head. "Apologies."

Just thirty minutes ago, I gave her half a pound of wight from the gray markets of Second Australia and four small, green tomatoes, but it is not enough.

Of course not. She has weeks of hunger.

"Smelling only. Never, ever autodevour. It is illegal. You know this."

A small thud comes from the kitchen. Marguerite stares at the porch's spongy, reeking, rotten wood until I tap the underside of her chin.

"Look at me." She lifts her eyes to mine, and I return a stern gaze. "You know the consequences, yes?"

She nods.

Four hundred years ago, green skin alterations were to perish for. You could get them for no cost. Ha, ha. Your favored show, Today in the Past!

I get to my feet and help her to hers.

"Come inside, my dear, have some ClearJuice."

THREE

THE FRONT DOOR creaks as I open it.

"Your door is hideous." Marguerite slips off her shoes and walks through.

This is true. As all citizens do, we decorated our door with intricate spray-painted images and words from Urban commercials, but our design did not turn out well. James of the Pillars is a horrid artist. I would not trust him to draw a straight line. And so, because our designs must be combined, our home never wins the annual prize: A week-long trip to work in Horizon. Second only to Urban's grandness.

I stand on the mat and take off my shoes. Use my foot to line them with James of the Pillars's.

Though I am only five months along, my stomach is immense. I cannot bend and scrub them clean anymore, so I stare at them and adjust them little by little.

Tiny jittering bubbles pop under my skin like spiders under their maternal's sack. I move the left shoe in front of the right. Make sure the heels touch the fronts.

Pop, pop, pop.

Crooked still. I can make this right. Better. I focus harder.

Forward a bit. Back. A bit to the right. There.

My shoulders drop. The bubbles grow smaller and smaller.

After the shoes are in a perfect line, I walk into our kitchen. The door locks behind me. A series of codes click, and three deadbolts turn.

Eww. I fan the air.

Marguerite's odor is concentrated in the small room, mixing with the vanilla-scented cleaning products James of the Pillars used. She reeks.

Soft music, Urban commercials, and the world news play at all times from the invisible speakers in one wall. In every room. In every home. They create a holographic screen during the news and commercials.

Gentle wheezes add to the mix. Marguerite.

She comes every Thurs and stays a few hours. To eat our food. To talk incessantly. To annoy me. Long ago, my husband and I decided to help her anyway.

James of the Pillars sits in the far corner of the room. Marguerite at the square, wooden table in the middle, facing me, kicking her feet. A patched, mostly gray dress hangs along her body, and a bit of cushion bulges from one of her thin slippers. Not my best sewing job. I will fix it later.

Her back is to our sink, and our two-burner stove sits to her left. During the snowflake season, it keeps her warmer.

She hums to herself while tracing the decorative lines in the wood.

"It is so nice. I like it."

I smile. Sometimes, she is not so annoying.

Years ago, I carved intricate Urban designs into the pine to make our marriage official. I spent weeks picking out the most beautiful work I could find, as that is my family's tradition.

"You must put your best into the wood. Into all you do, my dear daughter." My maternal carves the pine a few days after my parents' marriage. The high sound of her chisel is soothing, and I am entranced as I watch her tease out the smallest of slivers.

We bend down opposite each other, an inch from the wood. She flares her red-painted nostrils, and I laugh as she sniffs the pine deeply.

"Smell." Blows the sweet scent in my direction.

Dirt, a fresh breeze, her sweat, and a slightly buzzing life are in the table. I close my eyes, and for a long while, we rest, enjoying all the flavors of the fallen tree.

I blink, grinning at our table. On the other side is horrid plastic. Intentional. During audits, we flip it over and show that. It is safer that way.

Dim light comes from the paneling covering the ceilings and walls of our three-room home; it is warm because we saved enough to purchase wind-powered heating coils two years ago. The coils glow a faint orange and protrude from the walls in triangular designs. Unsafe to touch.

I put on my slippers—left one first—and walk to the right of the table, running my finger along the countertop's surface. Over the molder on top of it and onto the stove. A bit more countertop and to the fridge. Stop at our sink.

A small pinecone sits behind the faucet. I leave it there and scrub lavender sand into my hands to cleanse them. Relax as I inhale the pleasant, spicy scent. See Ancient Dream's twinkling lights spinning above me. Crunch into fresh wax beans filled with red sauce. Hear strong rhythmic beats mixed with dark cellos.

Urban.

Not now. Not yet. Right now, I use a bit of our water to wet the sand and wipe it along my nose. Marguerite is behind me, and I must lessen her stench immediately.

Sewage and lemons. Her maternal chose an excellent combination to hide her true worth. Who would ever get close enough to know she does not smell like a toxic waste plant?

As I scrub more, I stare at the wall in front of me, envisioning our bedroom on the other side. The books. The wrinkles on his side of the bed. The locked office opposite it.

Our home is like all others, except for the walk-in closet in our bedroom and the books. Urban-approved books are everywhere. In the kitchen, our bedroom, the toilet room. Protected in plastic wrap and stacked in bookshelves, the cupboards, and our dresser. Biology, chemistry, prosthetics, history, and so many more.

I have read a few to learn the past, look at the beautiful artwork of our ancestors, but most of them are not for me. They are for James of the Pillars—so he and the other Anomalies can create our future.

"We only have mango sand at my house. My sister's hands got so big... she is allergic to the others. I helped her with her hair. Her favored style has... three ponytails." Pause. Wheeze. "I do not know how to do hair well yet, but she... wore it anyway." Marguerite laughs.

"It is good mango is available then, little one."

James of the Pillars sits to my left, at the tiny makeshift table tucked into the corner of our kitchen. It is nothing more than a piece of black-painted circular wood atop a similarly painted barrel, but my husband did not want more.

I do not know why. Maybe when you have as much as he did, does, you tire of it and crave having less.

His head hangs. The missing patches in his hair are a stark reminder of our life. Every few seconds, he rubs his hair, and slivers of his dull, black curls float to the floor.

He is just 26-aged, but there is an immense wornness to him.

Oh, my husband.

I walk past our bedroom door and stop in front of him.

A needle pulls blood from him, pumps it through an attached tube, and gives his blood back without its plasma. The ClearJuice drips into the container built into the machine. Yellow. Poorly named.

He is as rundown as the rest of us.

But not truly. Never truly.

James of the Pillars holds a finger to his forehead and ends his first Innova of the day. His exhale is silent as the near-transparent film over his mouth hides his words, keeping Urban business in Urban.

Two more films cover his ears, eliminating noise. Innovation Sessions require hours, intense focus, and a place of silence. As he does not enjoy being alone, he does not always go into his office to complete his Innovas.

He lifts his head; a red overlay covers his eyes. His face is scrunched in imaginings and thought and anger that create deep lines between his eyebrows. It is extremely early, but he has already been laboring for three hours. He exhales. The red disappears from his eyes.

He has no rest remaining for this day.

A minute later, he blinks. When he notices me, he smiles and stands from the seat. I bow and smile back.

"Husband, here." I hold a Jam bar out to him, sweet with fruit and large white onions laced across its top.

My gaze crawls along the curves and angles of him— the tiny mole at the top of his ear, the awkward way he stands, not too tall, 68 inches, but gangly in the arms and knees, how he holds his head back a little, always ready to laugh.

That laugh. I adore that laugh.

The films split in half and flatten into his skin, each a soft, permanent alteration to his face. After five years together, I can hardly feel them.

"Let us give her six oz. Take her home after, my love." His voice has a rough edge to it. Weariness. Impatience. He is in need of rest and cheering and more rest.

I kiss his lips. Press the bar into his hand until he takes it from me. A small anchor inside me sits. Toilet. Now.

In there, I pull out a magazine of Urban's finest artists—Joshua of the Tiles, king of the haunting charcoal portraits. Ali of the Lords, master of the 5D sculptures. Ann of the Roads. I am not sure what they draw, but the mixture of small, sculpted rocks and pencil drawings is beyond captivating. I trail my hand along the page and return to our kitchen.

An unease whispers in my mind. I take the cloth my husband offers and wipe the seat clean even though streaks remain from when he did the same. When the trembling lessens, I hold his hand and sit slowly.

"Many apologies for my rudeness. Thank you for this." He leans down and kisses me. Lower to kiss my belly.

He tastes of dirt, vomit, and love.

"A grand morn. I am most excited to see you," he whispers this to our conceived and rubs my stomach a few more times. "I will be glad when you are birthed; I want to see far less of your maternal."

I push him from me. "Get away. Your voice sickens him. Feel." I pull his hand to me and press it deep into my skin. No movement. "See? You have paralyzed him."

We stare at each other. His laughter breaks through first. Good. This is a joke he does not know. I have memorized many books so I can joke with him.

His chuckle is quiet and breathy. Has always been that way. When we are old, I hope he will let me hear him fully.

Marguerite cackles loudly.

"What is so funny, little one?" I look at her, staring at us.

"I do not know, but I want to be happy, too."

This child.

He puts the bar in his pocket and stands.

The machine hangs from the wall next to him. After it makes a loud buzzing sound, the heat suction loosens. He pulls the needle out and dabs invisiband on his skin; it seals his blood in.

The machine starts its cleansing process as he pours the liquid into his cup. After swiping a finger across his forehead to snooze an Innova request, he shuffles over to Marguerite and tickles her cheek. She giggles and lies her head on the table.

He sits across from her, perched on the edge, and hands her his cup—tiny Js printed all over it.

She takes the ClearJuice but does not drink.

"Drink now. It will cool soon," I say to her. ClearJuice is best when fresh from the body.

We watch the wall's hologram. Today in the Past! is not on; the 3 and a half world news is. The newsperson highlights different continents and their regions on a public Need Map.

The information is limited, the trends simplified.

I view the same Need Map in more detail in my device. Rotate Valley's Map to analyze the sun's temperatures over the last months. Zoom in to focus on the week, and next, the day. 88.532 degrees Fahrenheit on average.

There has been a tiny increase in Lower Valley 4, but I do not believe a spike will happen in our region soon. How excellent.

Marguerite turns to me. "I do not under—"

"We are good."

More charts fill my vision. Water, vegetation, and wight levels from all over our world. Rows upon rows of information. Numbers fill my mind. I calculate the vegetation levels in Third Asia—50 million metric tons—and request more from The Dome.

Adding, subtracting, dividing. Continents, regions, cities.

Full access to the Maps is given to those who sort. Me. Others with similar abilities. We can see all our world, and that is comforting to me.

James of the Pillars sighs hard. "Of course they are in need."

First America. Along with many Third and Fourth regions, it is green. In need. Other continent's cities, mainly Valley and Abyss, are yellow. Soon to be in need. The remaining regions are red. Good for now.

One immense expanse of land, south of us, could always be red if it wanted. Could always be good.

"The Republic of United First Regions." He shakes his head. "Yesterday, they added two more fleets. A month ago, three."

"That is five fleets." Marguerite pipes up. He looks at her and smiles.

Yes, five more from Abyss. Many guards are leased from there; they train all their lives to get the chance to join the pawn lines.

As The Republic of United First Regions is home to The Dome's most powerful headquarters, it is heavily guarded, and all six of the First regions surround this massive campus.

Mighty sentries at their stations.

Within their walls, representatives from each continent convene and issue laws.

For the rest of us.

I blow out a breath. "As usual, First America requests much wight. Even after all these centuries—even after the Distribution War—they cannot tell a need from a want."

Greediest of all the First regions, First America requests thighs and hearts and shoulders from The Dome every three months to feed their plump citizens.

Marguerite pounds her fist on the table. "Second America is not so selfish."

James of the Pillars and I laugh.

"You are correct, little one. We are not." He smiles at her. "If we were one of The Dome's headquarters regions, we would have more say. All would have plenty to eat."

"All? Even those in Abyss?" At my words, he turns to me, scrunches his face. No answer. "You voted against giving them assistance last month."

Marguerite watches him. He pauses. "Those people do not even try to improve their lives."

"You do not know that."

"Yes, I do. You have never been there, but I have visited Abyss during many Imagine Trips. I have seen their laziness. Dirtiness. Criminality. They are not like us."

"And I am not like you."

We stare at each other.

Why can he never see how wrong he is? I allow myself this thought and push away the deeper one that plagues me, pushes me to defend the Abyssites, argue over them: in his true heart, does he think the same of me?

"You are hurting them," I say, but he is tense and silent now.

A few minutes later, he hands out tablets of Kuru Acid and lights the stove to make the morn meal. Making soothes him. After he drops the fluffy wight dumplings into a sweet and spicy potato soup, he takes one more tablet, just in case.

It will protect his brain from the wight's sickness. A lethal sickness for us all.

Marguerite is louder now. Angry at the news.

I wait until she finally quiets. "Husband, when First America travels up the Panamal, they will take much of Abyss's wight. Your vote could help those citizens."

He turns to me as he scrambles his meal. "Yes, it could."

"But you will vote against them." My voice rises. "Even though your parents are Commo—"

"Those people are not like them; my parents are Urban-born." He turns the temperature to its lowest setting and taps the spatula on the edge of the pan. Looks at both of us. "And those people are nothing like you. Know that."

I get up. Leave to tidy our bedroom. What is wrong with that man?

During your Gold Week, submit all of your Gold every morn to receive one premium unit in your local currency. We should not have to say this, but do not falsify your output. Your favored show, Today in the Past!

I walk to the room's far end, yank at the Sapphire blue cover, and tuck it in the corners. My stomach is heavy, and the band of my prosthesis keeps slipping down. It is an old model, and the vintage part costs much. Even with our savings, we could not afford it.

I will be glad when my new leg comes, but for now, I hold onto the support bar on the wall and move slowly as I convert our bed to a sofa. Something is wrong. A small lump sticks out from under the cover. I pull it out; it is a cranberry bar.

Why does that man hide food?

I tuck the bar deep into the crevice it came from, and when I am done smoothing out every wrinkle, I set the pillows down gently.

The sofa has done nothing to me.

Our filtering machines are next. James of the Pillars's is bolted to the floor at the far end of the couch. Mine is on the side nearer our dresser. I wipe all the dust off of our machines and check their tubes for nicks or wear.

Nothing. They are perfect.

The table now. Crooked. I place its legs back in the grooves in the carpet, and an anxious bubble pops inside of me and melts into a calm pool.

Onto the dresser. I straighten the long cloth that covers the top of our tall dresser and hangs over the sides. Its design is a chaotic mixture of gold triangles and swirls on a royal blue background. Not surprising, the chaos. It was made in Valley.

My pages of drawings and notes on Urban's clothing, food, and cultural trends are in its drawers, protected in plastic slips. I pull a few out. Vibrant reds, yellows, and most other colors pop off the pages. Dark shadows and gentle lights. I spent hours making them photorealistic, so I can dream through them.

I run my finger along the lines of the dresses and suits, feeling my rental dresses' fabric and James of the Pillars's clothing. Waterfalls of more.

I leave the small notebook out and close the drawer. Urban commercials will come on later, and I will have time to look at these pictures then.

One more thing: the teddy.

Today, it is holding a pinecone. I pick up the stuffed bear from the middle of the dresser and adjust the red ribbon around its neck. Too long on one side. I tie the strip slowly, savoring the texture. It is Horizon-made. Magnificent. Soft like warm cookies.

James of the Pillars bought it for our conceived a month ago. I smooth the teddy's ears back. Grin at its placid smile, the message sewn into its belly: *Hugs make me happy*.

I place it on the top of the dresser again, right where I picked it up. I am not in a hugging mood.

No hugs for you today.

Across from our bed is a long and wide walk-in closet: James of the Pillars's office. Its barrier is dark now but becomes transparent when it allows him through.

During shortages, I am permitted to go in there. "For my safety." The space is massive and silent, empty but for a chair, couch, and long table. When I was there last, I could not see my husband's innovations or plans, as they looked like blank pages, but he organizes in a horizontal fashion. Pages spread across the whole table.

His couch and chair. Oh, they were paradise. Sapphire blue dermer with black leather pillows sown with gold thread.

I smile, thinking of the drawer built into the bottom of his sofa. It was filled with the musky, sweet, rich smell of him. His suits hold his scent. Stunning Urban suits of many colors, including red. He is allowed to wear red.

And not one is a rental.

FOUR

MARGUERITE COUGHS. A deep, phlegm-filled sound. She has gotten too wound up at the news. I peek into the kitchen from our bedroom. James of the Pillars gets her a cup of water. He glances at me and smirks. Stirs in a spoon of powdered marrow to soothe her throat.

"It does help." I cross my arms.

"Uh-huh."

"You should not dote on her. She must learn her own limits."

He places the cup in her hand. "She will learn many limits."

Yellowed and tasting metallic, Marguerite takes a long drink of First America's used partially filtered water. We are lucky. Third America receives our used water and

Fourth America theirs. By that time, it has traces of feces in it.

"We have half a gallon left for this week, my love." He marks our remaining amount on the sheet above the sink and turns back to the news.

The newsperson points to many regions. "As you can see, First America, Third Asia, Fourth Australia"—they list other regions; the list is long—"need your immediate assistance. Go to your nearest branch of The Dome and send your cancered wight to help our Third and Fourth Region citizens. Be kind. Share."

"My paternal can help them." Marguerite smiles as she zones back into the news. James of the Pillars watches the screen a while longer and comes to our bedroom door. He caresses my cheek.

His hands are cold, and the nails of most of his fingers have broken off. Three charms dangle from his wrist. I glance at his barcodes. They are dark like mine but would glow if he ever took his Vow.

He will not.

I have no idea why he will not. Maybe he fears what The Dome will ask of him, but what more can they ask of him than they already do?

I want him to take his Vow. We could have a better life.

I could have a better life.

He hands me a small, warm container from his back pocket. It is a pain-relieving salve. My last one ran out yesterday. I open it, rub a little on the thick, jagged scars surrounding my wrist, and do the same to the other wrist. Minty vanilla soothes my pain. I hold it under my nose.

Sniff deeply. *Mm.* It smells like wealth and comfort. Excess. Urban.

"Many thanks." I screw the lid on slowly. Tighten it until it could not fathom turning more. None will be wasted. "How did you get this?"

"Chevaughn gave it to me. Yesterday, I mentioned you would be in pain today."

Oh.

He is allowed to ask his Keepers for small comforts for me. Tiny comforts and no more.

He looks out the window to the left of the door. "They wait so long. Often, I ask them for small things I do not need. Send them far so they can stop... waiting."

A trickling starts in my chest.

Tap, tap, tap...

The worthy move at their leisure. All else must wait.

No. I shake my head.

Tap, tap, tap...

No more.

A minute later, when the ache in my wrist has subsided, the sadness is gone.

I reach out to him, cup his chin, and run my thumb along his lips. "I will wait for your return. In the morn, you can help me apply this balm under my belly."

He quirks his eyebrows up, goes back to the stove.

This man.

I spritz my hair with vanilla peach perfume, place the container on the dresser, and go back to the kitchen.

Anomalies, Near Nobility produces the best brains to siphon. Put in your requests early so we can teach to your specifications. Your favored show, Today in the Past!

Often, this show gives random information. I do not know why they chose that title.

James of the Pillars makes two bowls, carries one, and sets it in front of Marguerite. I pick up the other and sit at the circular table in the back of the room.

The news comes back on:

"From this—" Screams. A woman, kicking and crying with blood dripping down her wrists, goes through The Dome's broilers. She shrieks once more, and her skin darkens and bubbles.

We shake our heads. Marguerite pounds her fist on the table again. "What an awful person."

"They always are." James of the Pillars scrambles his meal.

"—to this." A bell dings and the camera circles a magnificent table with a piece of broiled wight on it: Well-done, cut into strips, fanned out over brown rice, topped with vegetables, and grandly arranged on a plate. Red sauce is drizzled on the plate, and thin slices of garlic are sprinkled on top. We all stare.

James of the Pillars turns to me and licks his lips. Urban's wight. Delicious.

I lean back, forcing myself to relax. I was given the day off because The Dome's sorting machines are malfunctioning. I offered to do paperwork, but they gave the work to students instead.

Makes no sense. They will learn as they do more, while I must pay back each hour I am not working.

Breathe. I do and feel calmer. Watch my husband.

With two (he did not need two) Kuru amino acid tablets digested, his brain is safe to eat what he likes. What he is allowed. I shake my head, watching him finish making his morn meal. A towel sits under his plate.

He turns to me. Winces and touches his forehead as an urgent Innova is announced. He snoozes the loud shout into his thoughts. "I will not be available most of today." I did not think he would be. The most intense Innovas last many days. "Go on, wife, say what you choose."

He stuffs rogue crumbled brains and pieces of a small onion back into the two corn shells.

"You will believe eating someone else's brain can boost your creative ability, but not that powdered marrow is an excellent medicine." I sip the soup as he takes a bite and nods. "Beloved, listen closely: Brain siphoning is a myth told to you by a stupid child when you were a stupid child. The science has disproven it, but do you truly want to know how I know your logic is flawed?" He nods and takes another bite, staring into my eyes. "I knew Alejandro. He was brilliant. If his brain benefitted you, we would have seen evidence of that by now."

He chokes, laughing. "Is that so?"

"Yes. It. Is."

A third bite and the first shell is gone. Marguerite giggles as he moves closer to me, smiling and holding out the second one.

I settle back in the seat. Maybe that will calm our conceived. His kicks are like ships crashing to the earth. They will leave bruises.

James of the Pillars takes a bite. Half is gone. I do not know why he eats so quickly, but he crunches once more, and nothing is left.

He stops for a moment, confused as to why he has nothing to taunt me with—"you eat like a paper shredder!" Marguerite reminds him—and turns away to clean his plate.

After putting it away, he moves behind me and places the towel over my eyes. Under it, I can still see our home. The cracks in the walls are blended smooth; it is more beautiful in its blurriness.

James of the Pillars massages my shoulders and neck, and I relax even more when he moves to my head, circling his fingers against my scalp.

A while later, he whispers in my right ear, "We could spare 100 units for one of her medicines. Discuss."

I pull the towel away and look at him. "Hmm. I took inventory of our shared ledger yesterday. We do not have enough." I move closer to him. As my other ear is unhearing, the news' noise makes it hard to place sounds.

"We have enough for the month, and I am qualifying for a second position heading another engineering team. Also, I have been assigned extra hours because of a new… project."

New projects cause him much pain. And me. I twist the towel tight and rub the leg of my chair with it.

I do not want him to go.

It has been five years since he left to work in Urban. Since he spent months in his Innovation Room there. When requested, he must always go, or The Dome will not allow him to come back. But still, I do not want him to go.

He touches my arm. "I will return, my love."

I squeeze the towel in my hand as he moves in front of me. Rubs my stomach with one hand and taps his chest with the other. Too little blood leads to many kinds of pain, and more of our blood quota is given to me because of my pregnancy.

"We cannot spare 100 units, my dear." I run my hand down his dulled skin. "You cannot. You receive so little daily. Look at you."

"Look at her. What if she was your child? Where is your empathy?"

I remove his hand from my belly and press his fingertips to my lips.

"It is with you. You give too much. Are you attempting to autodevour?" I blow on his fingers, hoping my warm breath will relieve an inkling of his suffering.

James of the Pillars pulls them from me. "Send her away, then. Pray to the Inventor she makes it to her home."

"You know I do not believe in the Inventor, but I will ensure she gets there." He will no longer look at me. A grimace hangs from the corners of his mouth. *You deserve more, my love, and I cannot give it to you.* I turn him to me. He bends, and I kiss his quivering chin.

"Husband, know this: we are well."

He leans on the table as I finish my soup.

We relax until a news update shows on the wall.

The headline scrolls as the newsperson speaks, "The Dome is determining whether there is still a need for additional research or continued funding into The Blaze. Reports from the First regions show little progress—and most certainly no breakthroughs—has been made by the Anomalies."

"We are trying." He holds his forehead. Ruffles his hair as he stares at the screen.

Marguerite swallows a spoonful. "Perhaps you should try harder. Or find smarter Anomalies."

We exchange a glance, he and I.

This child.

He bends to my ear and whispers, "Do not ask, and you shall still receive."

I hold in my laughter. "Be kind."

He presses his lips together before talking softly, "Yes, we should try harder, but little one, intelligence is not all Anomalies provide our world."

"I know this. Commons are smart as well." She points to me. "My maternal loathes Anomalies… but you do not seem awful at all."

Awful? James of the Pillars?

I glance at his ears. It is a good thing his listeners are set to an extremely low-offense level. The Dome is always listening, and I do not want Marguerite to be punished for her honesty.

He helps me stand. "Why does your maternal think that? Anomalies save our world."

Marguerite shrugs.

I go to the toilet, wondering at her maternal's strange belief. When I return, there is B negative in the air. Warm and savory.

My husband is halfway out the door, and Marguerite's head is bowed. She stares at him still, muttering, near quiet for once. Her arm hangs in the air, hand outstretched toward him. The other pinches her dress, rubs its fabric between her fingers.

"Oh, that is how it is between us. You slink away like a scoundrel, with no farewell to your wife?" I smile, but he does not as he walks back in.

He wears a suit from Urban. A red glow comes from it. Like Marguerite, I stare. Vibrant yellow triangles on thick, flickering, layered, black fabric. Shimmering holographic words. The Dome's crest over his chest. No matter how many times he wears one, it is just as magnificent. Real, and here in Valley.

What if our conceived is like him? Oh, it would be so grand.

He comes to me. I bow my head, instinctual in the presence of an Anomaly.

"I… was going to… just go." After swiping his hand gently along my hair to lift my head, he does the same to his own, front to back. The gesture radiates confidence and a hint of snobbishness he does his best to hide. But when he wears his birth city's clothing, he settles completely into his true position in our world—a six-dot Anomaly. Brilliant. Rare.

Marguerite's eyes flit to every part of the suit and focus on the train trailing him, repelling dirt.

"You do not need to run from me. I know you are—" *more than me*. My voice is tight, laced with feelings I want to hide from him but cannot.

"I…" He watches me, and I drop my head.

Moments pass until I can look at him again. He tries so hard to be smaller, match us, but he cannot stuff himself into a life not made for him. He must wear these clothes when going to Anomaly functions, and one thing is undeniable: Urban fits him perfectly.

"You are most handsome."

"I am a shadow to y——"

I hold up a hand and shake my head. His words only make it worse. They will never be true.

"I want clothes like that," Marguerite speaks my feelings. Plain. Exact. I swallow them. The want. The awe. The pain.

I hug my husband, though the taste of rot fills my mouth.

He steps back. "I will be outside, my love."

I do not understand him. Have never understood why. But my life is what he prefers. What he craves. He could have everything, and yet he chooses *this*.

How lucky he is to have a choice.

Marguerite's head rests on the table as she hums a complicated piece taught to her by a neighbor. Her ClearJuice is half-gone.

I walk toward her, pulling our second chair with me as quietly as I can, and listen. Her perfect pitch is another sign of her intelligence.

I pause, close my eyes, and let her clear, sweet tone wash over me for a moment. Open them again.

She hums Antoine of the Glades's Sixth Sonata in A Minor and seems content to be alone more than most children I have seen. Though perhaps that is because she is rarely alone at home. As of her newest brother, K, she has five siblings. I assume with that many children to care for, no one bothered to give him a proper name. Still, with her desire to be alone, most likely, she will be a Third before booking one. I set the chair across from her and start my search for the B negative.

Where is it coming from?

I smell again. The oven. I open it. No, a cupboard above it. I pull out a small dish sitting on a towel. Steam seeps from under its lid.

I sit and place it in front of me. A note is taped to the top. It reads *A surprise for you and our infant*. Under it, sage and onions sprinkled on wight.

I sniff, *mm*, and take a bite. His tongue is a little sharp for my taste, always was, but James of the Pillars has cooked Alejandro just right. Slightly chewy. Soft, tender inside with a nice crunch on the outside. I take another bite. His swollen taste buds slide across mine, spreading seasoned oil and spicy onions. Tart. Earthy.

So good. Oh, so good.

I bend lower. Smell the steam of him. Catch a hint of that buzzing life that remains in all things. His flavor explodes in my mouth. Savory B negative mixed with cardamom and spicy Nyroot.

Brown eyes, tiny cleft in her chin. His infant has the same blood type. Salty, though, not savory. I met her once.

Will she need glasses like him? Always be one snipe away from being reprimanded like him? Make others laugh like him?

I chew him more, thinking on her. How Alejandro spread ointment on her elbows' fresh barcodes and cooed away every one of her watery hiccups. How he adored her. How she would have loved him.

I pause, a small, fatty mass between my teeth. Not savory at all now. I set my fork on the plate, the last piece of him still on its tines.

She will never know him. Not even wonder. His daughter will get a new paternal, and her old one will never be mentioned. I swallow him slowly.

185,000 units.

Would she think that is enough? Is there a number enough for memories stolen? How many have I taken?

I stare down at Alejandro. Close the lid on him.

"Little one, is that your favorite of Antoine of the Glades's songs?"

"No, it is my least favorite."

She continues humming, softer than before. I listen with no more commentary. Though she is in my home, this moment is a private one.

She stops humming and bolts upright so quickly that she blurs.

Whirring.

Marguerite and I stare at the door. No whirring.

We jump when three strong knocks sound through the window.

"I did nothing wrong!" A man screeches. There is a small scuffle, a grunt, and after, a groundVan's door slams shut.

Whirring. Silence.

Marguerite looks at me, her finger tapping like a hummingbird's wings. "The BloodBid only takes rogues, right? That man... did something wrong, right?"

I nod.

"I am scared of The BloodBid more than him."

"You do not know who he is or what he has done."

"No, but they did not have to be so mean."

She pouts a moment before gulping the last remnants of the beverage. The man seems to have disappeared from her thoughts. I stare at her throat. *Ding.*

Her youthful vocal cords could help her family immensely, especially when combined with her pitch and flavor. 125,000 units at least.

I am curious to ask her why she hums her least favorite song with such passion, but I will wait until I walk her home. She watches me, watching her. "I will donate my vocal cords… when I am older. I will never sell them. That will cheapen them, right?"

Her position is understandable, and she is wise to defend it, but these are the thoughts of a child.

Hmm, maybe tomorrow. Today, I will leave her in the dark. "Yes, Marguerite, they are priceless."

She smiles. "My eighth birth day is coming. Do you think… I will reach Vow age?"

A year after her new age.

She gets up in slow segments of movement. Stiff now, like a poorly maintained 100-aged woman. We do not have enough wight, ClearJuice, medical treatment, or anything else to give her a youthful vigor. Or to prolong her life.

"What makes you so sad?" She grabs the cup.

"My conceived causes me pain." It is better to lie, sometimes.

She pushes the chair in. It squeals against the worn, dingy tiles, and she hums the high tone by reflex. Soon, she transforms her leaning board into a walker. Its four wheels are still in good shape, but one of the metal handles will need another cushion soon. She goes to the molder next to the stove.

"What'cha want, marm?" Her face is serious. She wishes to become a happy-maker so she can 'talk all day and bring joy.'

"I wanna plate-uh." That small addition. The Western Urban accent. So grand.

She puts the cup in the molder and presses a button; it grumbles loudly, buzzes, and opens. When she turns to me, I scan the plate: It is scuffed, and a bulge disrupts its bottom. But that does not damper her enthusiasm.

Since she was two-aged, I have half-listened to her incessant chatter. I know her well. She wants to attempt a happy-maker move that would greatly impress. Her hand shakes lightly, but I do not stop her. I only observe what she will choose to do. She lifts the plate, looks at it, and flips it once. Smiles widely.

"I will not do more. If I fumble, you will have to purchase another... for your food and beverage."

I wash the dishes, grab jackets from our bedroom, and head outdoors. The front door creaks closed and locks itself.

We bow to James of the Pillars. He is sitting on the concrete of our side yard, slumped over in his magnificent yellow suit. It is far brighter than the most vibrant home's paint.

Crumbs fall into his lap. Collect there. He does not wipe them away. Does not notice his suit's beauty or savor its silky feel. It is nothing special to him.

He has worn Urban clothing all his life.

I go to him and drape his blue jacket over his shoulders; it flares and shifts to match his suit's color. He does not move, only stares at the ground, thinking hard, pushing dirt into his mouth as our ancestors did during the famines. He eats more than most people, as he enjoys the taste and smell of it.

After swallowing, he whispers to himself a while and holds a finger to his forehead. His eyes glaze over. Turn red as he joins a brief meeting. My husband leads the others, talking much as he pinches the dirt. Smells it. Eats it while he is listening.

I walk to Marguerite before pausing and watching him. A message pops in my head. I swipe my forehead and dismiss the weekly scheduled event: 7 and a half morn. Husband must be milked.

"Farewell, James of the Pillars." Marguerite sucks in a breath. "Enjoy the dirt!" She sounds bright, naïve, like a seven-aged child should, but when she looks at me, a soul far more exhausted than mine stares back. "I like dirt. I will join him the next time I visit."

"He will like that."

James of the Pillars's lips are bloody. He has not been careful of the tiny rocks. I trail my eyes down him. The suit hangs from him. He has grown thin these last few months.

I regret our conception was successful, but not for long.

We will have that better life.

I will guarantee it.

FIVE

MARGUERITE AND I hold our palms out to my husband even though we will not receive an answer in return. It will not be a grand day for him. He hates being called to duty, but going to the milking station is necessary. Anomaly females need his sperm.

A flash of Sapphire blue, then another, then another, move behind a home. The three of them step into the light, statue still in a triangular formation, arms to their sides, palms up. Their beautiful Urban suits flare and change color to match James of the Pillars's.

One walks to my husband and buttons his jacket. Goes back to the others.

They stand near fifteen feet behind him, waiting for him to ask something of them. Anything. The Dome refused his request to be alone in Valley, so his Keepers wait all day.

I do not know what to make of all my husband has, is, how little it means to him, so I push it from my mind and make nothing of it. I do not want to become bitterness and envy.

We turn toward Marguerite's home. She lives in the four-room section, one mile south.

It is 4 and a half, so the sun is not beating down on us yet, but every couple of minutes, she must rest.

Four hundred seventy years ago, citizens were allowed to have any life position they wanted. They languished. Most never found their purpose, and much potential was unmet. Be glad our world has The Vow. Your favored show, Today in the Past!

The streets are emptier than usual. Soft light comes from the strips implanted in the ground and casts a glow for the maternals, paternals, and children out working. The light reflects off the charms dangling from the parents' wrists. Most have at least two.

Some families gather dirt to put in their meals; others hum tunes as they work, and a third shout at one another, cursing the early hour, ineptitude, or broken tools. As we have done with Marguerite, a few families help—and get help—from one neighbor child.

I must make it back home by 6 morn.

We stop, and I adjust the strap of my prosthetic. Even with a cover under it, it twists and digs into my waist. Always a reminder of what I lost. And what I will have again.

It has been months, and I am still waiting for James of the Pillars's newest version to arrive. Still missing the magnificent prosthesis he made me. It was fleshy and warm, but The Dome took the leg and required him to innovate thirty new designs. They said he filed his paperwork late and punished him for creating without their approval, but it was not his fault. That stupid woman put his request in the wrong category.

And our lives changed. One errant request and The Dome began watching him closer than ever. Us closer than ever. Not only does he have listeners in his ears and viewers in his eyes—like all Anomalies—but because of her, he also has watchers on his hands monitoring his written messages.

My unease rises with the sun. It gurgles in my chest, growing stronger the closer we get to Marguerite's home. Still, to get this over with, I want to go faster, but I keep this to myself and walk beside her. For my patience, I get chatter. So much chatter. Marguerite does not waste one of her excruciating breaths. She talks on and on about every little thing.

"Rock Toes are the best candy. My dolly does not come apart. How strange. One of my medicines tastes yucky, like a dirty human."

All things I know.

I sigh. Loquamouths. Bottomless geysers of words that drench all near them.

"Are you afraid of The Wall?" At this question, Marguerite turns to me.

"I have never seen The Wall, so why would I be afraid of it?"

"No, I meant—" One of the wheels on Marguerite's walker hits a large crack, turns, and she pitches forward. I grab her jacket before she falls and yank her back. She rights herself.

"Many thanks. How much is my paternal worth?" She adjusts her jacket on her shoulders as she looks at me, having forgotten her question about The Wall.

I do not remind her, as I do not know my answer, but instead think on her paternal. "With cancer of the bones and so few birth parts attached. Is his blood sweet or sour?"

Marguerite gasps and crashes down into her walker's seat. Pulls a tissue from her pocket. Out comes ragged, body-shaking coughs. The jacket's pressure must have disturbed her lungs. After wiping the sweat from her forehead, she puts the tissue back and taps her thigh. "I do not know. I think sour."

Hmm. His possible numbers pop up in my head; I tell her none of them. It is not our way, and she deserves more than speculations.

"Hard to say. His worth depends on many factors: markets, Need Maps, blood type, flavor, etc."

She continues tapping.

I browse the homes around us, the art on the doors. Stunning. No two doors have the same base color. I look into the small windows, but only my faded and distorted reflection is there. Over time, the synthGlass has yellowed and become cloudy.

My hand itches to copy the doors' designs into my notebooks. Weave them around the eight faces I have drawn there. Meticulously drawn in each new notebook. They bring me pain, but I do not want to forget them.

Chittering and squawking fill the air. synthSquirrels, synthBirds, and other small animals move here and there. We do not need to feed them, but they are pleasant to have, so we pay to keep them installed.

Two young girls gnaw on a tibia until their paternal shouts for them to come inside.

At their age, these children should know better than to advertise their family has ever had a calf of wight.

Ding. 100,000 units each.

They stand, pull the bone back and forth, yelling, and only stop when the bigger girl wrenches it from the smaller and pushes her down. She gets up and shoves her sister back. Raises both arms above her head and lets her wrists go limp.

Echoing screams and overlapping cries ricochet in my head. Raised arms. Limp wrists. They are always in my nightmares.

The older sister raises the bone; her sister raises a fist—and their paternal comes out. He grabs the bone, slaps the older one on her back, and shoves them into their home.

Neither will have the tibia, which is a good thing anyway: They were doing it wrong. The bone must be broken and heated to get to the nutty flavor of the marrow.

The man's worth—his *ding*—fades from my mind. 140,000 units.

"What does my paternal's marrow taste like?" Marguerite taps her thigh harder.

"I do not know. I have not had cancered marrow."

She looks in the distance. "Will his wight make others ill?"

A boy with straight black hair and diluted ClearJuice-colored skin like the others runs screaming through their yard. *Ding.* Two-thirds his sisters' worths. He pauses only to kick off his shoes. Bolts into their home.

No conceived of mine will behave like these horrid children.

Marguerite pulls at my arm. I look down at her. "Will his wight make others ill?"

"It is extremely unlikely."

"Why?"

All these questions. Does her maternal answer none?

"Cancer is difficult to give to another. Possible but immensely difficult. His wight is good."

She taps the arm of her walker and stands. "It is not good for him!"

"I know, little one, I know."

Inside the home, there is silence—until the children come out carrying a heavy, locked basket filled with clothing, wight, vegetables, and water. Usually, there is a wheeled carrier for this basket, but they are being punished, so they must walk it a mile down the road to the Past-Knowers.

Marguerite sucks in a breath; her face is blank as she thinks hard. The look is familiar, but I do not know why. She coughs. "If it is good wight, why does it only go to the Third and Fourth regions?" She coughs hard again and goes silent.

I let her think on it. She shakes her head and walks in front of me. I smile at her back.

Why is always a grand question.

A moment later, I follow her. More relaxed the more steps I take. I have always enjoyed walking, so I tasked myself with taking Marguerite home. Even now, with my extra weight stressing my back and foot, it is pleasant.

We pass the children, who grunt along. The eldest sister holds the basket on her head. They bow to me as much as possible.

The sisters are too tired to fight anymore, and the brother has been punished for their poor behavior. He says he will fight them later. Do children ever learn the lessons you intend to teach them?

Near the garden is the large, multi-family home of the Past-Knowers: a well-kept, tall building with beautiful art on all doors. Inside lives the 50-aged and older—wise from their experiences. They are the third most important people in our world. All give to them and ensure their health and comfort because they have lived the past.

They can help us not repeat it.

Marguerite's breath wheezes and she pants heavily, but I do not stop. I wait until she holds up a hand. She must define her own limits, not crave for someone to define them for her.

We stop. She settles onto her walker's seat, next to the tall, flat, gray rock I sit on. The same one I sit on every Thurs when I walk her home. I am in peace for a moment as she stares at the bracelet around my wrist. She has always been fascinated with my charms.

"When did you get your eight charms, marm?" Her voice crackles.

"Some recent, some long ago. Most with my previous beloved." I try to envision his face, his smile, anything about him, but I do not remember what he looks like anymore. Or how he laughed. Or how I felt when I was with him. I only see James of the Pillars.

It is odd to mix old lives with new ones. Old beloveds, old children, old feelings. I am glad our world does not mix anymore. What use is it to revisit a past completed?

I adjust my leg. Sweat has gathered in the prosthetic. "Do not call me 'marm' in public. I am Common. 'Marm' does not befit Commons." She smiles at me and nods.

The wind blows, cold despite the rising sun. I pull Marguerite's hat down to cover her ears, her jacket up to cover her neck. If she catches another illness, she may not live to see the next week.

"What did you feel when you received them?"

"Proud. With these charms, we could survive hard months and long shortages."

"My maternal has one charm." She scratches her earlobe. The top half was sold long ago. "She purchased it after my birth and cried after receiving it. She still cries." Marguerite taps her thigh more. "Will you get a ninth?"

I zip her jacket up further. "I may get another charm, but I have not decided yet."

"Oh, well, if not, I will be very happy." She stares off into the distance, her eyes wide and open, her mouth pursed and closed—and pokes my protruding belly button. "Why are you so immense? My maternal was never so." Poke.

"Stop that, silly." I grab her hand and rest it on my belly. Place both of mine over hers. Even through her gloves, her fingertips are as cold as the wind during the snowflake season.

The children come upon us again, wiping sweat from their faces. Their flavors are much stronger than most, wafting in the air: one is sweet, another bitter, and the third savory. O positive.

They are talking loudly, playing Okwu. Laughing now. Patiently waiting their turn to speak so they will not lose points.

Marguerite offers a word as she moves toward them, smiling brightly. It is a grand word that would get many points in the game.

The children stop. Stare at her. Harder at her walker. Its arched handles. Its seat in the middle. Its four wheels. They set the basket down. The girls kneel to me, with their hands in their laps and their eyes downcast. Each with only one birth leg. Gray dresses. Hair styled in the same way: two braids combined at the back to create a heart above their free-flowing back hair. Dangling cowrie shell earrings that end in a dark pink lotus bursting out of a thick circle.

The boy—far shorter than his sisters—uses a stick with flat pieces of wood at both ends to hold the basket. He sets it down and holds himself in a plank position on the ground. Lowers his eyes. His shirt gapes. A long, old keloid scar crests along one of his shoulders; his birth arm was harvested long ago.

Sweat rolls down his hair—shaved all around with a shiny bun at the top. His seashell necklace bares the same flower, the same circle that cannot contain it.

They do not move but wait patiently.

It is good to see they have *some* respect for their elders.

"A grand morn." They rise after my words.

Greet Marguerite next. Each holds their palm an inch from hers. Anomalies touch; we must preserve space.

The younger sister's lip curls, and the brother narrows his eyes at her gasping breaths.

"I can help you." Marguerite gestures toward the large basket.

"How, übel?" The younger sister's voice is loud. "You cannot even walk yourself, let alone carry this."

"Do not call me that." She looks at the eldest, who looks the most tolerant, and spreads the handles of her walker longer and wider and lowers the seat—smiling hard all the while. "None of us will carry it. You can… put it on the top of my walker and roll it. I will sit in the seat." She gasps quietly. Cuts it short. "It will work… I, I read this method in a book."

"It does move smoothly. We shoul—"

"No, brother, come. She is defective and smells like year-old garbage." The oldest girl fans the air and lifts her hand, palm up. They help her put the basket back on her head and assist her in supporting the weight. All three flash their palms quickly and walk off.

"May you break your legs and be slaked!" Marguerite shoves her walker away. It slams into the side of the rock next to me and tips over.

I have seen a slake. Heard the screams. Piece by piece, the baking takes days.

She stares at the ground as she rights her walker. Sits beside me while brushing rock dust from its metal. Putting the handles back to their usual size. "I did not want to help them with… that stupid basket, anyway." She winces at each inhale. "I like being alone."

68

I wipe the dust from her fingertips. Push her slumped shoulders back and lift her head. "Being alone is a gift to the strong. Know this."

I glance around. Hold her palm up. Press mine to hers.

'And in other news, protests against the infant registry are spreading across our world.' Faded images show from my device, as it has determined I am sitting. A kaleidoscope of citizens from different regions and continents plays over my vision. Small batches of them with shaved heads, nearly naked bodies, and loud voices. They stomp the ground and hold up signs. Others carry infants with large numbers written on their foreheads, backs, and stomachs.

"Infants should not get barcodes; they should be at least... three-aged." Marguerite holds up three fingers. "I will protest."

"That is grand, but I hope one day, you will have no need."

Marguerite stares at my belly, smiling once more, her eyes Terrain-large. "You are as big as my tía... who double conceived."

"Mm-hmm. In this way, I am an anomaly. Different than others. It is how I was birthed. Most females—even Anomalies or those carrying conceiveds of Anomaly bloodline—do not have such huge bellies." I pause, rubbing my stomach, reveling in the prestige of my husband. In the possibility I will birth an Anomaly. Maybe... maybe even a six-dot.

I cup her hand again, and she raises a finger on the other.

"Are you going to poke my belly?"

She shakes her head and yet moves her finger closer. *This child. What am I to do with her?* She sets her finger on her thigh. Stands. We continue to her home, strolling along side by side.

"All Anomalies live in Urban. Lucky them." She gets that faraway joyful look on her face once more.

"Most live there, some in the First regions, others elsewhere. James of the Pillars lives here with me."

"Will I become an Anomaly?"

"No, you are born of two Commons. But your pitch is a sign you will receive a good life position. In the past, it was rare, and so it remains."

"James of the Pillars has... Common parents?"

"Yes, he was raised by them, but he was born of two Anomalies. His birth parents perished."

"Oh, that is sad. Why can I not become an Anomaly?"

So many questions.

"You do not carry the Anomaly gene, and your brain will collapse itself rejecting an implanted one."

"Will your conceived become an Anomaly?"

I shrug. "We must wait until his eighth birth day."

"How did you meet James of—Are we defective?"

I pause, my breath coming in tiny heaves. It is an excuse. I am thinking of an answer that fights the one drilled into my head. Finally, I say, "Just because you are Common does not mean you were made wrong."

"Well, I am glad we are Common together. Do we belong here?"

Again, I fight an answer given to me long ago. "I do not know. Valley is the floor, and The Dome has large, dirty feet."

Marguerite wobbles a little. "I am glad to live on the floor. It means we… are the ceiling of another room." She leans into my side before holding herself upright. "James of the Pillars is an Anomaly. Why does he live in Valley?"

"My husband lives here because love doomed him."

She pauses, continues walking. "Why did you doom him?"

We have arrived. I stop where I always do—ten feet to the side of her home—and let her go to the door alone. At the threshold, she turns to me, waiting.

"He begged me to."

SIX

I MUST BE back by 6 morn.

This repeats in my head while I say a quick farewell to Marguerite and turn away. Behind me, her maternal comes from their home.

Xaia's shoes slap on the ground and drag across the concrete. No steps to struggle down. Four-room homes do not have a porch.

Like me, she is missing a birth leg. Her right, while I am missing my left. Unlike me, she is also missing her other leg and an arm.

We rarely meet, as our working hours are so long. And, of course, because she despises me. But today, I do not have the strength to move quickly so she will not see me, so I close my eyes. Her face lingers in my mind. Marguerite looks much like her.

Xaia does not say anything. I open my eyes, unwilling to keep acting like a child, and turn to her. Hold my palm out.

Ding. 65,000 units.

She is looking in my direction but not seeing me. She does not return the greeting. Her eye is a washed-out dark brown, like mine. Vacant and very unlike Marguerite's gray eyes. The other eye is covered with skin, a gaping hole underneath. I am glad I did not have to bear her scowl, but this look is much worse. She is desperate. Beyond exhausted. Running out of everything needed to care for a perishing husband and daughter.

Oh, Marguerite.

"She has had half a pound, potato soup, two fruit bars, four tomatoes, and a glass of six oz." Xaia does not react to my words, only stands there. Still. Head held high.

The pole chafes, its wood rough against my young skin, and I cannot move. And the wide bands hold my arms at my sides, and each one binds me to the pole stuck in the floor. They are tightly wrapped around my forehead, and my flat chest, and my wrists, and my knees. I stand naked in front of my maternal, staring into her eyes, and her gaze is clinical. And her face is comatose. And when she unties me, the bands leave grooves on my body.

I cover them with my clothes, but the feel of them remains.

As she hugs me, I rub my head against her and try to wipe my skin's memory of the binds' feeling.

"Stop that. You are not meant to forget." My maternal kisses the binds deeper into my forehead and hums my favorite song.

The gentle notes fade as I stare at Xaia. Twenty-five-aged to my thirty, she is haggard and sagging at every angle. Patchwork synthSkin covers her. Most likely, none of her birth skin remains.

I peer into a window, clearer than most. Deep bags under my eyes. Lines above my eyebrows. Dry, ashen, peeling skin. Better than her, but not immensely so.

In Urban, she would be beautiful.

In Urban, I will be beautiful.

Finally, she nods. "Many thanks."

She goes back inside and closes the door softly. The deep, undisturbed resignation of her magnifies the sound of the door closing. It is much louder than when she slammed it in my face five years ago—after seeing my six charms.

Five years. I cannot believe it has been five years since I first delivered Marguerite home. I stare at the door for a few minutes, following the magnificent lines and perfect brush strokes, thinking on her maternal.

Xaia is a proud woman, a grand maternal, and a thread's snip away from breaking.

I adjust the belt around my waist and begin the mile back home. The door opens once more. I turn to it. K, Marguerite's youngest brother and hater of pickles, stumbles after someone nudges him from inside. He secures his balance and toddles to me. A three-aged child, he is learning responsibility and courage.

When he reaches me, he lowers to the ground, hands on the smooth concrete, back straight, eyes downcast.

Most boys his age hold the greeting sloppily and fall soon. He does not. She has taught him well.

I acknowledge him. He gets up and greets me. Digs into a small unzipped pouch at his stomach and drops a balled-up piece of paper and a vial into my hand. Like Marguerite, he is missing a pinkie, but his walnut complexion is richer than hers. *Ding.* 12,000 units. A little more than two gray market arms.

"From my mat-mat." He looks at me with scrutinizing, intelligent eyes. He does not know what she despises me for, but he knows I am unwanted—unforgivable in his maternal's eye. When he tires of staring at me, he goes back in. The door closes.

I open the crumpled paper and read the stunning cursive:

You. Oh you, wicked woman.

You are not a Donation Facility. Do not feed my Margee again. As you well know, I do not believe in your methods of income, and I am not a taker of false charity. Here is payment for your "generosity." Know that if you come within a mile of my home without my express permission, I will report you to The BloodBid—and rid our world of you.

I shiver, but not from the gust of cold wind ripping through me, and walk again. I do not understand Xaia's dislike of me; I did what was needed to survive. How can she not comprehend that?

Still, her words bounce in my head as I walk. They all sound like *not worthy.*

Halfway home, I stare at the vial. It is James of the Pillars's design. Red cap. Illness free. Cold. Up to five days. I do not know how it works exactly, but it is comfortable to hold.

I open the vial and smell her flavor. *Mm*, a moderately sweet A positive. Nowhere near as pleasant as Diane Candies or Marguerite, but lovely nonetheless. Pockets of undiluted sugar cane, immensely sweeter than her natural flavor, checker her blood.

Adrenaline. From her rage at me.

I put the cap back on and slip the container and note in my dress' pocket. Zip it closed. It is a little before 5 and a half, and sweat drips down my back.

I continue walking, fanning myself. Down a cross street, a woman sways and stumbles while walking. I watch her, hoping she will turn off and go into one of the homes. She trips and falls to the ground. Slowly gets back up.

Other citizens jump out of her way. Terrified. She is not drunk or mentally ill but sick with The Blaze.

Autodevouring became illegal after a town of five thousand worshipped and ate their own wight. Ugh, how horrid. Do not follow their example. Your favored show, Today in the Past!

Rather than walk faster, I move to the farthest side of the road. Go another way. Go another way. But she turns the corner, growing closer to colliding with me.

I keep my eyes trained on the ground instead of on her dark green skin. Still, I see her. The woman sways in my direction, turns, and falls on me. I jump back, and she collapses—perished before she hits the ground. A sourness, stale with a hard, piercing edge to it, pours from her.

I move away as fast as possible, watching as her face bloats more under her matted blonde locks. Her skin

76

only has a few splotches of pink left. Dark pink like uncooked wight.

Her lips are frozen in a fish's pout. Thick black veins shove them outward. Those same veins cover her body, dividing her skin into pieces. She has scratched deep welts in her skin and, like all others, has perished with her eyes wide open, clouded and blind when they had sight three days ago.

Alejandro bubbles up from my stomach and into my throat. Savory, tangy, acidic chunks. I swallow him back down, but I cannot unsee her.

Her open shirt. Her barcodes, now masses of oozing flesh, are burned beyond recognition. An upside-down triangle broken into pieces carved into her stomach. A message under that symbol: *Crush The Dome.*

The woman has gone without her daily blood filterings intentionally. She is a rebel. Their bodies are found when least expected, and they are dangerous. Teeming with contamination—bloated, unsafe.

The Blaze has consumed her, as it did billions of our ancestors. In a few hours, she will explode from the building pressure. I mark her location in my brain's device and continue home. A groundTruck will collect and dispose of her soon.

I must be back by 6 morn.

SEVEN

JAMES OF THE Pillars is not in our yard, but he has dug a deep hole in the semi-soft dirt and written musical notes and engineering formulas around its edges.

Left tiny bits of them for others to see and for me to hide.

I want to pass the hole. Leave it as is. Go inside and replace the sweat-filled sand between the silicone and shell of my prosthetic and rest the aching arch of my foot, but I fear someone will find what he has left behind.

I do not know what will happen, but Urban will punish him if their business leaves Urban—and I will lose him.

I walk to our invisible fence; it lights red and allows me in.

He has tilled the soil and watered the row of vegetables. A few small tomatoes and carrots will sprout soon, even though the dirt is salty and our water is not clean enough to grow plants well.

An update pops up on a Need Map. Green now covers 30 percent of Second Europe and Second Asia. An immense temperature spike shut down the plant houses in their Valleys and Abysses and perished the plants. They will request food from us first and look to other regions if they need more.

Those plant houses were not made of the best materials; it is no wonder they failed.

I scan the Map a minute more as my heartbeat grows faster. After I swipe my forehead, the update goes back to the miserable place it came from. No more. Not now.

I focus on my monthly Share meeting later today, where I will trade food with my friends. It is always pleasant, and the short walk to my friend's home, three blocks from me, will calm me.

The formulas around the hole are complicated. The script childish. I brush my foot across his handwriting and push the pile into the hole. Stomp on it so the sides cave in—but there is not enough remaining dirt to fill the emptiness. Pathetic.

A pounding heat floods my body, and the mess on my shoe grows filthier the longer I look at it. In my mind, it spreads over my shoe and climbs up my leg. I stomp the hole again. The rebel woman, the hidden musical notes, Marguerite, the lack of dirt.

Stomp. Stomp. Stomp. Stomp.

There is more. Urban is more.

I will have more.

But do you deserve more?

That voice. My voice. Always whispering in my mind.

Are you worthy?

Yes. Yes?

Maybe.

Sure? Common, Valley, lying wife, what makes you worthy?

I… I do not know. I stare at my dirty shoes. Can I be worthy if I do not know why I am?

When I am about to scream, I walk up the stairs to our small, bright yellow home with the dreadful door. The second stair sinks under my weight. I leave my shoes on the porch, lined up front to heel, and slam the door shut. It locks behind me. I open it and yank it closed again. It locks once more. Locking means nothing; it is an illusion. No window, room, or life is locked. The Dome will enter. To take.

Sunlight bathes our home in a warm glow. I close my eyes and take measured breaths. The inferno simmers down, blue-hot lava burping up every once in a while. I inhale. Exhale.

Again.

Again.

Open my eyes only when the eruption has gone back to its usual state: scalding embers waiting to explode into a fiery tornado.

I pick my plate up from the table, flip it, and spin it twice on my fingertip. Most likely, that was the happy-maker move Marguerite wanted to try. I smile and place it in the cupboard above the tiny refrigerator, next to James of the Pillars's cup. Put the vial in the fridge and lean into the cold air. Glance at the pinecone there. Stare at Xaia's blood. At my charms. If not for them, we could have been friends. But

'In Valley, you never do well for long.' My paternal's words echo in my head as I pull out my ClearJuice and close the fridge. She is wrong. The charms were needed.

I rub lavender-scented antibacterial sand onto my hands and throw the small ball into the recycling to be cleansed.

"Stop," James of the Pillars whispers from our room. I go to him. He clutches our blanket, his breaths quick.

"Wake up." I pat his nightstand.

His eyes flutter open, frantically search the room before settling on me.

"James of the Pillars, it is me. You are okay."

He pauses a long time before releasing his grip on the cover. Reaches out and grabs my hand. A long while passes as he holds onto me.

Finally, "The door is innocent. I interrogated it this morn, my love." The panic fades from his drowsy voice.

Napping during his thirty-minute filtering is needed, but it is not always successful.

I sit on the bed next to him. "I am listening."

He sits up and wipes his eyes. Holds me from the side. "I know ya are, my love." He doesn't say anything more about his dream, only closes his eyes and hugs me tighter. Whispers, "I'm glad ya still wit me."

"I have no intention of leaving."

"Please don't." He loosens his grip slowly before letting me go.

Is that what he is haunted by? Something else?

Husband, what is it? But I do not ask him this. I have tried many times before. He will tell me when he is ready.

"You know what you need?"

"Tell me." He opens his eyes and smiles.

"The best ClearJuice in our world."

"But the kitchen is so far, my love."

I put the back of my hand against my forehead and close my eyes. "The journey will be difficult and possibly longer than your break will allow, but I will manage." I open my eyes and sigh heavily. "For you."

He laughs.

I go to the kitchen and fill his cup with my ClearJuice. Pour slowly, making sure the liquid reaches the line I've marked—not over, not under.

Right at the line or they will take him away.

The voice, always the doubt and fear, whispers in my mind.

Do not go over.

My hand trembles.

If I fill it just so, to 6 oz. exactly, we will be good. I will be good.

I check the line a fourth time and stir in a pinch of cinnamon. Breathe out. Once more. The quivering under my skin calms.

Our bed creaks as James of the Pillars gets up, his filtering done. Throughout the day, The Blaze's contaminants build in our blood. Fresh blood must replace it, or we will perish in three days.

I shake my head to clear it of the rebel woman so I can focus on what is to come—the shower. It is dry now, but it will not be for long, and I am most excited.

Ouch.

I rub my stomach; our conceived hits out a second time. Little violent one. He is strong, and his feet and elbows are painful. I rub the sore area as I add a sprinkle of cinnamon to the top, right in the middle, and go back to our room. Pause in the doorway.

James of the Pillars stands in the leftmost corner, facing the wall, his head angled to the right. Praying. In the Inventor faith, they are taught to focus on the thin space where the two walls meet—the present.

His breaths are short, and his fists are clenched. It is difficult for him to stay there. Here, with me. In the present. The left wall, the past, can be so easily lost in. It is vast and filled with all that happened before.

But the past is not his main enemy. The right wall, the future, is what swallows him whole.

Rarely do I find him staring at his past. After five years, I still do not know much. He avoids it meticulously.

I walk in. James of the Pillars does not turn to me but continues staring at the chipped paint and cracks in front of him.

"When we are perished, our names will go on The Wall. Do you think we will be remembered as merciful or as monsters?"

I walk to him, turn his head to the present. "Only now, my dear. We do not know the future."

"Are you sure?"

"Yes, it is as blank as this wall."

"How do you know this is true?"

"I do not, but we have learned from our mistakes. We will not forget the past, so we can write on an empty future."

I hug him around the middle, press my body close to his. Bury my nose into his shoulder blade. Slight tangy sweat. Him. All of him here with me.

I stay there long after I have kissed the back of his neck. Nuzzled the glowing red words stamped into his skin there; those same words are etched into my and all other citizens' necks. He stares into the present a bit longer, lowers his shoulders, and turns around in my arms. Smiles.

"Oh, scary." I lean back. It is a grimace with a bloody smile stapled crookedly over it. I nod, bowing to him as he runs a finger down the four raised dots at his temple. Kneads the last one softly.

"Think less, my husband."

I move my hands behind his head before wrapping one of his curls around my finger. Jerk a handful down to touch the back of his shirt and cover the words there. He exhales and closes his eyes. I swipe my finger back and forth across the soft, raised skin before letting his hair go. A few curls sit in my hand. I let them float to the floor.

Since he is an Anomaly, those same words are branded into his forehead—'Property of The Dome.'

He opens his eyes. The dimple on his left cheek deepens as he smiles harder. "What would I do with you gone?"

"Eat brains all day, clean less, and drink myths." I hand him the cup and kiss him passionately. Rub my thumb along the thick, black edge line across his chin. "But sadly, there is no myth in this cup."

"How unfortunate. Next time, do better." The dimple is like a tiny bullet, drilling in now. "Why were you angry at the door?"

"A rebel fell on me. Disgusting. And I dirtied my shoes outside."

He looks toward the outdoors. "Oh, that is my fault. I will clean them at my next break."

"Thoroughly?"

"Always."

The fear slithers back down, clinging to the sides of its bottomless trench. "It is a grand day to be alive, my dear."

"Yes, it is. Every day is." He smells the drink. Licks his lips. "Mm, cinnamon. Many thanks."

"You are welcome. Do you know the day?"

"I do." He kisses me with equal adoration. "Only one day of the week elicits such excitement in you." He takes a large gulp while stretching one arm high above him. Bends. Rests one hand and two lips on my stomach.

"It is Thurs, and this day brings your maternal great joy," he says through my belly. "Why is that, my little one? It is because it is…"

"Double Water Activation Day!" We say in unison.

I will take a shower at 6 morn, and he at 11 eve. Taking a shower alone is a grand luxury. It is a wonderful day.

He stands, and we make an exchange. I hand him my prosthesis; he gives me the crutch, leaning against the wall next to him. Shoos me away. "Go. Enjoy. I will make a morn dessert to celebrate."

I lean forward and stare into his dark brown eyes. Closer until the sliver of gray that circles the brown is revealed. Closer until my breath is against his lips. "When you return next morn, let us cheer each other."

"I am most excited." He kisses my ear. Presses himself to me, closer until I swallow loudly. Steps away.

Waiting for the morn will be a gentle torture.

I walk into the toilet room fifteen minutes before 6 morn. It smells like sanitizer, but still, I scrub the sink, toilet, and showerhead. Undress. James of the Pillars has put a chair under the water's spray. I hold the support bar and sit slowly, resting the crutch against it. Gently massage the deep bruises the belt has left. Pain shoots through my belly and into my chest. My breasts have grown three sizes and hang low. I hug them to me—grateful they are with me and not skewered on a stick or frozen in a plastic-wrapped package with three other breasts.

No. No more. I shake my head of these thoughts. A moment before the water turns on, the scent of frying wightcakes fills my nose.

Four hundred seventy years ago, there were no Commons. Only Anomalies. Before The Blaze struck our world, all had the creative ability. Can you believe that? Your favored show, Today in the Past!

Mm. The water cascades down my body, warm enough to be comfortable. I clean myself in a minute so I can enjoy the remaining nine. I close my eyes, and the chair under me disappears as I drift off into the deep recesses of my mind.

James of the Pillars and I are well off. We live in his home at the top of Urban. He only eats dirt when he wants, as he does like the taste. My prosthesis is flesh-colored, flexible, and I walk with ease. It feels more like my birth leg than any ever has.

My husband holds our two-aged child, whose head bobs up and down as he dozes and sucks his thumb. I kiss his fat cheek and press his head to James of the Pillars's shoulder.

We go to Ancient Dreams regularly and enjoy our world of centuries ago. The dining room's magnificence surrounds me again:

Cream-colored walls with gold trim, intricate arched doorways and windows, a chandelier above each of our tables. Splashes of light create glittering diamonds in the room, and I have on semi-glossy black heels with my blue dress. There is no bracelet on my wrist.

I am there, and I am one of them—an Urban citizen.

Whirring drills against my ears. Pushes my heartbeat higher.

Cold slams my body. The water has gone off. For a moment, my eyes see only a world of excess—love and comfort and prestige. The walls are a freshly painted cream color, and the outside of our home is not brightly painted; it is nothing more than a place to sleep, eat, and cheer. It is not a symbol of hope. It does not have to be. I want to be there more than anywhere. I want to be worthy.

When my lips tremble with cold, my vision of excess fades, and I crash back into our home in Lower Valley 7: cracked walls, thick synthGlass that blocks out my neighbors, chilly wind, a tiny toilet, and stained floors. It is too much of too little. Melancholy creeps in as it does on Double Water Activation Day. Sets its heavy weight on me. The droplets of water cool on my skin, raising goosebumps on every inch of my body. I detest this life and want another.

Humming. Perfect pitch.

James of the Pillars's tone is deep. Indescribably handsome, passionate, and competent. He hums an unfamiliar song. A new song. Complicated with many tones dipping, sliding, and jumping into one another.

We will have that better life.

He is my key to Urban.

I partially dry and dress, grab the crutch, and go through the kitchen. His eyes are closed; he is immersed in his humming. Does not hear me going to our room. The tall dresser is against the wall that is shared with our kitchen, so I write his humming on the notebook I left there. Each note is easy to hear.

Music swirls inside of me. It fills my brain and lifts the melancholy from my heart. I write quickly, capturing every note my husband offers. When he effortlessly hums C5, I lose track of what I am doing at the high tone and scramble to remember what I have missed.

He stops humming, but bits of it are still in my head, fading quickly. I write faster, sprinting across the page before I forget the complex melodies that are far more skilled than Antoine of the Glades's. When I have written all I can remember, I stop.

The later notes are sloppily written. Hideous. But they are there. Pages of his composition scrawled in a most embarrassing script that would make any of the low-class ashamed.

I fix the barely legible sections and fold the notes. Tuck all but one page in the left pocket of my dress. In my right pocket, I tuck the first page.

"My love?" I turn around. James of the Pillars's face widens in surprise and contracts in guilt at the same rate.

In his hands are two plates, held low. A small, circular, steaming wightcake with boiled ClearJuice sweet sauce leaves the scent of wealth in the air. The circle is perfect. The designs are not. On top of the cakes are clumsy blobs of black mud. Mine is AB negative. With our savings, we splurged a bit and purchased a few pieces of this wight, as this rare type is my favorite.

I bow. Sit on our sofa. A specially designed cushion that is higher on one side supports my pelvis. James of the Pillars hands me the plate. His own wobbles, tilts, but he catches it a second before his food hits the floor.

He positions a pillow behind me, and I sit back, comfortable. "Many thanks."

He motions to the mess atop the cake. "I-I tried."

He does that a lot. A lot more than I assumed an Anomaly husband would.

Still, I sniff deeply. *Mm*. "It is magnificent. Well made."

"You are welcome."

He leaves and returns with my prosthesis. Thoroughly cleaned. No sweat remains in it. Only fresh sand. I put it on as he sits at the other end of the couch. We watch the children's show for a moment, turn toward one another, and play a silent game where we mirror each other's movements as we eat.

I do not tell him what the Need Maps told me: another shortage is coming, and we will have to give much more this year. I only smile harder. Laugh longer.

Later. I will tell him later.

The game goes slowly. James of the Pillars uses a spoon, while I use a fork. Spoons are easier for him to manipulate; his eyes and hands do not mesh well. Every once in a while, he bumps his mouth with the utensil. I bump mine too.

On our last bite, I give him my fork, and we use our hands.

A nibble before he sets his plate on the table. "What do you have in your pocket, my love?"

He did see me. "Nothing of importance."

His gaze narrows, focusing on my dress, and his face hardens a little. "May I see?"

"No, it is my concern." My heart thumps faster.

"I do not believe it is. What do you plan to do with your concern?"

"I—"

"Submit it to The Dome?" He comes closer and puts his hand out. I turn away, but he is faster, even with so little blood. James of the Pillars grazes my pocket the first time and hits his hand on the sofa's arm. He does not react to the pain that must be thrumming through his arm but pulls the sheaf of pages from my pocket and skims them. When my husband is done, he rips them. Holds them.

He will not leave them anywhere, as he knows I would put them back together. I have done it before. He gestures to my other pocket. When I shake my head, he looks away.

"I will never submit… anything. To submit these pages would doom me to a misery I have not experienced." He picks up his plate. His hand shakes.

"I understand."

"You do not. The price is too high, and I will not pay it."

"Tell me then, what will it cost?"

"I cannot. Before I could, but I cannot now." He swipes his forehead. "You know I am bound by Anomaly law. And Urban law. All business remains within."

He points to his ear. Of course. I had forgotten for a moment. His listeners. The transparent films that blur when he mouths words.

The Dome may need the Anomalies, but they have never trusted them.

The page in my right pocket digs into my hip. What kind of wife would hide this from her husband? An unworthy one.

Still, I say, "We could live well, my dear."

"Truly? Is that all ya care about?" His low-class accent slips into its original, relaxed Urban, as it does when he is greatly pained. He stares into my eyes. "I-I don't know what else tuh do." He glances down. "Am I not enough?"

I pause. "You are, but this life is not."

"I choose this life, mah love."

He is right. I do not understand him. "If I could choose, I would pick another life. This one was given to me, and it will always be a horrid, festering gift. Why would you choose this?"

He lowers to his knees and speaks in the low-class accent allowed for everyone's use. "I choose you. You are worth every sacrifice. If you must be here, in this existence, I am most pleased to be here as well." He kisses me and places both hands on my stomach. The pages make a barrier, rough compared to his palm. He presses his lips to my belly button, staring so hard it is as if he can see through my skin.

"May we, my love?"

"Perhaps." I put my hands over his, and our conceived kicks.

James of the Pillars swallows hard, closes his eyes. "I want this."

"Well then, perhaps you should take your Vow, and you can have what you want. We can have what we need."

He pulls away and grabs the plate. Stands. Glares at me. Sighs and steps away. He looks at the pages in his hand with equal measures of a snarl and a longing—and crumples them.

I stare at my plate. His misery is my fault. Without me, he would not live as a four-dot. He would have his six dots, the immense privilege that comes with them, and Urban.

He will never say it, but I know. I know. I am a burden, a heaviness he does not know how to lift and throw aside.

I was born wrong, and to love me, he cannot fully be himself.

"I apologize."

"You have my trust. Do I have yours?" His face is soft now.

"Yes, my dear."

I ignore the page in my right pocket. Its existence is evidence of how much he should trust me.

I hold myself still as he stares into my eyes, his gaze moving back and forth. Searching.

Finally, he pushes his last bite onto my plate. "Nothing good will come from a submission." He rubs his hair. "Taking my Vow will lead to horror. Only horror. Trust these words."

"What can be more horrid than this life?"

His face goes blank. He presses my fork into his plate. Scrapes it across. The high-pitched noise screams through the room. Like the sounds at my position.

"Stop that." At my words, he sets the fork down. Bends.

"I apologize, my love, I apologize. I did not mean to…" James of the Pillars hugs me. His arms are tense. Still, he hums "Uzuri wa Kawaida"—the song he wrote for me when we met.

Its creeping melody glides into a faster pace and, a second later, crawls once more. Quiets the guilt and screams to their usual volume: a soft, burning breeze.

When I no longer tremble, James of the Pillars goes to the kitchen. His footsteps echo as he paces the small area surrounding the table, muttering to himself—to someone called "you."

There is a loud pause. A clang when he sets his plate down. The scent of burning pages and repressed potential fill our home. I hold my nose. Still, I taste it on my tongue: Bitter, thick, slimy. A maggoty mass that rots forever, unable to decay to nothing.

A door closes. From the toilet room, his drowned sobs torment my ears.

The price is too high.

It always is.

EIGHT

REMEMBER THAT IF your personal ledger has no units in it, you will not have access to your shared ledger. Your beloved cannot monitor your private account, so always be responsible and work hard. Your favored show, Today in the Past!

Our Share Meeting was canceled, so I walk from my friend's home holding a bag of unshared onions. Turn my face to the sun as I do. It has fully risen, and I marinate in its warmth a moment.

When I reach our home, I set to work, stirring a few more strawberries into the bowl. Adding some onions, more sugar mist, and a hint of water. Taste. Hmm, a bit more mist.

It is done.

I pour the mixture into a one-inch tall pan, lace the top with onions, and put it in the oven.

Our kitchen fills with the smell of fruit and sweet. There is nothing to do, and so I sit a moment.

Close my eyes until the timer beeps.

These will be the best Jam bars I have ever made; I will make sure of that.

After I have cut them and put them in the fridge to cool, my access card, as gray as my dress, vibrates. Words scroll across its top: "Your travel request has been accepted."

I head out to catch a hoverBus.

Because I may carry an Anomaly, The Dome granted me access to the wight market on the line between Terrain and Valley. Usually, James of the Pillars purchases the wight, as I am not fond of the task, but I would never skip the chance to go to one of the markets in the largest region. Would never give up a chance to leave Valley.

A small group of people, most of whom are my colleagues, stand at the stop, waiting for the hoverBus. Concrete, small bushes, and a tall, thin pole is all the stop is made of.

Some are pregnant like me. A few rub their bellies with joy, most with exhaustion. Flat rocks provide pleasant seats. Other people wait a few feet from us, in a large marked triangle that will lower and give them access to the groundTrains—sleek carriages with 12-foot-tall ceilings that travel hundreds of miles an hour.

A handful watch me as I approach.

They have seen me walking with James of the Pillars. I stand straight. Hold my palm out to all of them. They return the greeting.

To be the beloved of an Anomaly is a grand honor.

I slow down as I get closer and hold my back even straighter. Scowls and panicked nerves emanate from them.

"When will the machines be fixed, miss? I must go back to work soon; I am running out of units to pay The Dome. I must purchase more food before the shortage." A man bombards me when I reach the bus stop.

To be the beloved of an Anomaly is a grand annoyance.

Ding. 40,000 units.

At the man's words, the group's tension rises further.

"Do you think it will be a horrid one this year?" "A shortage is coming? I am not ready." "How much do you think the other regions will ask of us?" They hurl questions, fears, at me from every direction.

Dings. Their possible numbers pop up and block out their worries: 60,000. 45,000. 25,000, oh, how horrid.

Three hundred seventy years ago, The Dome created the sorting machines to distribute blood and wight to citizens. How lucky for us all. Your favored show, Today in the Past!

I focus on the first man as the questions pile atop one another. Red permapaint sits in the grooves of his nostrils as it does mine and all other Auctioneers.

One keening voice pushes through. "I do not have anything to spare, miss."

I train my eyes harder on the man's nostrils, the color, to block their mountains of terror out.

At nine-aged, we received our paint. That day, our life positions were assigned based on our natural ability to smell the different flavors of blood. Most discerning children become Wight-Harvesters and Tasters. Far fewer become Auctioneers.

I shade my eyes against the sun. The people in front of me are clearer in its shadow. Exhausted. Disheveled. Though they have groomed themselves well, their unraveling nature sits in the slump of their shoulders. The panic in their words. The rising resignation in their eyes.

I do not want to see this anymore. Them anymore. Me anymore.

"I am not sure when the machines will be fixed. I—"

"What do you mean? Are you not the beloved of 'the grand James of the Pillars'? Has he not told you? I must feed my son." The man is rawboned. Thin in every area that should not be thin. Black rot fills his mouth, and his heavy makeup covers the deep green underneath. It gives him a somewhat normal complexion and strengthens his skin, which is partly translucent because of The Blaze.

I close my eyes. Looking at him hurts. But he is seared in my mind. A teddy torn apart.

He stands on two creaking, worn prostheses instead of two legs and a pelvis. A crutch is under one arm, and the neckline of his sweater sags. Underneath it, he has the same scars as my maternal—jagged, puffy ridges above the areas where his clavicles used to be.

His complexion is a kaleidoscope. Like Xaia, massive sections of his skin have been harvested and replaced with synthSkin that does not match his original coloring.

I open my eyes. He is pointing at me with an ancient prosthetic arm and glaring. Pulling an older teen closer to him with what remains of his birth arm. A tether at their waists connects them.

His rage slips, falls into the desperation it is trying to burn away. The man's eyes are as large as a child's and trained on me. "What about my son, miss?"

There is nothing I can do for either of them, yet here he is, pleading for anything. I stay silent a bit longer before looking away, to his boy.

Ding. 110,000 units.

He is close to a healthy weight, of a regular complexion, and whole-bodied. He has five red bars of increasing height stacked side by side on each of his cheeks and makes odd noises, twitches, and mumbles incoherently to himself. Or no one. Or everyone.

Like his paternal, his clothing is a patchwork of grays, poorly fitting, and the graffita designs are blurred and broken. His skin glitters. The tiny energy-harvesters placed all over his body take his electricity and store it in two clear, flat batteries—one attached to his chest and torso, the other on his back. Both programmed to zap someone if they try to steal the energy. He is lucky to work as a Battery.

I look back. The man's eyes are locked on mine. "My son, miss."

"What about your son? How dare you speak ill of an Anomaly, Abyss filth?" A woman far from the man looks like she may attack him.

"Yes, what arrogance. What can you do but what any Auctioneer can? Sort blood and read Need Maps."

Another man sniffs hard. Waves his hand dismissively at what we can do before pointing at the paternal. "Do you know how to fix the machines? Can you innovate better ones?"

The man shakes his head. "N-No, I do not, cannot, bu—"

"I voted against allowing you people out of Abyss. You do not even look healthy. I thought only the healthy ones were allowed out." A different woman crosses her arms over her chest, moves further away. "You will bring horrid strains of The Blaze. More shortages. I know it." She snarls at him, his son, and others from his city. Their thick makeup clearly marks them as not-us. Some twist their faces in return, but others lower their heads.

"New strains? Untrue. You speak from fear, miss. We are worthy citizens who work hard and contribute the most wight to our world," a woman shouts. Her makeup is more natural, thinner than the man's.

And her words are true. I have heard there is a white groundVan on every corner there, collecting them.

"I think they should be allowed tuh visit." A man sitting on a rock shrugs. The front half of his hair is braided in intertwined horizontal designs hanging to his ears. A short row of triangle-shaped gold beads decorate the ends of the braids. A bald stripe splits the front and back half of his hair, and the back is cropped close.

He sits on a towel to protect his clothing from dirtiness.

Ding. 710,000 units.

Unlike our dingy, faded gray garments with light colors at the hemlines, his are exceedingly clean and vibrant. Several colors, slightly pulsating graffita designs of many triangles, and bold words grace his outfit. Only a few patches are of a duller color. Horizon-born. Common like us. I study him, enchanted by the brand-new fabrics and designs. "What harm do their visits do us?" He glances at the woman.

"What harm, sirn? Look at him," the first woman is quieter when asking this, respectful now.

The man shrugs again. Horizonites have a pleasant, laidback manner and few worries since their city is one below Urban. Why fret? He has access to filterings, water, and grand medicine at all times.

Arguments break out as the people fight over how soon the shortage will come, how much better their bid numbers are than others, and whether those from Abyss should be allowed access to other cities.

James of the Pillars and I fought over this decision as well. He voted for their restriction. As one of his votes is worth fifteen of mine, and many Anomalies agree with him, I believe they will lose the ability to travel.

Maybe the same will happen to us in Valley. I close my hand into a tight fist. Stupid Anomalies. They do not understand what they are voting against; they have no idea what it means to be locked in. How small it makes your life if you are never allowed out.

The Dome has issued a new law. Listen closely.

Silence.

Distribution Law #180-76: Cattle flesh is restricted to regions and cities with enough energy to support the animals. Any other citizens found to be conducting illegal markets or auctions will be bid without question, mercy, or units paid to their families.

"Excellent. We'll eat well." The Horizon man wipes dust from his pants, oblivious to our glares.

Only First, Urban, Horizon, and Upper Terrain citizens will be allowed cattle. A shame. I like pig and cow.

We wait a moment to make sure no more news comes, as it reports at any time, and our conversation shifts back to the first question about the malfunctioning machines, the shortage.

"The Anomalies are not trying hard enough. You heard the news. Why should they? They are doing well. She is doing well." A man gestures to me.

He is wrong. I *seem* to be doing well. Seeming can never be doing.

"The Anomalies do care; they are trying their best. You must be patient." Another man looks around for support.

In the silence, a woman glances at me and clears her throat loudly. "Please, miss, tell us, what's taking so long? It has been hours." At her polite tone, the crowd calms.

Why does everyone believe I know these answers? I know nothing. It is hidden behind Anomaly law—as James of the Pillars reminds me every day.

"I am not sure. I apologize. The machines are choosing wrong or sorting wrong or... something." I turn from her to the first man. "And if you speak poorly of my beloved again, I will ensure The BloodBid comes to collect you. You have forgotten your place."

I stand taller. The crowd quiets, avoiding eye contact with me.

"The Anomalies are trying their best. My husband is trying his best. He does not know how to try less than that." They stare at me, and I look at each of them. "They *will* fix the machines so we can return to our positions."

Soon. Please soon, my husband.

I know they would never believe me, but I am as upset as they are. Each hour we do not work, The Dome removes units from our personal ledgers to pay for our absences, and I am not exempt.

Some of them nod, and the man squeezes the teen's hand. His son leans into him, releasing a shrill sound and flapping his hand rapidly. The light from his battery glows bright under his shirt.

When it is full, The Dome will distribute his electricity to every regions' Urban.

Still, a few of them regard me as if I broke the machines. Hard glares until the polite woman gestures for the paternal's arm. He hesitates before motioning for her to come closer.

Another woman steps several feet to the side, whispers, "Careful. You know he is very"—she looks around—"green under that makeup."

"Don't be that way." The woman flexes his hand back and forth, holds his inner wrist to her nose, and smells it deeply. Terrain-born. They believe flexing the hand will bring forth the better blood.

She smiles. "I wanna say... 20,000 units."

"What, that is all, miss? I am a sweet O positive." He pulls his hand away and speaks to the man in the black vest next to him. "Please do me the grandest of favors, mister, and tell me of better numbers. For my darling son." The paternal's anger and panic drip away. He holds back a grin.

The man walks to his other side and sniffs his wrist. "Empathy in care. Objectivity in numbers. That is our mission." He glances at the woman. "Half 20,000 units by my assessment. She tells lies." They laugh, and so do a few others.

Add your conceived's wight to their registry. Relax knowing you have completed their checklist. Oh, and be specific. Fat ratios and lengths are appreciated. Your favored show, Today in the Past!

None of us will give him his true number.

I sniff him next. I would assess him at 40,000 units, but I offer a meager number. He smirks at me.

Everyone but the non-Auctioneers relax. They look at us as if we have gone mad, and we let them. This is our way, and so we continue.

Ding. 156,000 units.

A girl with one red line down each of her fingers keeps track of our assessments. Adding and subtracting. Calling out the new totals much quicker than other Calculators I have seen. By the time the orange hoverBus lands, our combined worth is Abyss negative, and we are at peace.

A paradise of Commons.

"Please be silent," the driver tells us after we have sat down. Our joking subsides, and we slip into our thoughts. I settle in and close my eyes as the Terrain bus rises. It is warm, clean, and the seats are plush. Best of all, it is excellent to only sit next to two people.

Their *ding*s are crowded out by a richness like thick, freshly made stew circulating through the air. A few people are on their Gold Week.

I cannot wait to have my conceived, so my Gold Weeks will continue. It is grand to be rewarded for our unfertilized eggs.

Numbers pop into my head—plus, minus, balancing—as I attempt to anticipate how bad this shortage will be and how we will survive it. I breathe out, pull the silky air in, and push the gnawing worry away. It fades as Ancient Dreams floats into my thoughts.

The patrons wear vivid colors, gold decorations, and headwraps. Others are in muted color-shifting tapered pants, layered dresses, and skirts. All with short trains trailing them. Most of their barcodes glow, but I am as welcome as any other Common citizen from Urban, and—

I open my eyes when the person next to me taps my shoulder.

"I have asked you three times. You and your immense belly have made me miss my stop. Let me out."

I get up and let the woman out of our seat.

She sucks her teeth. "No wonder you learn nothing from your husband. You do not listen to him." She gets off and glares at me as the bus lifts. I hold my middle finger against the window, and she stomps off.

I settle back down, my hands on my belly, thinking on her words.

Stupid woman. I do listen to my husband.

The seat warms more, and I forget about her. Terrain's hoverBus is much slower than Urban's, but it is still a quick fifty-mile ride from my home. Not enough time to dream more. In a few minutes, I reach my stop at the line between Upper Valley and Lower Terrain. Around me, others walk through. Onto their business.

104

A shimmering is ahead of me. I walk to it. Hold my hand near the invisible barrier between the cities. Watch the people in the market.

I have gone through many times before and, every time, wonder: will it reject me this time?

NINE

I TOUCH THE barrier. It lights red and lets me through. I step back, into Valley. Forward into Terrain.

One step can change everything.

I walk fifty more and reach the market. Many flavors of wight hit me: Lots of A positive and O positive, O negative, AB negative, *mm*, and so many more. Numbers are everywhere. From the citizens' bodies. From the wight on the tables.

I push their worths away. Quiet the *ding*ing that is now a loud roar. It is exhausting. Crowds are exhausting.

For a few moments, all the magnificent smells fade into a coppery nothingness. I suffocate the guilt turning their flavors bland—no matter how fresh they are—and continue shopping.

Terrain citizens fill most of the market. Polite, friendly, and somewhat thin, they greet me with wide smiles.

My cheeks ache as I return every one. The day brightens, as it always does when around them. Only those of the hardest hearts can resist a Terrainese smile.

The market is enclosed in a squat, metallic building dominated by an immense hallway with many doors to smaller rooms. Everything about The Dome's facilities are sterile. In this one, the temperature is cool, and the walls are designed in rows, some pushed out, others pushed in like a zigzag. They reflect a distorted version of my body—slices of me shift back and forth as I move.

A few trios of The BloodBid, Commons like us, are stationed at the hallway's beginning, middle, and end to ensure no laws are broken. Their clothes, hair, skin, and irises are red. Permanent alterations to their bodies.

Only a few in our world are allowed to wear red or The Dome's crest. It is imprinted on their uniforms' chest. Nine triangles close enough to form a larger triangle. Five red triangles on the left, a diagonal strip of three golds in the middle, and a red one on the right. "Terrain" is written below the crest. It is also along their backs.

They move silently, slowly. Watching us.

We bump into one another to avoid them. Trample others' space to create a wide circle around them. Trails of furtive glances are all that is left behind us as we scurry along.

I scurry. Maybe if I match the pace of the other dancing feet perfectly, The BloodBid will not pick me from the pattering waves.

I focus in front of me, attempting to ignore the dread, a barbed chain tightening around my spine. On both sides of the hallway are toilet rooms stationed 100 feet apart. Only a few flies hover. Hints of stale, hardened sourness waft through the air. Nearly expired wight on sale for a low price. I never purchase these. Today should be their last day in this market. If they do not sell today, some will be sent to Valley, most to Abyss.

I smell deeply. In… five days, the flesh will show black spots, but most are fresh. How pleasant. I adore this market.

Some sellers have precut wight while others take custom requests. As they cut, the table drains each piece of its units and deposits them into The Dome's underground filtering system. The birth flavor stays with the wight because of the Hasp enzyme. It is absorbed into the body after the auction and requires a heart rate of at least 200 beats per minute to activate.

The tubes below the semi-transparent ground fill with red. I watch them until my vision shimmers. Travels back to my youth. No. No more. I shake away the sucking thoughts as my stomach rumbles——hungry and nauseated in the same amounts.

I walk down the aisle. Signs hang from the ceiling, the offerings inscribed into the thin metal: 'Hearts,' 'Brains,' 'Thighs,' 'Feet,' 'Candies.'

I go to the candy. The table's tent board reads:

We have Dianes. Join us, and be grand.

An assortment of shapes, colors, and prices litter tables, and a man and woman monitor the booth.

A little girl bites into a bar covered in caramel. In her other hand, she holds six more by their sticks. The intricate holographic "N" on the gold and black wrappers shimmers as she eats. Other children and adults order from the sellers. They hold their elbows under The Charge and greedily grab the amount the sellers give them.

"I did nothing wrong!" A man shouts from further down the hallway. The citizens give him a wide berth, and the girl and I watch him a moment. A member of The BloodBid places a white patch on his forehead, and he falls unconscious on the ground. They drag him to the side of the hallway.

"What is that? Is that good?" I greet the girl. She bends low, straightens, and holds out a messy palm with a wide smile.

Ding. 220,000 units.

She shows me the candy's inside. "See?"

A deboned, half-thawed finger is in the middle of the caramel, surrounded by chocolate crunch.

She takes another bite. "It's called a 'Melting Finger.' Very, very good, but you must eat it quick, miss."

"Yes, or you'll get punished for getting candy on your clothes." A boy with one long, thick, black braid turns around, bows low. Unbends. His skin is like chicken broth with a bit of tomato boiled in. His worth is a bit less than the girl's, and there is a deep sadness to him. Like Marguerite's, but more desperate.

'We must survive, my angel.' Another voice. Always in my head.

I adjust my prosthetic. Relieve some of the pain of it.

The boy greets me, and a second later, pulls a whole candy free from its stick. He jostles the turquoise medallion dangling from his neck as he chews hard, eating as quickly as James of the Pillars. After his first swallow, he points to the far end of the table. "There're 'Twisted Skins' over there and 'Rock Toes' next to them, miss. The big ones cost eighty units each."

These children are Terrain-born, two cities shy of Urban, and it is evident in their somewhat laidback speech.

"Many thanks, little ones. Drink water with your candy." They nod and head to the walls for a sip of water. Red dots crawl through the crowd, lurking, circling us. I push them from my mind and browse the table. There are many options. I skip over wight-free, but circle back when a seller waves me over.

"C'mon, you look like someone who is adventurous and enjoys trying something new." *Ding.* 250,000 units.

Hmm, I do like trying new things, and the Terrainese do carry Dianes.

Since the tiny cost will not help us during the coming shortage, I purchase a wight-free candy. The taste is as magnificent as I remember—until I swallow. It is bland. Still, I grab a few for Marguerite and James of the Pillars. Some small 'Rock Toes,' a handful of 'Twisted Skins' of various ages, and other candies go into my basket. I will get two 'Melted Fingers' when I leave. One hundred units altogether.

Do not forget to put Kuru Acid in your infant's bottle. Their bodies can create it, but they must consume other citizens' acid to remain healthy. Your favored show, Today in the Past!

110

The crowd parts, and we bow low. I strain my eyes upward.

An Anomaly girl walks through, flanked by her three Keepers: one in front and the other two on each side, slightly behind to ensure she does not fall. They are clad in black. Arms at their sides, palms up. Her eyes are glazed over red as she strolls along, recording the market and applying possible solutions virtually.

About nine-aged, she is dressed in the finest Urban clothing. The vibrancy of her dress' color nearly blinds me, and still I stare. Multicolored bands with a base tangerine color wrap around the many small puffs of hair parted into her head, and five dots sit on her temple.

Large, gold earrings of an intricate circular design with small chandeliers hanging from them adorn her ears. A gold necklace that ends in white seashells wrapped in small gold beading cascades from her neck, the shells larger near her navel. Her tangerine dress—Egyptian blue ruffles to her elbows and lace sleeves with neon graffita woven into them—is immense beauty surrounding her dark brown skin.

The girl is on an Imagine Trip and will visit each city in Second America. *Ding.* Freeze. Calculate. 25,600,000,000 units. Her number is nearly unbelievable.

She breathes in deeply. "Am I allowed a piece?"

She focuses outward and turns toward the table. Between her eyebrows are three white dots, painted down, big to small. Another is on her chin. Her eyes are bloodshot, surrounded by puffy bags, and her lips are pursed tight.

The sellers smile wider as she and her Keepers stop walking. A boy groans softly. The prices are ten times what they were seconds ago.

The Keeper pauses. "Yes, that—" All three of them wince hard and grab their foreheads. "No, I'm sorry, marm. The Dome said no. Ya diet don't support it. Maybe... in two months."

"Just one, just one, I ain't had a piece in so long. Please."

"I'm sorry, marm."

The girl looks at the children next to me. A few of them look up with their chocolate-covered mouths, sugar-dazed smiles, and zoet-stickied fingers. Wave at her.

She sighs and nods. "Buy 500 fuh 'em." She gestures to the children and continues walking. Her eyes unfocus, and we rise only when her two-foot train has passed.

The sellers freeze, looking at their ledgers, then jump a few times. "Children, it's free candy day!"

"Her dress is Terraintastic. She's got much luck. Get some sweets for your conceived, miss!" A different little girl holds her hand full of candy sticks out to me and runs off. A new batch of children and adults rapidly replace her.

I watch as the crowd parts further in the market. Touch the page deep in my pocket while I marvel at her dress's splendor.

"Before you go, miss, we have a special on our newest beverage, 'The Carotid Countdown.'" The woman smiles widely at me, her teeth straight and white.

Ding. 230,000 units.

The candy's prices are lower once more. Okay, one more sweet, and that is it.

I transfer the units and grab the lightly ticking beverage. When I touch it, a ten-second countdown appears on the tiny, squishy bottle. The ticking grows louder. I look at the woman.

She shrugs. "No one knows exactly what'll happen when the countdown ends. Sometimes, it explodes. Other times…" She shrugs again.

The man laughs. Leans toward me. "Few wait to find out."

Hmm. I wait the ten seconds. The bottle and the liquid harden. The smell is not so sweet anymore. I bite the top of the bottle, break off the semi-hard liquid inside. A gentle fizz bubbles in my mouth, and relaxation flows over me. I close my eyes.

Open them.

How grand.

I browse the other bottles. Different sizes, colors. Just. One. More. Then I must go. This time, I drink the beverage immediately. The fizz explodes in my mouth, nearly painful, and spreads into my nose, eyes, lips, and ears. Sweet and relaxing. I swallow. It settles the worry churning in my stomach. The nagging voice always reminding me catastrophe is an inch away. I do not want to move. For a short while, I want to have no cares.

When it wears off, I get one of every non-melting candy for James of the Pillars. They will keep until he is allowed to eat them.

After pausing to stretch my back, I move down the aisle and purchase one heart, three packs of breasts, two Tallizin™ thighs, a kidney pie, many small packs of dried meat, and a jar of pickled pinnas (the earlobes are my favored part). I bypass delicacies, as I have already gotten much candy. Three thousand units later, my cart is nearly full. It hovers next to me.

The girl is long gone, but the magnificent tangerine lingers. I pull out the page and read his song. James of the Pillars's voice, his high, layered notes, are loud in my mind.

He is stirring a concoction on the stove. Humming as he smoothly rocks his hips from side to side. He laughs loudly, watching an awkward, fluffy-haired, short woman who teaches at an impoverished school for young children. I do not understand the humor, but he adores these ancient comedies.

What would he have called this piece?

Someone bumps me and knocks the page from my hand. Before I can pick it up, a foot kicks it a few feet away.

I hold my belly, pain gathering in my lower back, and push people out of my way.

No, no, I cannot lose it.

I cannot lose Urban.

I will not.

When I get close to the page, a child tramples it, running to the candy table. Another kicks it even further. On purpose, it seems.

Wretched boy. Most likely from Valley.

I lose sight of the page and search harder.

James of the Pillars will not hum new songs again.

I scan the ground, bumping into people.

I will not lose it.

"Watch where you are going, miss."

I give the person a hideous look, and they move out of my way. Shoes, pant legs, and arms swing in my vision.

Where is it? Where is it?

Someone runs past me. There it is. Unmoving. The commotion chaotic around it. A piece of it stuck under the front of a recycling kiosk. I barrel through a woman.

"They are rude, aren't they?"

Her friend nods.

There is some truth to our nickname, "Vulgar Valley," but I do not have time to care.

I go to the page; the thick plastic is crumpled, but inside, the note looks intact.

I open my legs wide and squat, holding onto the top of the kiosk for support. My prosthesis digs into my belly, and my conceived shifts to my right side. Pressure builds in my pelvis, and I wet my undergarments, but I lower more and tap the ground. My knee aches as I search for the page, unable to see it behind me.

I will be most excited to have my body back.

Finally, I feel it. Hold the page tight while my heartbeat slows. I grit my teeth and make the slow, shaky climb back to standing.

Someone snatches it from me.

"Give that back, you—"

I do not know what the rest of my sentence was going to be. It is consumed by terror. A red-tinted hand holds the page. The intricately designed hair of a woman stares back at me. Her head is down, and gold corsets are weaved through her intertwined braids.

Young, so young. Fresh into adulthood. A Martinet. They only look harmless. They are trained even more than other sections of The BloodBid to enforce the laws and stop crimes. Or start them.

Ding. 920,000 units. Yuck. B positive. I detest this flavor.

Her head whips up. She grabs my bicep. The deep scar on it explodes with pain. Even more when she tugs me toward her. "Where'd you get James of the Pillars's composition?"

She pushes me to the floor. My knee crashes onto the smooth concrete. More urine wets my clothes. Well, I hope it is urine.

"I—I" I whisper. "I am his beloved, marm."

The Martinet laughs. "A Common?"

A blur. A white patch moves toward my forehead. I lean back as it whirs lightly.

How does she know the song is his?

"I am his wife, marm. He is a busy man; he asked me to write it for him."

The white patch gets closer. Closer.

Stops when another red hand grabs hers and twists it hard at the wrist. She drops the patch. It retracts and disappears under her shirt.

"You didn't view her citizenry." The Martinet's leader yanks her shoulder, turning her to face him. "Do it now."

Her eyes glow a brighter red as she scans my profile.

"What? His beloved is a Common?" She looks at me, her eyes glued to my belly. "She's not mentioned in his profile."

"Common beloveds are not. They're a stain on an Anomaly. Which is why our first rule is to always check citizenry." Her leader puts his hand out to me. I take it. He pulls me up and pushes her down. She bows to my belly as he presses a palm to it. "Are you injured?"

116

I am sure my knee is bleeding, but that is not what he is asking. "No, sirn, my husband's conceived is excellent."

"Are you sure?" He reaches out to me.

I block him. Drop my eyes and swallow. Pat my vulva, thighs, and butt. I look at my hand. Show it to him. It is wet but not with blood. I lift my eyes.

"I'm sorry. Very sorry." The Martinet touches my belly, too, his worth near hers. Both of them touch it as if it belongs to them. I belong to them. So many hands certain they have every right to touch. I stay silent instead of telling them they do not.

Her hand is warm, shaking hard on my belly. She bows to my conceived once more and stands. Apparently, he has forgiven her from my womb.

She gives the page back. My hand is trembling, too. I put the note in my pocket, but I cannot stop the tiny earthquakes of my nerves.

"I'll inform James of the Pillars of this Martinet's actions and pay for your next physician's appointment. She'll be severely punished and auctioned. A portion of her will go to you." He is not looking at me but staring at my stomach.

"If you do not mind, sirn, I will tell him." I stand straighter. "He is busy on a new project and may take the insult better from me. Perhaps I can convince him to punish only her—and not the one tasked to train her."

The leader glances at me and bows lightly. A nod of his head.

They leave. The BloodBid handles their issues quietly.

My cart rattles as I hold its lip. Little balloons of fear swell and burst in different parts of my body. I check myself again. There does not seem to be harm, but I schedule an appointment with Physician Nore anyway, and continue shopping. We will need the wight.

I pass one of the candy sellers as they go back to their booth.

"Before you go, miss, we have a special on our newest beverage, 'The Carotid Countdown.'" He points to their table.

"You already spoke to me!"

I am worthy. I am worthy. I am worthy. I am worthy.

"Oh, um, yes. I remember." He smiles even harder and disappears into the ocean of people headed to his booth.

I walk on, turn a corner, and go down a long hallway. Come to an arched doorway ringed in red and swipe my access card to purchase brain from the restricted area. James of the Pillars's list of needs for this month is already at the forefront of my device.

The room is immense, dark, and quiet. Near empty of people.

Floating glass containers with red bases fill the space, clear solution swirling inside them. I lean against a wall and watch the brains rotate in the liquid. Stand there, staring until each one grows blurry.

I do not know how much time passes before I skim the brains' features: Anomaly or Common, IQ, Age when perished, Temperament, Blood Type. So many options. After listening to a few of their speeches and comparing their features, I get stuck between an Anomaly and a Common.

A hundred years ago, the Anniversary of Anomalies was established. Fun. Laughter. Citizens, enjoy the free holiday off.

Anomalies, if you are needed you must report immediately. Your favored show, Today in the Past!

Finally, I choose a woman. 110-aged, Common, patient with a streak of rebellion, of an average IQ, A negative.

James of the Pillars's list does not say he needs creativity or immense intellect but grit, problem solving, and wisdom. The woman is more than worthy; her bio card says she spent much of her life at Near Nobility— one of the best siphoning schools in Valley.

I put her brain in my cart, thinking of the best way to tell my husband a shortage is coming, and head home before its cold gel warms.

TEN

IT HAS BEEN a month. I sit on the couch, poring over Need Maps at 1 and a half morn. The room is mostly dark, comforting, but I cannot sleep.

I will not be able to sleep well for the next six months. Though the Anomalies fixed the sorting machines weeks ago, James of the Pillars must still leave for the new project.

Already, I feel his absence. A coldness in our home. Every joke I must answer myself. I do not want him to go, and I know of only one way to get over this missing—get under a distraction.

On the Map, the continents of our world are highlighted in different colors, and I choose various regions for more information. Blinking dots signal real-time updates and important information.

Studying the Maps calms me, as I feel less alone, stuck, when viewing more of our world.

Diagrams overlay my vision. There is more green on the Maps, more need, than there was last month. We have not had to distribute much in three years. This may be our time.

Intense heartburn wells in my chest; the medicine does not work as well as my physician said it would. I glare at my stomach. Four more months, and I will be free of him. I shake my head to focus. Stare at the regions.

In First Australia's Horizon, an earthquake splintered the underground electrical grid, and most of their facilities shut down. Their Anomalies will be punished for the poor design. Their representative requested energy containers from First Africa, but they refused, and so their wight spoiled in the large facilities.

Disagreements between these two regions are ongoing. Centuries before, either food or energy was not shared, but I am not sure who began the fight. History depends on who had the freedom to write it.

Third Europe's Terrain has requested an immense amount of wight after a new species of fome bugs were found in their food. Not many perished, but the insects' saliva caused much illness.

I zoom into the now-orange area: quarantined. The population is large, and there is not enough cancered wight to send, so we will send uncancered wight, too. Most likely, First America will send cattle. They like to keep their wight—and send ours.

Denise of the Pines has unveiled her newest design, Mirrored Paradise. This scooped neck, color-changing dress suit is just 330,000 units. Available now. Your favored show, Today in the Past!

Oh, finally, I have been waiting for her release. She handstitched every line in the original design and has been torturing us for months with a shape here, a color there.

An image of the suit comes to the forefront of my device, rotating so I can get lost in all its angles. Praise floods the forums under it. I turn those off so I can savor her design—and not see citizens buying it directly from the comments.

Different sizes are overlaid on models. One is pregnant, and the layers look beautiful on her. I sketch the magnificent lines in my notebook, take a snapshot, stand, and superimpose the blue dress on myself.

Do you want a dressing room for 60 units?

I nod twice, and our bedroom slips away as a twinkling, gorgeous room rains around me. It solidifies into a large cream-painted space with gold trim and hanging plants. I look into a trifold mirror spanning the far wall.

The tiredness and discoloration of my face is gone. It is plump and glowing with health. My hair is pulled up into a stunning triangle-shaped brown bun with gold beads laced throughout it. The back hangs down to my shoulder blades in three fat braids ending in puffs.

The fluttering strips of blue fabric glimmer in the light. Like my skin. Stunning, smooth, near-black lacquer. I close the cuff links over my wrists and adjust the small clasp purse at my shoulder. Denise of the Pines's signature is stitched down its band.

When I move, the fabric's gentle swishing echoes in the room. The dress flows down my hips and covers my prosthetic. No one would be able to see I am missing a leg. They may believe my limp is temporary.

The long lapels are snug around my neck, sown along the plunging neckline at the back and front. I put my hands in the suit pockets and strike a pose.

James of the Pillars appears behind me, staring. Comes to me and spins me in my soft dermer slippers. I pull him close and peck his lips. He tastes my vanilla peach lip gloss as he trails a finger along the inside edge of a lapel.

"This ancient thing? Husband, it has been in our closet forever.'

He closes his eyes as we sway. I watch him, my fingers craving to draw his lines as I have done so many times while he sleeps. He smiles. I press my nose to his throat and smell the intense crackling life there. Feel his steady heart. Hear my song from there.

He opens his eyes while humming the last note. Our child, little chubby thing, waddles in, grabs his index finger, and pulls him away. James of the Pillars winks at me. Matches our two-aged child's unsteady gait. I laugh loudly and turn back to the mirror.

Smiling harder than I ever have.

Do you want more time for 100 units?

I shake my head twice.

Ready to become more beautiful than you have ever imagined? Purchase Denise of the Pines's newest masterpiece, Mirrored Paradise, for 330,000 units.

I shake my head four times.

Purchase declined. We have archived Mirrored Paradise for you, but come back soon. It will sell fast. You do not want to risk your beauty, do you?

A gorgeous dark gray, gold, white, and orange gown flows like a slow-motion waterfall onto me, and its train follows my twisting. My bun tumbles down into shiny, small, dark gray twists that loosen into large curls. The darkest twists are tied into a ponytail at my neck, and the rest flows freely, lightening to white at my mid-back.

A matching headscarf floats from the ceiling and settles on my head. The intricate designs are perfectly set in the velvet fabric.

It is not too late. We also have a Toghu from Denise of the Pines's vintage LeJohn collection. Her award-winning collection, we do not hesitate to add. Do you want to purchase this majestic piece for only 200,000 units?

Even though a generous fifteen-year payment plan appears under the mirror's message, I shake my head six times.

Purchase declined. Come back within a week. We hope these masterpieces are still available for you.

The room fades. I sit in our empty bedroom, giggling softly. How grand my life will be.

I save the dimensions, sewing patterns, and variations to write them in my notebook later. We are lucky Anomalies are allowed a fun position alongside their life positions; they create beautiful things from their leisure.

I pull up our resource ledger. The patient voice tells me detailed stats of our income, costs, and savings. Though our savings are nearly gone, we are still doing well. I think on the dress—330,000 units. It is *only* 300,000 units more than our monthly housing costs. And with that thought, I switch back to the Maps.

Lose myself in the numbers, figures, and charts. The predictability of adding and subtracting soothes many of my jitters.

I jump when something soft slides across my foot. James of the Pillars is sitting in a kitchen chair across from me, shirtless, with a warm, wet towel in his hand.

"Oh, Oracle, what do the Need Maps tell you?" He smiles as he glides the rag around my foot, over my ankle, and up my calf.

I tell him what I see, relaxing into his touch, though the news is not good. "The shortage is closer, my dear."

A slight pout pulls at his bottom lip, and I laugh. It comes out before I can catch it.

Though my husband left Urban eight years ago, it is easy to remember he grew up in Pillars, one of the wealthiest neighborhoods there. He speaks of shortages as if they do not come randomly, quickly, and often.

"You laugh? I do not understand why. Do you think the network I have set up to assist you will be enough this time? Should I get more Commons? I do not know how many more will volunteer, but I can purchase some. They do not cost much." Yes... it is clear he was born in Pillars. He rubs his hair hard, spiraling into an anxious vortex. "I could put in a request for you to come to Urban with me before the shortage begins."

I do not get excited at that proposal anymore.

Travel between cities is forbidden for everyone except Anomalies and Couriers. All citizens are accounted for during a shortage. His request will not work. It never has. I am legal only in Lower Valley 7, and even James of the Pillars cannot change that.

"My dear, be reasonable. You know they will not allow it. I am unneeded. If I perish, they will open me, take out our conceived, and distribute my wight to whoever needs it most."

He stares at me, horror atop the light scars on his high cheekbones, a light shake to his head. Those with privilege doubt how our world works; those without know.

He blinks. "Still, you cannot stay here. Thieves, violence. No, not now. What if your walker breaks?"

It rests against the couch. At seven months, I am too immense to safely move around with only my prosthesis.

"It will be okay. The walker is strong, and violence does not happen as much as you think. I have stayed through other shortages. Worse than this one will be, most likely."

"You are too calm, my love. Violence is often the result of lack. I do not want you or our son to be injured."

He snoozes a meeting. Wipes my foot. Absentmindedly rubbing hard.

Soon, he drops the rag into a bowl. "A member of The BloodBid could provide far more protection. They are pleasant and dutiful here."

Terror causes my foot to spasm in his fingers. Luckily, he is not looking at me. His viewers would capture my fear.

I choose my words carefully so James of the Pillars's listeners will not hear my ill opinion of The BloodBid. "Oh, the Commons will help me. Do not trouble yourself. You have taken care of all you can." I laugh. An airy, skittish sound.

His head jerks up, puzzled at the unfamiliar sound I made. I flatten my expression. "It would be no trouble. A simple request, and they will send their best to monitor you all day."

No! I let a breath out slowly. "It is okay, my husband. There is no need. I am sure they have more important matters to attend to."

"What's important tuh me's important tuh them."

His words hang in the air. One second, three, seven.

He glances at me. "But I will follow your lead." His distressed expression clears some. "Close your eyes, my love."

I do. He massages my leg, squeezing the pain from my arch and the stress from my calf. His warm palms caress my skin, and his thumbs press circles into my sole, gently rubbing in calm.

I do not go to Ancient Dreams but stay here.

The First regions ration our precious lakes and bravely protect The Dome's second headquarters in the Russian Republic. Take a second to reflect on your contribution to our world. Can you do more? Your favored show, Today in the Past!

He pauses, and I pull my foot away when he slides his finger along the middle of my arch. He holds it tight as I laugh, tickling my foot more. When I open my eyes again, he stares at me, a gentle smirk on his face.

"We have 30,000 units in savings remaining." Talking about numbers relaxes me even more than his massage. "If there is a shortage, we will have to spend much of it on food and your housing. I can put a third of my daily units in, but that is all. Discuss." I pull my foot away again. James of the Pillars presses his lips to the skin where my toes were and sits next to me after releasing it.

We take a picture of our personal ledgers and combine our devices. Go over our shared ledger. There are 50,000 units in mine. 1,200,000 in his. 30,000 in savings.

I stare at the massive number in his account. It is so much, but even as it sits there, I know it is already spent, and none can be transferred until he has more than his expenses.

He winds his fingers in mine. "Valley's security systems are being updated again." Anomalies receive these updates before other citizens. We pre-ordered this version a month ago. "The newest security system should be shipped in two weeks. Will the shortage have already begun?"

I shrug. Need Maps do not work that way. I can only estimate. The Dome will make the official announcement.

"They have added more features since you last saw it, my love." Images and text scroll across our vision: enhanced fingerprint recognition on all windows and doors, the ability to more accurately detect fingerprint copies, and automatic theft reports sent to The BloodBid.

The system is much better than our current one. He squeezes my hand. "Mind the mail."

Mind it? What an odd way to tell me to—oh, I see what he is saying. He will send something to provide more security.

I squeeze his hand in return. Hold it. Message received.

"As for my room in the Innovation Facility, I will request the tiniest space, and I am near certain I can get 200,000 units from other Anomalies. With the stipends from the Anniversary of Anomalies, that should be enough to pay for my room for two months. I have not heard of any increases."

"What if there are no Anomalies that need your assistance? What about your home in Urban?"

"I do not know. I will find a way to pay what remains for my home." He stares in front of him, planning. "I hope they will not insist I take a larger room. I do not need much space to think."

His hope is futile. I do not know why he hopes. The Dome always assigns him one of the largest rooms. 'For his comfort.'

Though James of the Pillars makes much each day, as a double citizen, he must pay three sets of living expenses: ours in Valley, his Innovation Room in Urban, and his four-bedroom home there.

I do not know how much that sums to, but his home is, at minimum, three-quarters of what he has in his ledger now. These rules annoy me, make our lives much harder, but what honor would he have if he did not support his birth city? They supported him for eighteen years.

"I will make more, I promise. Some of their brains are useless; they always need mine."

"Perhaps do not tell them that when you offer the labor."

"Grand advice. I will try to remember that. Your sleep?"

Screams tear through my head. I lean on him. Hug him tight. "I get so scared. I will be scared. I am always scared, my husband. When my eyes close, there is only horror."

He pulls me closer. Kisses the top of my head. "What more can I do? Will more songs help at all? I can record more." He hums a Common tune; it quiets the wails.

"No, the ones I have are perfect. They do help. Many thanks."

I do not tell him more. He has already made immense sacrifices to stay in Valley with me.

His body jolts. I watch as the life melts from his eyes, the red overlay covers them, and the films slip over his ears and mouth. For a long time, I rub his arm, snuggle into his chest's warmth. Every part of him is taut with stress. Urgent Innovas do that to him.

When he is finished, he shifts and buries his nose in my hair. I listen to his heartbeat.

Two hundred fifty years ago, the siphoning schools were created. Are you Common? Can your brain benefit an Anomaly? Apply to join now. Intense criteria must be met. Lifelong training mandatory. Your favored show, Today in the Past!

"I do not want to go." His words are quiet, slow; his heart's pace fast.

"I know."

"I must."

"I know that too."

My husband rests his cheek on top of my head and wraps his arm around my chest. "Our son's name. Any ideas?"

"Not a one. I do not care and so have no preference. You choose, my dear."

"Really, no opinion?"

I shake my head. "Any name will do. He is our property."

"True, but do you not give your favored item a special name, chosen with care?"

"You name. You care. I will birth."

He groans and lies next to me, the top of his head touching my thigh. Staring at the ceiling. I put two fingers to his wrist and my other hand on his chest.

"Your parents can help. We do not have long to decide on his name. His registry must be completed."

"Not now. Please." I close my eyes and rub large circles into his chest to remind him to stay calm. Every couple of rounds, I massage his shoulders. Time ticks by less hurried, as we do not talk, only breathe.

Eventually, "My love, I must go now."

I keep rubbing. He does not move.

Finally, he sighs and nods. Custom for Anomalies. They learn this gesture as children.

"The new designs await." James of the Pillars sits up, and I open my eyes. He kisses me. "I will send wight home each week, and units when I am able."

"Do you think the clinic on 200th St. will still be open during the shortage? What about Physician Nore? Am I still on the high-priority list?"

Nothing is guaranteed when shortages come.

"Yes, you are. He'd never risk… I wouldn't let anyone hurt…" A muscle tenses above his shoulder.

"I know you would not." I press deep into the muscle. A hard knot under his soft skin. "Will you visit your parents and brother there?"

"My parents, yes, but not my brother. First Australia has leased him for a year; they need a Grand Anomaly

131

right now. I would have loved to visit with him, though. Will you be okay?"

'Give all a chance to tell you who they are.' Wise words from an anonymous woman. Circa 2035. Ha, ha. Yes, we do see the irony. Your favored show, Today in the Past!

"I will be well. Do not worry, my dear." I smooth the emotions from my face. "Send me a message whenever you need, but know I will not read even one. As you know, I will be far better with you gone."

"You are too much." He gets up from the couch, laughing. Kisses my stomach while pressing both hands on the sides of my belly button. "I love you, my son. I will see you soon. Know that I very much wish I could be here when you join our world." James of the Pillars lowers his voice. "Please give your maternal an easy birth and do your best to look nothing like her." He blows on my belly button as if it is a candle.

This man.

He hugs me around the middle. Straightens.

"Many loves, my wife."

"Many loves, my husband."

I touch the page's plastic as I watch him go. Though the composition is no longer in it, it still comforts me.

He walks slowly on those knobby knees, and the gaping emptiness in my chest grows the smaller he gets. These will not be our problems forever. Someone knows how to submit his song.

I will find them.

ELEVEN

"DO YOU KNOW anything about Anomaly law?"

This has become the only phrase I've known for the past week. In the spare hours after my position, I have searched all over Valley to find someone who knows how to submit James of the Pillars's page.

The woman in front of me, sipping from a mug of tea, ended my search.

Ding. 3,200,000 units. Magnificent.

Her tea is a dark brown, but her teeth do not stain. They are sealed from imperfections. Her top-floor suite is immense, triple the size of my kitchen and bedroom combined, and decorated in matte magenta and black.

Her bed is against the wall to my right, behind a black curtain, and her dressers are to my left, made of polished magenta-stained oak. A white trim decorates the floorboards and door borders.

It is beautiful.

She nibbles a cookie I brought her. Magenta-colored fennel seeds atop a cocoa-flavored breading.

A tiny waterfall of sweat runs down my back. It is not hot in her room. I glance from her lips to the cookie. "Past-Knower Sauda, are they… to your liking?"

"Not particu*lar*ly."

'Not particularly'? How can that be? I checked her bio many times before our meeting.

"I could get you othe—"

"No. Your question is an easy one. Recently, I found cocoa burns my throat. How fantas*tic* the changes of aging."

Her enunciation is sharp enough to pierce a whale shark's skin.

Oh, I am watching the past this moment. I smile at her, all of my teeth showing.

A magenta robe covers her black, layered jumper, and gold bands decorate her arms and neck. One thin band around her head with spikes connected near the top. A lethal crown.

The circular tablecloth is black with magenta swirls throughout. I resist the urge to touch the fabric; it looks exquisite.

"I will make this quick, young one. It has been many, many decades since I worked in Urban, but I do not think the pro*cess* has changed much." She adjusts. The cushion inhales where she is not and molds to her new position. "Urban changes only when it absolutely must."

Her face is a tapestry of brown wrinkles. Each one a sign of her adoration for life. Each one stunning. She is near 80-aged, and her room's beauty reflects her wisdom.

I wish I had a better question. A harder question. I wish I wanted to know something more worthy of her sacred knowledge.

But I do not.

Three hundred sixty-five years ago, The Dome declared the Rightful Accusation Law after The BloodBid wasted much time on millions of false reports. Never again. Only report true crimes. Your favored show, Today in the Past!

She rings a bell sitting on the table next to her, and another Past-Knower, far younger than her and worth less, comes in and sets a batch of magenta cookies down. Ginger and heavy cream by their smell.

They bow to one another. After the man has chomped through a cookie, he leaves.

I glance at the crumbs on the floor. So much mess. And yet, a Past-Knower likes my cookies. I breathe out the excited rush and focus on her words.

"With your marriage, I do not know what will *hap*pen should you submit anything to Urban, but I will not keep the knowledge from you of how. That is not my place." She crushes the cookie into the tea and leaves it there. "It is my place to give the lessons I am allowed. What you learn from them is your choice."

"Do you advise against it, marm?"

The cookie bits bloat, bang against each other, and fall apart while she thinks on her answer.

"Urban has many *hid*den rules. Anomalies even more. It has been a long time since I have received questions

135

about a Stained Anomaly marriage." My smile falls a bit. I swallow the miserable, outdated term and fix the grin to my face stronger. She blows the tea for a minute. "I do not know enough to guide you one way or the other."

She takes a sip.

Long and slow.

I think on her words. A long time even for a Past-Knower of her age? Oh. I had not thought of that, but it does make sense. We are all born with Common genes, and they often cancel out an Anomaly gene. Most would not choose to combine the two.

She sets the cup down, bits of cookie paste on her upper lip. "But I ask you this: When this my*ste*ry is solved, how will you know if you have won? Lost? Sometimes, young one, it can be hard to tell."

I nod as she drops another cookie into the hot drink. It floats on its back, covering the liquid's surface.

"For a Common, the process is long, complicated, and will take months to complete. Are you listening?"

I hold my pen over a piece of paper, ready to write down every instruction she gives.

"Yes, marm, with every red cell of myself."

TWELVE

TWO DAYS AFTER talking to Past-Knower Sauda, the additions to the security system arrive. I've been minding the mail closely—as the inspectors at the Communications Facility do—and received a package of infant clothing, the deep sludge of Valley gray halted by small bursts of color along the hemline.

Fifteen tiny wires of a matching gray are sewn into the clothes, positioned in four sets of lines next to one another with one horizontal line through them, so I know how many there are.

I spent much of my position's breaks in the toilet room, pulling the three sets of wires out of a pant leg, arm, and collar.

At home, I sit in our dim room, unraveling the gray thread to reveal the true colors.

Now, only to put them in.

The instructions James of the Pillars sent are easy, but the assembly is difficult. I insert the tiny board into the security system's underside and tweak the fuses carefully so they don't break, as James of the Pillars's color-coded schematic shows. The lines are not written by him but a computer.

A fingerprint is on the top right side of the page, so I assume these wires will improve our scanner's identity system. Sweat beads on my palms. I wipe them on my dress and continue working.

Go slowly. They will take him away if you make a mistake.

I check the instructions for the twentieth time, making sure I use the right wires. Making sure they are going in the correct place.

What is he doing in Urban?

How will he be when he returns?

I stare at the schematic, thinking of him poring over its design. Finding a way to use a computer without alerting anyone. I must install everything correctly.

After I've set, tucked, and checked the wires, I open the hatch in the corner of our bedroom and install the system, following the instructions.

The hatch glows red, and I close it.

Turn the lights up a few notches before lying down and watching Urban's commercials. I will not get any more sleep tonight; the screams are rarely quiet when James of the Pillars is gone.

Instead, I pull out my notebook and open to a clean page. Always a comfort when I cannot sleep.e

I draw the dresses, fabrics, and beauty of Urban. Hold the pencil lightly, sketch the soft lines of the seams, slowly fill in the dark shadows of the clothing's folds, and meticulously match the magnificent colors.

On display now is a male in a matte orange pantsuit that shifts to a matte purple as the light hits it.

I take a snapshot when his clothing is in between orange and purple; it will be a challenge to get the colors right. He stands in front of a table, a covered platter behind him, tendrils of steam coming from it.

I stare at his clothing. His hair. It is dyed orange and shaved in eccentric triangles of lightly varying lengths. What artistry. He poses, spins slowly, and smiles at the camera. I request a copy of the suit be sent to my device, so I can view it later.

When he finishes presenting the clothes, he moves to sit at the table—squat slow, slide in. The table's top is sculpted in triangles so small you can hardly see them, and his face reflects off the polished Purple Heart. A most beautiful wood.

He lifts the lid, takes a bite of mashed kale and chews.

1, 2, 3…

I write it all down.

Sun, 5 Sept 2493
Designer: Denise of the Pines
Chews: Thirty
Clothing: Orange matte pantsuit with a 1 ¾" Jakkar stitch down the inseam. 2" stitch on the outseam. 5" black Plinot lace around the ankle, wrist, and neckline, which is also between the tiger stripes on the outfit. Orange shifts to a deep eggplant purple

Train length: One foot long. Black with orange and purple stripes

Shoes: Glossy orange. Two-inch wedge heel manufactured by Santos on the Strip. No strap. Uses heat suction

Lips: H2341 Mauve (mid-gloss)

Model: Rashad VI

Sex: Male

Height: 5'3

Citizenship: Common. Birthed in Urban. Neighborhood of Hilda

Costs: Rashad VI (20,000 units to lease for the night), Table (40,000 units), Mashed Kale (7,000 units), Platter (12,000 units), Suit (150,000 units)

He struts off, and orders pile up in the comment section. The camera swivels a few feet to the side, and another Intimate, Rashad VII, takes his place.

—+—

The BloodBid woman's hand arrives two weeks later. Boneless. Small. B positive. Eww. My least favorite flavor.

For a moment, I see it attached to her wrist. Feel its warmth as it shakes like my own. The moment ends, and I cut it into cubes. I get lost in the cutting, the perfectly straight lines, and only stop when a loud beep comes from the wall.

The news:

"Severe shortages have been declared in multiple regions of our world. Distribution Law #90-25 has gone into effect. Each citizen of First and Second regions must distribute 25% of their resources

to aid others; those from Third and Fourth regions must distribute 35%. Consult your ledger to see the changes."

Our fridge is half-filled with wight, and James of the Pillars has reinforced the bolts, so it cannot be removed from the counter. I enter the lock code, unwind the chain, and stare at shelves of citizens, bundles of parts. Hear their numbers, their worth, their teeth chattering in terror, echoing, layering on top of one another.

I close the door on their teeth and shake my head.

No more.

My breaths are sips. Quick as I remove the bars across our cupboards and take inventory. Near full, we have as many dried vegetables as we could get over these last three weeks. When prices rose, all citizens knew a shortage was coming, and they flocked to the markets and gardens.

Since the other Commons have their own families to care for, James of the Pillars requested the network help me only if I am in dire need.

That is what I requested of him. I will not be pampered like I am the dynasty elect of The Korean Independent.

The Third Booking Market opens in three months. If you require a Third, plan your marriage ceremony for this month. A reminder: when you select your Third, check their fertility levels, disposition, and genetic history. Your favored show, Today in the Past!

It must be a slow news day. Everyone knows this.

My position's hours have doubled to fund the new machines' builds, but my rate has halved. I grow resentful of the Anomalies. Of James of the Pillars. I wish for smarter ones, faster ones, more creative ones.

I resist my desire to send him angry, impatient messages but do not always succeed. Some of my anger seeps through the encouragement, smileToons, and jokes.

Not this morn. It is early, and as usual, I send James of the Pillars three messages through my device. Too many, and he will not have time to read them.

I go to our room and sit. Pull out a notebook and pencil.

I think hard on the message. My tongue peeks through my lips as I concentrate. I do not have any joke books now. Our home must only be filled with important information, so I try to remember a most clever one. I cannot, but a riddle I read long ago pops into my head.

He will not guess this one. He really will not. It is grand.

I write and cross out the riddle a few times. Remember it better. Write out the best version. At the bottom of the page, I sketch a laughing shoe with three shoelaces. It makes no sense, but he has an odd humor.

My dear James of the Pillars. I must ask you a question. It is of the utmost importance and is somewhat hard to ask, but here it is:

Why would a Wight-Harvester call a jaffaroon a jaffamoon? :)

I laugh more, picturing his arched eyebrow. That cute dimple on his cheek. I will not receive a message immediately but get a dozen delayed replies at the end of the week.

The Dome allows him outside communication for fifteen minutes a week. A luxury, and we are luckier still. They made an exception and allowed us two screen calls. I will save one after our conceived is birthed.

James of the Pillars will want to see him.

THIRTEEN

THE WEATHER HAS grown colder over this week. Yesterday, snowflakes fell. I sit in one of the three long lines at the Donation Facility, my belly larger than ever.

They are kind and have allowed me a modified wheelchair. It moves easily through the light snow and relieves the spasms that tremor through my lower back when I stand for too long.

James of the Pillars has sent Marguerite a bit of extra wight, and I have come to collect it. The nutrients will do her good. The line stretches down a city block, so I wait, thinking of her hanging clothes with Aniyah, the girl she has been watching forever. I am not sure which of them asked first, but their connection is strong.

That day, a basket sat on Marguerite's lap. She handed a garment to the older girl, who hung it. They laughed and took their time.

I do believe they may become beloveds, as they grow closer every day. Even more so with the shortage, which is already not treating Marguerite well. The anonymous donations of Urban medicine are slow-coming, and her home is chilly no matter how many holes her siblings fill.

At her maternal's wish, I do not feed her, only give Aniyah a small lunch bag to share with Marguerite. As Aniyah's parents have steady work, her family should be well during the shortage.

'Once a week, and no more. It is cold.' That is what Aniyah's paternal instructed her, but she forgets his words. Runs the half mile from her home in the four-room section to Marguerite's twice a week. Always with food and a small gift hidden under her coat.

I smile. The long line and cold snowflakes disappear as I think back a few months.

They are sitting in our living area.

"I did not innovate the design, but I made this for you." Aniyah gives her the handmade dress or trinket. In return, Marguerite tells her about the history of the fabric or metal. Or some other random thought that enters her random mind. A few dresses are dolly-sized, and the girls sit on the floor, dressing the plastic families.

Other times, they attach a trinket to toy hoverCars and zoom them around the room. Each model revs, jumps, and putters, attempting to follow Marguerite's directions, which are so haphazard they become confused. Aniyah laughs hard as she chases the toy around the room. She jumps on our sofa and bumps into the table, forgetting it is there. Neither she nor the toys can keep up with Marguerite. Eventually, pieces shower down from the sky after they've crashed into a wall. Or into one of the girls.

Slowly, touching shoulders, they pick up the shattered bits, playing Okwu as they do. The game takes a long time, as Aniyah forgets her word or that they are playing at all.

When they are done, they walk to their homes. Aniyah sets her hand atop Marguerite's as it grips the walker, and that chatty girl tells her wild, true stories of the past. As they continue, she reminds Aniyah of events to schedule in her device.

Though they move at a sloth's pace, Aniyah is always happy to walk the three miles when Marguerite visits us. This is their usual way. I know because Marguerite tells me this every time she visits us.

Every time.

They are well matched, those two: Marguerite is impulsive, brave, and loud, and Aniyah is disciplined, strong-willed, and quiet.

A cold gust blows up my sleeve and chills me. The thoughts fade away, into the present.

—✛—

Marguerite has gone ill, so they do not walk anymore. Aniyah walks there alone and helps care for her. Her lungs have worsened. So has her grief for her paternal. When I am able, I screen call, but she cannot talk much now. The torture of her silence is in every wide-mouthed gasp.

Eighty years ago, rogues created an illegal market to regrow birth parts and sell them again. All were violently farmed. It was horrid. Save yourself the misery, citizens, and work hard at your positions. Or else. Your favored show, Today in the Past!

Instead, she coughs and lies in bed with the covers to her neck. Marguerite's twin sisters, her middle brother, and Aniyah tell her stories of their day. They perform happy-maker moves as Marguerite's grandmaternal puts food in through a tube donated by someone in Urban. I do not know these citizens who care for a little, defiant, chattermouth Valley girl, but I hope to find out one day.

Each call, Marguerite shows me the bracelet Aniyah made for her. It is gray and orange, and it hangs from her bony wrist. Her eyes dance with unspoken words as she repeatedly points at Aniyah and grins hard. Should they become beloveds, they will, most certainly, marry of love.

I smile. It is always grand to marry of love.

Finally, after two hours of waiting, it is my turn. Another citizen and I enter the Donation Facility. The man scans our barcodes and, a second later, hands each of us wight, vegetables, and a water stipend from The Republic of United First Regions. He looks at the man next to me, who frowns at the tiny amount on the stipend. "What? There is water on the ground. Next," and looks past us.

I shrug at the frowning man as we step out of the room. Xaia.

She is a few steps down the hallway, laughing with another woman. Her hair, so like Marguerite's, is gone. As are the rest of her teeth. Sold.

The woman points in my direction as she tells a story, and Xaia follows her outstretched arm, deep crinkles at her eyes as she smiles.

When she sees me, her happiness collapses—into a snarl. Her friend steps back, the look is that savage, and whispers, "Who is she?"

I pass by, so slow on my walker, craning my ear, wondering at her answer.

Nothing. She continues their conversation as if it had never been interrupted.

I glance back. Stop myself a second before giving her a most-awful glare. Lucky for her.

She is Marguerite's maternal, and while she means nothing to me, she means a great deal to that irritating girl.

I push Xaia—and her silence—from my mind. I do not care what she thinks. I really do not. She means nothing to me. Why would I care what she thinks?

When I turn the corner, I shake the locked container. Pieces of wight and vegetables rumble within. I hope it will last.

The Dome has cut James of the Pillars's rate. Until the Anomalies create a working design, they will continue to be paid less.

I reach into my coat's pocket and touch the plastic. Bits of his composition fill my mind. Though I have studied it meticulously, I cannot remember the entire thing. Only a few notes. The Blaze's fading happens more with music, but I remember enough.

When the notes loop a third time, Past-Knower Sauda's voice replaces it:

It can be hard to tell. Her words echo in my head, but his humming grows louder and relaxes me.

FOURTEEN

A FEW DAYS later, I walk into the kitchen, ready to fall into bed. The door locks behind me, and I reach for the extra locks above. They are not there. I turn around. The kitchen is not as I left it.

No, no, where is it?

I go to our bedroom, nearly slipping as snow falls from my boots.

Pages litter the room. Our mattress is cut open, its innards snatched out, and the sofa's arms have been split open and searched through. Linen is all over the room. Puffs of cotton. Shreds of sheets. The pillows' stuffing lies on the floor like it was meant to sleep there. Dresser drawers, the alarm clock, most of our clothing. Gone. The rest, scattered throughout the room.

James of the Pillars's books do not sit in tall stacks anymore. They have been ripped from their protective sheets, flipped through, and thrown in piles in various corners. No food hidden inside any of them.

None of that matters. Where is it?

I rifle through the mess with my foot, finally landing on his first favored book: an infant's tale from his paternal. I hold onto my walker while lowering myself. My knee yells at me to stop, but after a brief argument, we reach the floor. Flip through the blocky book.

Some pages, with their fading images and few words, stick together after all these years. I pry two of them open, my breaths short gasps.

Is it—yes, there it is. His composition. In its plastic. Perfect. Still with me.

My hand shakes as I read its notes. Harder when I think of what this could have meant.

The end of my chance.

Past-Knower Sauda said no duplications are allowed, and the submission will only work if I complete it.

I cannot lose the page. I must move faster.

I set the book down and use our couch's cushions to rise to my knee. Move around our room, pushing some of his books aside. A few of the heaviest ones are missing. I stare at the largest pile, trying to determine which ones are gone. Avoiding.

The kitchen is next. I do not want to go in there. Not yet.

The thieves threw my drawings all over the room. Colorful scraps all over. Pages of Urban's dresses, pants, skirts, rooms. The daily numbers and measurements I meticulously tracked. All ripped up. I won't be able to put them back together. They are in small pieces.

What odd thief would spend time shredding them by hand? I do not know, but I hope they are also stupid.

Only exceedingly stupid thieves would sell James of the Pillars's books, as all are registered to him. I hope these thieves sold them, so they will be bid.

I pick up his second favored book: a thick tome on genetic cleansing. Indecipherable symbols, small text, thoughts in a most handsome writing, and a few notes in James of the Pillars's wobbly, sloppy, beautiful script.

Some of the golden-edged pages are missing, and the red spine is broken. How could they do this to a book? To him. He will be devastated at its destruction.

I hold the book open while looking at the cover. Run my hand along the authors' names: Jamesina of the Pillars and Danton of the Waters. The pages slip from my fingers, and the book sprawls open, flat, settling on the dedication.

'To our sons. May they become the grandest of Anomalies. And if not, we *will* love them less[1].'

At the bottom of the page, the footnote reads: [1]winkToon.

I close the book and smile despite everything. His parents did not leave a winking symbol but wrote out the word. That proves it; his humor is hereditary.

I hug the book to my chest, set it down, and leave our room. The kitchen is waiting.

One hundred eighty years ago, in 2313, we closed the immense hole in the ozone. Our ancestors were desperate. Let us learn from them. Remember: everything is recyclable, including your teeth. Your favored show, Today in the Past!

I creep to the kitchen, rifle through the cupboards, and slam them closed. The final set bounce back open, and I slam them closed again. No, no.

I scream. Just once.

Always just once.

And stare at the wall, trying to unsee what is before me. The fridge is empty. Its skull smashed in. Its cord cut.

The cupboards are empty. Their doors hang askew. I look around. Their locks and bars are missing.

Mess. It is everywhere. All the wight, vegetables, fruit, and vials I stored are gone. I lean on the table, my heartbeat chaotic. Pieces of our chairs are strewn all over the kitchen. For a long while, my mind is blank.

What am I to do? The shortage will only get worse.

I close my eyes.

Breathe. My maternal's voice.

I breathe. In. Out. Rub my fingers against the table. Feel the lines I have carved in it. Feel my maternal's hand guiding my small one so many years ago.

"Breathe." She guides my hand in strong, smooth lines as we sculpt her wedding table for hours.

Each time, my hand is tense. Quaking. My movements stiff. "I do not want to ruin it, Matty."

"You cannot. There is nothing to ruin. We are imperfection and still grand. See." She drags the knife across the wood, erasing days of painstaking work with a jagged, horrid line.

Tears well in my eyes, spill down my cheeks. "But… it is not perfect anymore. I want it to be perfect."

"Impossible." She turns me to her. Hugs me. "Breathe." I do. Deep inhales I blow into her chest. "Do not focus on perfection, my dear daughter, unless misery is your wish. Dents, crookedness. They are tests. Without them, how will you know your love is true?" She holds me tighter to her heart. Its beats thump against my cheek. "How will you know you are alive at all?"

I put my hand to my chest and breathe until I can think clearer. Focus on my options.

My bracelet dangles from my wrist. Adding another charm to it would help, but The Dome will not allow me right now.

Exchanging units for cleaning would also work. We are allowed such exchanges during a shortage.

Also, there is some food in James of the Pillars's office. I did not put much though, as I did not want to risk losing it if the barrier rejected me. Still, that is promising. My walker and I go back into our room. Pause at his office's black barrier. Step forward and walk through when it goes transparent.

Nothing has been disturbed. Three of the wine bottles are where they were, in a nearly complete two-foot mansion that has not been moved an inch.

The fourth bottle, a lifetime dining card, and many crumpled notes sit next to it. Paragraphs of apologies from Ancient Dreams. They sent the remaining three bottles after that horrid night.

A large pinecone sits on top of the mansion's ceiling. I stare at it.

Breathe. I do not have to make a decision right now.

Back to the kitchen. One bag of food is with me, most of which is dried vegetables, wight, and fruit. If I eat small rations, these will last two weeks—enough time to think of other possibilities.

I peek out the front door and head to our backyard, which is filled with deep snow. It is easy to get to because neighbor children shovel and salt the ground each week. I pay them with James of the Pillars's sweets. He has a great many stored now.

The small pieces of fresh wight I just bought are tucked under my jacket, and they look no different than my large belly. I never thought I would feel lucky to still have two and a half months of pregnancy left.

Footsteps and deep holes litter the snow, so I bury the wight behind our small garden's barrier. I wish I would have thought of this earlier. I would have far more food left.

In the kitchen, a message pops up in my device:

'Second notice: Theft report has been auto-submitted. Thank you for using Knight's services.'

I must have missed the first one. This is a good update to the system.

I program new lock codes for the door. Check the bars on the windows. What happened to the security system? Did I install the upgrade incorrectly?

Oh no, the upgrade.

The theft report. I sign back into the portal and cancel it. We do not need anyone to investigate the system.

Too late. The report was submitted an hour ago.

An hour. Wait, I have time. Since James of the Pillars is not here, and I am not listed as his beloved, they will take their time arriving. Even better, they may not come at all.

I spend the next hour removing the upgrade. Maybe this will reset the system back to its defaults.

You will not see him again. The tingling fills my body.

You will lose Urban. That nagging voice.

You will always be wrong. I clean. Everything.

First, the kitchen. I use the long, clawed stick to reach many places and scrub until I am lightheaded. When every surface sparkles, I find the vial of Xaia's blood on the floor, resting in the space under the counter. It is cold, and I put it inside of our molder, which has not been damaged. So ancient even thieves had no desire to take it.

I clean. Our bedroom. The floors. The walls. Anywhere I can reach. As I scour our home, I search for more food. James of the Pillars hides food even when there is no shortage. But I do not find any.

An hour later, I bend despite the pain in my back and push our dresser in front of our bedroom door. When I am done, I sit on the edge of our bed, holding a book I grabbed from our toilet room. I cannot understand much of the massive tome on water and muscles, but my ignorance is comforting now.

Seventy-five years ago, Ancient Dreams hosted the first of the Anomaly Galas, and more are happening this year! Priority is given to five- and six-dots. Happy-makers, the competitions to serve them begin soon. Your favored show, Today in the Past!

When my device rings at 6 morn, my brain is fuzzy. I do not want to leave our home, but I must go to my position.

155

Already, their *ding*s are sounding in my head.

The next morn, I return home. The investigator's report is short. It says we have an ancient security system and made no other conclusions. They did not even check. From what I can tell, they walked in and walked out.

How grand is their apathy.

I collapse onto our bed and use much of the rest of our units to purchase a thicker bar for our front door. I will call my husband tomorrow.

"Theft? My love, I am coming home." James of the Pillars stands from the high-backed chair in his room. It is the best chair I have ever seen and must be made from the happiest wood that could be found. Blue dermer is on the headrest and armrests, black leather everywhere else.

Real cow skin.

No cracks or dryness in it. Supple. His Keepers massage oil into his chair every day.

I want to touch it. Him. I want so bad it hurts. And I am glad for that ache. Without want, there can be no hope.

I motion him to sit. Calm himself. They will end our screen call early if he gets too upset.

"No, no. It is all right. I am well, and so is our conceived." The dim lighting in our kitchen is swallowed by the bright lighting of his room, which reflects off little. Matte cream paint, black trim. The massive space is empty, his bed and bookshelves hidden in the walls.

"Do not come. I can handle it. You must finish the project."

He rubs his hair and sighs hard. "But—"

"No, stay there, my dear. I am excited for your return. I, I want you to return."

An Anomaly woman walks into his room. James of the Pillars stands, bows low to her. I do too. He rises. I do not.

"You may unbow." Her voice is breathy. I straighten.

She greets only him before stepping forward and whispering in his ear. My husband's face twists as if he has smelled something putrid. She must have brought awful news.

She is beautiful. Her skin the darkest of vanilla.

Ding. Stutter.

Ding. Glitch. A lightly pounding headache.

46,900,000,000 units.

I gape at her, most embarrassingly. Six dots stretch down each of her red-tinged temples. The woman is a leader of The BloodBid. *The leader* of them all, judging by the dark red circle surrounding The Dome's crest on her chest. She is one of the most powerful people in our world.

Oh, I never thought I would be in her presence.

Still, I avoid her piercing gaze. Though she is in Urban and cannot harm me, grinding fear cramps my stomach.

She watches as I straighten my clothing. Pat my curls down. I wish I believed in the Inventor. Maybe they could help me look less a disaster.

Healthier. Like her.

Ornate like her.

Glowing gold streaks weave through the red, fat, and skinny twists in her hair. Two twists swoop along her forehead, and the rest are fashioned into triangular ripples of water tight to her scalp.

An alteration turns the white of her eyes black, and her red irises analyze everything.

Leaders of The BloodBid are well-versed in detecting lies.

She stalks back to the door before turning that scalding look on my husband. Unlike me, he does not shrink away. "James of the Pillars, I need ya."

"May I have one more min——"

"No." She flicks her hand, and the screen goes black.

FIFTEEN

A WEEK HAS passed, and I lie on our bed, staring at my resource ledger. Aniyah sewed the mattress back together after we stuffed it with a few of my neighbors' long pillows. It is more comfortable than James of the Pillars's couch, which is magnificent when I am not pregnant but is so soft it leads to immense back pain now.

Repeatedly, I move numbers around, growing more certain I will not have enough. Our filterings, water, waste removal, heating, and housing costs are paid, but I am lacking enough for the electricity. Without it, I cannot run the filtering machines or the tiny fridge a man dropped off a few days ago.

'James of the Pillars requested I save for this months ago. It can fit vials and some wight. I apologize it is not larger, but know I am available when you need, miss.'

'Many thanks.' I plugged it up in James of the Pillars's office.

Forty years ago, remarriage was outlawed. Remember to grow your bonds. Support your spouses. Share in their sorrows and joys. Your favored show, Today in the Past!

Though James of the Pillars sends wight and warm infant clothing to the Donation Facility, the food does not last long, and he cannot send units yet. He and the other Anomalies are working nearly all hours of the day, but the project is failing. And failing. And failing.

If he would take his Vow, we would not have these problems. The price cannot be as high as he says it is.

I do not dwell on that thought. Instead, I think of ways to get 3,000 more units. It is only a month into the shortage, so people may be more giving. Like Aniyah's parents. They may have units to spare.

But I will not count on that. Over the next week, I knock on door after door. Dozens of them. Touch my stomach and smile.

Rattle these words off in a loving voice, "My conceived has the Anomaly gene. His paternal, James of the Pillars, is a six-dot. It would bring me great joy to see his birth." Smile wider. "In return for units, I can cook, clean, or draw you a grand picture. Cleaning is my specialty."

Some respond with, "If your conceived's paternal is an Anomaly, why do you need my assistance?" and slam their doors, but most soften to my need.

On the last day of the week, an older man near Past-Knower age requests an image of an infant perro. Long, floppy ears. Black coat with a patch of white diamond fur on its forehead.

A slobbery, loud, messy animal. Eww.

Ding. 255,000 units. His home smells of sweet O negative; it is everywhere. Still, after my thirty years, I do not know why some people's flavors are so strong.

He does not say anything but stares at me. I know what he is about to ask. They all ask. How tiresome.

I glance at him. "Ask, mister."

"What is my worth?" He swipes his sandy curls out of his eyes, dark brown under eyelids beginning to sag. "I will pay you, of course. I have always been curious what it is. If I knew my worth, I would know how important I am. My purpose." His calm demeanor gives way to a shrug. "That must be an odd question, huh?"

"No, not at all. Many want the unknown to be known, but that service is not on offer." They do all ask. How annoying. "It is against an Auctioneer's honor. The image, I can do."

He smiles a little. "Okay. I guess I will know the number one day."

I nod as I straighten the stack of blank pages I have bought with me, thinking on his words. "One day, an Auctioneer will tell you your worth. And after, you will be drained, dissected, and devoured." I tuck a rebel page into the others. "Your worth will not matter then. You will not matter. Until that day, tell yourself."

Next, the colored pencils. I sort them, light to dark, one parallel to the next until they stretch across his table. "Send me an image of the perro you want." He does, and I begin.

Sculpting big eyes, a photorealistic shiny coat, a silly smile on the creature. Feathering in gentle colors mixed with deep tones. It does not take long. I have been drawing most of my years.

"Wow, miss." He runs his fingers over the drawing. "Many thanks."

"You are welcome. A grand eve to you."

He adds 100 units to my account, and I go to the next home.

And the next.

And the next.

At the end of the week, I have 2,000 units.

There is another way to get more units, but I am avoiding it. Have yet to succumb to it.

I cringe and shake my head. No, I will not think of that.

I continue on. Get a few units from each of my friends at a Share Meeting, but they do not have much. Neither does the network of Commons.

2,150 units.

My panic grows. I hold it in. I must focus on getting more, but that more will not be from Aniyah's parents. They have not been paid yet.

Your electricity bill is due in two days. The voice from my device infuriates me. So calm while I grow closer and closer to terror.

I go further, request short-term access to other areas of Valley. Rub my stomach longer. Smile harder. A near Terrainese grin, but there are hints of Valley hardness in mine. Still, I try.

After receiving your premium unit, the rest of your Gold Week will be sterilized, shipped to First citizens, and converted into their currency. Do not forget to be grateful they sacrifice a unit. Your favored show, Today in the Past!

Dozens more doors, dozens more requests for their worths, and I have reached 2,600 units—so close. So close.

When the bill is overdue, my breath wheezes like Marguerite's. My skin itches everywhere there is skin, and I scratch myself like I have spent hours trapped in a bush of poison ivy. The light green tinge can't be seen, but I know it is there.

James of the Pillars, husband, I wish you were here.

I have not gotten one message from him. Why? This is not like him. What could be happening that I have gotten no messages? Did something happen to him?

Maybe, maybe, he is being punished. I do not know how Anomalies are punished, but I am sure The Dome has many waiting.

He has left you. You have lost him. It is your fault.

Stupid voice. Lying, stupid voice.

My breath picks up, my heartbeat with it. I believe that voice. It is mine.

But another grows, a whisper.

No, that is not right. He would not do that. Not like this.

I shake my head. I must stay focused. Stay calm.

The second day. My vision is blurred. Dimmer. I wipe dust from my eyes. The muscles in my eyelids are becoming stuck in an open position. Still, I hold in my nerves. Some of them. A sprinting heart will only cause The Blaze to spread faster.

I keep walking through Valley, rubbing a towel along the walker's handles. Walking has grown hard. My heartbeat pounds all day, laboring to pump blood through my fat veins. They bulge from my face, splitting it into horrid lines no amount of makeup can hide.

In the mirror at home, I press on the lines. Usually, they are rigid tubes like metal straws, but sometimes, they bubble out as my blood struggles to push through.

Bumps all over me, slowly smoothing back down.

I send James of the Pillars another message. Nothing. This is not the life I envisioned with an Anomaly husband.

This one is no easier. It is far worse.

More is so close to me, but I cannot have it. No matter how fast I run toward it, it keeps moving away. I scrub the cushioned part of the walker's handle until it flakes off and shows the yellow foam underneath.

My disappointment with him rages in me and focuses into one word—useless.

James of the Pillars is useless to me.

I shake my head of him. Again. Again. He is still there, but I do not have time to dwell.

I cannot stop. I will not. I am too close to Urban.

As if you are worthy of Urban. Look at you.

Shut up!

But I do look at myself. My lips have become like a deformed fish's. Pressed together as the veins around them have grown so large. It has only been a day, and I am hardly able to speak. My eyes, they have sunken in. Eventually, I look into the mirror only to slather makeup all over myself. Keep The Blaze in.

Our conceived is kicking and hitting against me as the toxins attack his amniotic sack, trying to get in. This is hard to do as my blood does not enter the sack.

If I perish, they will take him out of me. Cleanse my wight. Auction it at a steep discount.

164

I do not want to perish.

I do not want to perish here, in this life.

I go to my position.

Luckily, I have not been banned from my work. I spend my days doing paperwork with others who are ill. Urban despises doing its paperwork and has sent three warehouses to us, so extra hours are available.

I am fine with this. I enjoy doing paperwork, as it is further away from the farms.

The second day wears on. How quickly I have forgotten how to lift my head. I keep it low while walking and flinch when people jump away from me. Take the long way around.

There is a wailing in my head, a banging that wants the door to open. Despair. Me, losing Urban when I am so close.

I silence it; it hurts too much to hear it.

Small amounts of units trickle in from the network, but they are not enough.

Please, I do not want to perish here.

In the eve, I trudge to someone's home. Slump against my walker. My energy has nearly disappeared. Each breath creates a sweatiness on my forehead; my throat is crowded with veins.

One more day.

The rebel woman. She pops into my mind. She did not have a full day. She perished in the early morn.

No, no. That will not be me. No, I will not let it.

I must get more now.

200 units. I can get that.

I say the loving words. Push them through any resistance. I cannot smile anymore, and so I wave softly.

No.

No.

No.

The last home in this block.

"James of the Pillars, really?" Their eyes turn black as they check my registry. The couple look at each other and nod. Synchronized. Beloveds. "We have said no to many, but not to you. Never to an Anomaly."

They do not talk of the extremely low possibility that our conceived will be an Anomaly, but hope and excitement fill their eyes. A fevered obsession too.

They smile and chatter as they transfer 1,000 units into my ledger. Eight hundred more than I need.

How grand.

Our conceived will have two horrid nicknames in his registry, but I have more than enough for the filtering machines. I will keep making more.

Two weeks later, I lie awake with a finger stuffed deep in my ear, but it does nothing. The Urban commercial—the man's screams—transfers to my device and shrieks through my head. Quick inhales pour from my mouth as I am transported back there.

Once you go to the farms, you never leave.

I sit up in bed and check the incoming donations in my device: halved. Everything is halved. James of the Pillars sent half? I watch the news, but there are no reports the project is going worse than it was before.

What has happened? In case he is despairing and needs my encouragement, I send him a message. End it with "smileToon" written out.

Look around our home. It is filthy. I scrub more, but it refuses perfection.

—✛—

A week and a half later. Even less. A quarter.

I am not in dire need yet, so I do not ask the network for assistance. Instead, I work longer. When I am not at work, I ask questions of my neighbors.

One woman has added a small, fake flowerpot to her bright teal porch. I pause, staring at her door before knocking. It is newly painted, and her artistry is beyond all I have seen in Valley.

When she greets me, all I can say is, "Your door."

"Thank you." She smiles widely. "Come in."

Ding. 108,000 units.

I step into her kitchen and sit. Plastic sunflowers, calla lilies, and chrysanthemums are scattered around the room. Paintings of different regions of our world hang from the walls. Realistic but drawn slightly crooked. Colors brighter than they would be. Shadows longer than I can verify. Stunning in their detail.

She consults with Anomalies to make the paintings originals.

"Want some ClearJuice?"

I nod. The woman pulls a pitcher from the fridge and fills a cup, moving gracefully around her kitchen. One birth leg, one not. It was harvested from the mid-thigh down. She does not hide her prosthesis like me but proudly shows it off, wearing shorts though the weather is chilly.

The design is familiar. One of James of the Pillars's older models. It will shift color as she darkens to an acorn in the sun season and back to her original lightly burnt honey in the snowflake season.

Will mine shift colors as well? Will it be less conspicuous than hers?

The leg blends in decently with her skin but nowhere near perfectly. Twelve repeating numbers, each set like a zebra stripe, wound around the SynthSkin: manufacture date, batch number.

The unlikeness is intentional. The Dome did not want James of the Pillars's designs to compete with the identiPros. Perfect replicas of birth parts. Expensive.

She sits and hands me the cold glass. Intricate red swirls of permapaint fan out from her eyes, onto her temples. Few have paint like an Artist.

Males, are you worried about your sperm going to waste? Females, your ovaries? Do not. Before your auction, we will transfer your testes and ovaries to a zero male and zero female. You are welcome. Your favored show, Today in the Past!

I smell the ClearJuice. Rotten bananas and month-old curdled milk flood through my body. Tiny bits of stale, hard sourness under that. Always there. I hold in a hard gag and hand it back to her.

"Something wrong? It is fresh."

I can smell its freshness. Life wafts from it. Most likely, pumped yesterday. "That is not it. It is B positive and sour. Many thanks anyway."

Confusion crosses her face. "How—Oh, of course, you are an Auctioneer. It is my husband's ClearJuice." A blush brightens her mid-brown cheeks. "He does bathe." She smells it. Shrugs. Drinks it. "I have not pumped today, so I do not have anything else to offer."

Unfortunately. She is a semi-sweet B negative. Her ClearJuice would have been a most pleasant broth.

"That is fine." She sniffs the drink once more. "Your husband's flavor has nothing to do with his bathing habits or personality traits." Many people believe these are related.

The woman laughs. "Good to know. It must be... fascinating to be an Auctioneer." She leans forward, whispers, "When I was young, I used to be terrified of you all. I thought you were spies for The BloodBid. Just knew you would accuse me of a crime to take home more units."

Sigh. This again.

Anger boils in me, but her pleasant Terrainese-like personality sets it at a simmer. "Long ago, *some* Auctioneers did that. Stupid ones. Sending citizens to collection is of no benefit to the one who sends." I shake my head. "We are assigned who we auction; we do not get to choose. They were disgraceful and have made us all look bad."

"Oh, okay."

"Have you received fewer donations?" It has taken far too long to get to this question, the reason I came here.

She wraps her hijab tighter around her neck when a breeze comes from a window.

"No, the same amount. My daughter sends extra from her position as a Translator. She has always had an adventurous spirit, so it is grand she can live off-continent. Get out of Valley." She looks out of the window, into the distance. "As a Translator, you know?"

Yes, I know.

She tells everyone this all the time. It is the first thing that spills from her mouth. I do not understand why. Her position is far more impressive than her daughter's, and she does have many other children.

Still, it is good fortune her daughter gets to live in Second Europe. I have heard they have magnificent fruit shakes, and all citizens get them for no cost.

I get up to leave. As I do, my stomach grumbles hard.

At the sound, she asks, "How is your conceived?"

"He is doing well."

She reaches for my belly but stops herself so abruptly, her six charms knock against one another.

"May I?"

I nod, sit again, and she continues forward. Sets her hand on my stomach.

"I used to make the most terrible noises with my children, too. It is grand to be older. I do not have to be pregnant anymore. Gets tiresome, you know?" The woman rubs my belly gently.

"I do know."

"The second was painful, the fourth enjoyable, but after him, I did not want to ferry anymore. She looks out the window again. Stares off for a long while. "I had many more after him."

170

Her weariness disappears, replaced by a smile. "My daughter speaks dozens of languages. She sends me pictures." The woman shows me images of Second Europe——its Urban, Horizon, Terrain.

Slightly different architecture, similar to ours. Across the water. Far from here.

"Your door is most magnificent. You did not win the trip to work in Horizon?"

"I did, but I was sick that week. The flu." She looks down at my belly. Laughs. Deep wrinkles show at her eyes and mouth. "I grew exhausted, but each new infant gave me hope. Maybe they would have the chance to see more." She smiles at me. "Your infant will know more."

"If he is an Anomaly, he will."

She kisses my belly. "Even if not. My daughter is a Translator, you know?"

"I do."

She tells me about her paintings as she rubs my belly.

Her hand does not feel possessive but supportive. I let her dream aloud, about places she will never see.

SIXTEEN

I DO NOT want to think what is happening in Urban that James of the Pillars would send so few donations. Usually, there has only been a week when they were reduced, but it has been a month.

The rag has a hole in it; I scrub more. Waves of fear roll through my body. My ledger is near empty. Just last week, The Dome announced a tax on water that must be paid upfront.

How much will the network bring?

Will Physician Nore be able to see me?

I clean the smallest crevices, trying to push the worry away. It does not go away, but I do find the bottles' missing doorknob in a crack in the cupboard.

Underneath the kitchen's windowsill, on the outside, I find a medium-sized stay fresh tube running along it. Its packaging is painted the same yellow as our home.

I peel it off and close the window. After unrolling the tube, it is near four feet long. Labeled in wobbly letters, with next year's date. I open it. A fruity smell comes out.

Oatmeal and strawberries.

I drink it slowly.

Paradise. My stomach's grumbling stops.

But this was not hidden for me.

Why does he hide food when we will need it?

What good will it do if only he knows where it is?

Irritation wells up, but every sip of the tube keeps it in check.

There must be more.

I look around the kitchen. I did not find any before, but perhaps I was looking in the wrong places.

He has not hidden food in the dressers or couch. Too obvious. He has hidden it in plain sight.

I turn in a circle, surveying the kitchen. The heating coils. Yes. I turn off the coils, let them cool, and look behind them. There are tubes strapped to the walls behind them. Six tubes with reflective surfaces to throw back the coils' light.

Each day, I drink from one of the tubes. Pureed wight, mashed potatoes, and oatmeal. Other foods too. They sustain me as the shortage worsens. It does not seem like it will be longer than others, but many more continents are in need this year. Bugs, power outages, and new strains of The Blaze spread across our world.

That is why it is best to stay within your own continent. Your own region. Your own city. Safer.

I look around our home. No. No, it is not always best.

Fewer and fewer donations come in—until finally, I receive none. The garden has closed, saving all fruits and vegetables for Urban, and my personal ledger is close to negative.

The time has come. I contact the network.

"A grand morn to you, miss."

Every day the next week, a citizen drops off a bit of wight or vegetables. They greet me the same way and rub my belly as they hand me a few vials for my filterings, so excited for James of the Pillars's conceived to be birthed. I write down everything they give me. I will not be indebted to others.

A quarter of everything goes into his office. The rest is hidden outdoors, in the cold. I sit on the plush Urban couch with both of his suit's arms wrapped around me. The three wine bottles are across from me, still arranged in an unfinished mansion on the right side of his long table.

The fourth bottle has not been opened. I leave it closed. Wine will only fill my stomach for a short while, and I want to enjoy it with James of the Pillars.

Yet… curiosity grabs me.

I fit the fourth bottle into the others and complete the structure. The designs carved into the glass are so intricate I cannot fathom them. Swirling triangles of gold against the red glass.

Each bottle has a fluorescent piece of The Dome's crest on it. When the mansion is complete, the crest sits centered on the front wall.

I put the doorknob in and turn it. Oh. Lights come on in the mansion. They flicker gently, and red and gold fill the room, dancing on the pinecone.

It is magical.

It is perfect.

Six-dots, you—uh, apologies, wrong channel. Still your favored show, Today in the Past!

Over the next week, I watch the mansion's lights a few minutes every day.

—✛—

"I cannot help you any longer." The man's words slam into me one day. Tears stream down his face. "Your infant. He is precious. So precious. But I... I have been forbidden to assist you."

His body shakes. "Please, please tell James of the Pillars that I apologize, and I will take whatever punishment he sees fit to give me."

"What, wait, who?"

He does not answer but runs out of our door. The first of the network.

"My daughter. She is gone. I can help you no more." A woman kneels at my feet, her hands vibrating against my belly. "Miss, I, I—"

She is the last of the network.

—✛—

"Citizens, a mandatory audit has been issued for the under Americas. Prepare your markets, auctions, homes, and Donation Facilities according to the stipulations you have received."

Of course, an audit.

It has been a month, and few will share after this announcement.

The Dome has ordered representatives from First America to inventory and inspect our food, so they are on their way from The Republic of United First Regions, traveling up the Panamal in lavish hoverBuses.

They will take much food. A shortage only means more food for them and another cost for us.

Though I am always prepared for audits, I do not know what will happen. I have not gotten a message from James of the Pillars in this last month. Instead, all I have heard is

Assistance denied.

I am avoiding what may need to be done, but my device continuously reminds me I am getting closer. It nonchalantly informs me that my fifth application for a food stipend has been denied. That I am doing too well.

Why would it be anything but nonchalant? It has not opened my cupboards.

I set up automatic submissions and scrub small areas as I dress for my position's overnight shift. Our home may be cleaner than it has ever been, but there is no more food hidden.

I drink water and leave our home.

On the day I am so nauseated I auction a young teen for far less than she is worth, I put on my jacket, boots, and hat, and catch a hoverBus to the Wight-Harvesting facility in the center of Valley.

I do not want to do this. Have been avoiding it. But there is no other choice now.

The building is immense, clean, and sterile. Multiple floors. Light-gray metal with horizontal lines across it.

A stream of *ding*s and numbers flood my mind. Fade away. We are sorted by blood type.

I wait on the first floor in a soft, luxurious chair. Happy-makers in gray toghus glide around with gold platters, silently offering us small drinks and fancy, little triangle-shaped sandwiches with The Dome's crest toasted into the top and bottom.

They are delicious. I try each type and eat the ones with a slice of carrot, blue DiamondJar sauce, and bits of wight until the ache in my stomach goes away.

A woman stops in front of me, smiling. "Wanna massage, miss? Music?"

You can get that?

I nod, and the happy-maker swipes a finger across her arm. The chair reclines and vibrates. Firm rollers slide up and down my back. Headphones come from behind the chair's top and cup around my ears. Soundproof.

A menu of music shows in my device—I choose my favorite Class-hop song, "Graceful Infinity."

My heartbeat slows as the intense beats and violins fill my mind. I close my eyes and breathe out. It is much better here than years ago.

After a few songs, I turn off the music. The chatter and laughter around me are far more interesting. I talk with the others.

Did you know some of our ancestors used to bury their wight? That means plant it in the ground and let it rot. In fancy boxes of all things. Your favored show, Today in the Past!

Groans and head shakes ripple down the lines.

"What was wrong with them?" a man whispers to a woman.

"I do not know. Something severe."

"Yes, very severe."

My thoughts fade into the ancient past. When The Blaze first hit, nothing would rid them of it, and the more desperate they became, the more destructive.

"They tore up everything—the air, the water, the dirt."

"We fixed the air." The man sucks in a lungful just to prove how much we improved it. He purses his lips, smug.

I am not sure why. *We* did not fix it; our closer ancestors did. They had lost access to the dirt, too.

Before them, in some lands, large holes six feet deep were reopened as they sought the wight with jewelry, special teeth, or were buried in fancy boxes. Many fell in, hurt themselves, and they would be robbed, too. Murdered. Blood transferred, and The Blaze spread through their world faster.

Most dirt was covered with concrete to prevent such greed and destruction.

I keep dipping my hand in my pocket to touch the page's plastic. Though the composition is no longer in it, it still comforts me.

Pulls me away from thinking about then—and now. I have been here before. I do not want to be here now.

Hours slip by. My turn.

Ding. 335,000 units.

The person sits behind a large, ornate desk. I sit across from them, the long line of citizens behind me.

"What do you wanna sell, miss?"

"The left forearm."

"With or without the hand?"

"Without."

"Dominant or nondominant?"

"Dominant."

"Okay, so you wanna sell the dominant forearm and keep the hand. Is that right?"

"Yes."

"Do you mind if I verify the muscle fibers?"

"No."

They wrap a cuff around each of the largest parts of my forearms. A moment later, the left one beeps, and they remove both of them.

"You can get 500 more units if you bundle sell the hand today." They smile widely. Terrainese. They run all Wight-Harvester facilities and enjoy doing transactions face to face. I adore this about them. I think on the offer.

"Many no thanks."

"Do you wanna trial an identiPro for 180 days?"

I pause. Those are grand, and I will have six months to figure out the first payment.

The cost shows in my device, and my eyes widen. Even more than on the Urban commercials.

199,999 units. The payments will be immense. Still, I do enjoy a trial, and the seven-year repayment plan is generous if I want longer.

I close my eyes to think on it. Soft beats in my head start, fade lower, and a video of a heavily pregnant woman plays in my device. She is sitting on a large, blue lily pad, floating in a lake. Shaved head. Crisp, snow-topped mountains surround her, but she does not look cold at all.

Gentle music comes from the near-transparent guitar she is strumming. When she plucks the strings, they sound like violin notes. The video zooms in, pans across her arms. I do not know which is the identiPro and which is her birth arm.

But, I do know this: her dress is most beautiful.

A matte powder blue strapless gown called Existence. Simple. No frills. Tight. An overlay hugging the woman's deep brown skin. One of Denise of the Pines's most memorable designs.

The woman looks off into the distance as the benefits of her identiPro drift with the clouds, then disappear, leaving only her, smiling softly.

The video glides along an extremely long tendril of the lily pad, bobbing in the water. At the end is another large lily pad, which is connected to a smaller one.

Back to the woman. She is looking at the lily pads, far from her. A shadowy figure is on each.

She looks away, keeps strumming as she stares at the mountains.

The video fades away, and I open my eyes.

Think on the offer more.

For a long time.

"Yes, I want the trial."

The person continues, "Excellent. The first monthly payment'll be automatically taken from your personal ledger if you don't cancel within 180 days."

They are patient and smiling as they type on their holokeyboard. "You'll receive 1,500 units for the forearm, miss. Yeah, that's all. I apologize. Please sign here."

I sign.

"Thank you fuh growing the harvest of our world." They smile and guide me through a door.

I emerge from the harvest feeling better than I have in a long while. The medication given to me removes all of my pain, and my belly is nearly too full. After the procedure, we were allowed to eat from a large table and take some home.

The identiPro is grand. My left forearm is identical to my original arm, barcode and all.

As I walk down the warm, dimly lit hallway plastered in holographic screens showing smiling people eating, running, and laughing with identiPros, I flex my birth fingers; the muscles in the topmost forearm of the identiPro ripple as my birth ones did.

I hum a little, not well, and stop in the middle of the hallway, moving the arm. Touching it.

The same small veins. The same thick scars at my wrist, still painful. The same short hairs on the top and infant smooth skin on the underside. The same lighter patch of skin from when I fell while scrubbing the tops of our cupboards as a girl.

Two years ago, The BloodBid celebrated three hundred million collections. If you see a rogue committing a crime, report them to The BloodBid immediately. Your favored show, Today in the Past!

I will have my leg again, too. That identiPro will be as beautiful as this one.

I get lost in the looking, poking, my happiness, and drop the small container of dried vegetables. It breaks open, and the flat, vacuum-sealed bags scatter all over the floor. I squat to pick up the container. A Terrain woman, speeding down the hallway, stops. Gives me a massive smile.

"I've done the same, miss. Please don't strain yourself." The woman stoops, grabs the container, and rushes around, picking up the bags.

Ding. 310,000 units.

A message appears in my device: 'IdentiPro: 180 days remaining.'

She says something, but I do not know what. I stare at that number. Watch the timer tick down.

Will I be able to make the first payment?

The hundredth and fiftieth?

After a while, movement gets my attention, pulls me from my darkening thoughts, and I look up. The woman patiently holds the container out to me, smiling all the while. I take it from her. Her upbeat demeanor silences the worries. Their joy truly is infectious.

"Enjoy your identiPro, miss. We look forward to your payment in six months." She uploads a gift card for five packs of infant diapers and three bottles and puts her palm out to me. I do the same.

The countdown continues. This forearm is not mine, but it will be. The submission will help me afford it.

And after, I will have all the things I want.

All the things *I* deserve.

SEVENTEEN

BODIES HANG FROM the conveyor belt. The lucky ones swing by their necks—the unlucky ones by their wrists. The belt moves forward, and the already perished bump the screaming, kicking still alive. More citizens crowd below in long lines, only a short wait for their turn. Their screams echo through my head as they are herded into the farm, shoved from behind. Roped to one another. Cursed. Zapped with electricity if they fall or hesitate.

Hundreds of bodies turned into wight. Hundreds of barcodes scanned. Hundreds of citizens yanked up by unforgiving machines.

Like the woman, unfamiliar and held aloft by her wrists. She screams as the conveyor belt turns violently, and blood drips down her arms. But the pain is not why she shrieks. She will be farm-to-plate, and so she watches as the bodies in front of her are drenched in oil, seasoned, and consumed in flames—knowing their screams will soon be hers.

"Husband." I wake up. Tears stream down my face as they have most morns these last three months. My shaky, staccato breaths and thudding heartbeat are not loud enough to cover the screams of the farms. The smell of fried skin. The bodies drained of blood and separated.

I rub the thick scar around my wrist. A matching one sits under my bracelet. Even after all these years, pain pulses through my hands; it is carved into the scars. I reach over to the other side of the bed. Empty.

But all of him is not gone. James of the Pillars's humming comes from my device. Relaxes my nerves as it spins a web of safety in the dark, early morn.

My position will start in a few hours, so I lie in our bed, bathed in the gentle candlelight of the room, hugging myself, breathing deeply a few minutes until the bile scrapes back down my throat. Though the pillows make our bed comfortable, they do not rid me of my terrors. My memories.

Coughing and gasping come from the tiny, semi-transparent bed next to his side. I roll into the cold space and jump out. Thirty minutes over four hours, I am late.

Ding. 50,000 units.

Black, thick veins stick out of the infant's skin—his brown color is mottled with green—and his eyes grow

184

cloudy. He wriggles as sickly blood fills his body. As The Blaze's intense, telltale itch tortures him.

His small filtering machine sits on a tall table; I put the needle cuff around his elbow before sticking my arm through its upright hoop. After it reads my barcode, the needle descends, slides into my vein, and sucks in my blood.

"Units not accepted." Scrolls along the top of the hoop.

Cough. A wet gasp.

Stupid machine.

I stick my arm through it again.

"Units not accepted."

Large patches of his skin are green now, darkening every second. Big, black worms in the white of his eyes. The small, red veins have turned into fat, painful ones.

I run to the kitchen and open the fridge.

I have bartered the other vials. Only one remains—Xaia's.

I grab it. I need warm units.

Think, think.

A noise outside—footsteps?—no, cannot be. I turn the stove on. A page I read in one of James of the Pillars's books pops into my head.

Yes, that could work.

Quick gasps come from our room. I move faster. The Blaze does not know mercy.

I grab a large metal soup spoon and pour enough of her blood into the spoon for a filtering.

Do not spill.

The vial's cap snaps back into place as I hold the spoon high over the flame. If any of it boils, I cannot use this batch. Careful. Careful. There is only enough for one more filtering.

I breathe out slowly. Dip my finger in until it is body temperature.

Silence from our room.

I walk to that silence.

He is a darkening green all over. His eyes are stuck open with nearly white irises now. He is still.

No. No. Not like this.

My hand trembles as I touch his chest. It is softer, bulging slightly. Does not rise a millimeter.

I shake him. Nothing.

Shake him harder. He spasms. A gasp.

The machine reads my barcode, and the needle descends into her blood. This should not work.

Please work. Please work.

A pause. It activates.

The filtering process starts, works quickly, and he calms.

Again, a sound from outside the window. Footsteps? No, I have grown paranoid in my loneliness.

I stare at him as he stretches lightly.

A month old, he is a healthy, pleasant infant who cries little and possesses gray eyes with flecks of dark brown.

He hiccups. Cries a bit. Rubs the tears away with the butt of a palm. I put my finger in his other hand and watch as the black under his fingernails recedes and returns to pink. He holds tightly. His palm is soft and warm, and his gummy smile is like my own. All else is like James of the Pillars.

How unfortunate for me. Until we are perished, my husband will never let me forget this fact.

I smile down at him—snatch my finger from his grasp. He startles, and I turn away. I have never loved one of my conceiveds, and I do not intend to start now.

I send a report detailing his malfunctioning machine. In it, I mention the infant is of Anomaly bloodline. They send a message back near instantly, and

"Error: Incorrect units inserted," shows on the hoop, then "Recalibrating…" then "Recalibration complete."

After the tubes clean themselves, I filter him again to make sure my units work. He falls into a deep sleep. I go to the kitchen, open the small compartment in the wall behind our sink—where I put the composition—and go back to our bedroom. Sit on my side of the bed and hook myself to my filtering machine. Much larger than the infant's.

Three tubes come from it: The first is fat and unbreakable. It goes into the ground and connects to The Dome's industrial filtering system. The second is small, clear, and pulls out my contaminated blood, and the third, like the second, pumps in clean blood up to my daily earned amount.

I relax as the contaminants are removed. Look at him.

"I do not love you, but I will not be late again. Know this."

He is tiny. His blood must be filtered every four hours, or he will perish. I set a third alarm in my device. Stare at the page's notes. Every morn and night, I touch it softly and thank it for what it will do: afford us the life we truly deserve.

The life I truly deserve.

The bed is inviting, but sleep is not. When my eyes close, the farms open. Still, I lie down because my bones are tired, and my heart is exhausted. I pull the note from under my pillow and unroll it. The thieves did not destroy it, luckily.

James of the Pillars wrote me a small essay that begins with

You have slept on these names. Considered them in your dreams. My love, if you choose none, I fear our son will be called Sidewalk.

I go through the list again. We must sign the infant's name into his registry before his second month. If we are late, he will be assigned a name.

Over our five years together, I have gotten used to James of the Pillars's writing, so each name is easy to read. He has gone through all 50 letters of the alphabet and put five names for each letter. Next to them are their historical meanings. I read the list again, as writing this much must have been excruciating for him, but none of the names matter to me.

I do not care what the infant is called.

I put the list in my pocket and lie back down. This day will wear on without anything to alter its trajectory. It will not stop, only turn to night and then day once more.

I spent yesterday ridding our world of citizens collected by The BloodBid. Their cries do not stop, and my comfort does not console them. Not a one. And yet, the worst is not the ones who plead or curse but the ones who do neither.

The ones who stand in silent resignation haunt me. This was always their fate, and they accepted it long ago. Their emptiness forces my thoughts back to the first day at my position—and to my paternal who rid me of my leg.

⁛

"An auctioneer." The man sat at a desk at the training schools; I offered him my arm. He stuck me with a needle and put my blood into his database. "Your Vow."

It was bright in there, but I looked into his eyes as my maternal taught me to. "I vow to auction as only I can. I dedicate my life to the nourishment of our world."

"Accepted." He handed me a paper.

The other children, nine-aged like me, stood in front and behind me in perfect lines. A few rocked back and forth with anxiety, but I did not. My paternal taught me to look confident, as if I knew nearly everything there was to know, but I was still open to learning more.

At precisely 7 morn, they herded us into a room barely large enough to seat us. Bright. Everything in The Dome's wight facilities was bright. The paper listed my name, position, and pay rate.

Two large vials per day.

Low pay because I could not smell the nuances of infant blood, only report there were gaps in the flavor. Stupid nose. Stupid gaps. My stomach grumbled with worry. How would I assist my family with just 1,000 units? One hand costs that amount.

A girl raised a finger high into the air. She had talked non-stop about the lecturer's success since we first arrived and asked many questions.

"How did you become an Auctioneer for Urban?"

The lecturer ignored her.

"When will we get a pay increase, sirn?"

He cracked his neck and spoke slowly. "When you're thirteen-aged."

"How much?"

"Enough."

She raised her finger a fourth time. He gave her a stern look but allowed her to continue, "You are an Auctioneer for Urban."

"Yeah, we've established that."

"I have heard you sell to only the best in our world. I admire you and will be like you."

The man spoke even slower, not looking at any of us, "No, you won't. I'm Urban-born. You'll only rise high enough tuh hit the roof The Dome has built for ya—and it's not even tall enough for you to stand in." He laughed and tapped on a holokeyboard. Thick scars wrapped around his wrists. "Know these two things, lil one: I'm only here because we have tuh put in charity hours, and… flattery's an unpleasant trait." The girl sat back in her seat, but her admiration was undeterred.

"First training'll be six hours. After that, you'll begin your positions. Ya listenin'?" We nodded, and the training began. We learned to assign the dates of the citizens' auctions, interpret the vast, ever-changing Need Maps, complete the time-consuming paperwork, and ration wight to the cities that needed them.

After that, the lecturers taught us how to decide who would go to the gray markets, who would become premium-cut, and finally, how to call the bidding numbers in the most alluring way. My position was simple. I would excel easily.

When the six hours ended, they took us to another room one by one. While no one could fail their life position, you could be given an assignment with lower pay.

Inside, the room sweltered. It was even hotter in our full-body suits. The goods stood in lines, chained to one another, intermixed, though many came from Abyss and Valley. Two or three were Commons from Urban, and four were rebel Anomalies caught before missing their filterings too long.

They huddled together, morbidly obese males and females, whispering in low-class accents, none of them better than the next.

Some sobbed and hugged others. Some carried infants or stood next to young children. Most of them were silent. A few made guttural noises that echoed in the room, wincing at each croak, flailing their pudgy little hands around. Their vocal cords had been heard, removed, and auctioned earlier.

And the Anomaly rebels? They had muzzles over their mouths, ropes around their bodies, and new barcodes branded into their skin. They would not perish from their auction but face a worse punishment unknown to us—hidden in Anomaly law.

All were naked, shaved, cleaned, fattened up, and oiled down. Stripped of everything and transformed into breathing slabs of wight.

Ready to auction.

Reverse tiered seating—highest in the front and wrapping around the stage as it lowered—held a group of citizens as different as the goods, empty-handed and clinical.

Ready to bid.

"Be silent, still, and separate, please." My voice, young and high-pitched, rang out clearly as my paternal had instructed. Courtesy and comfort were of the utmost importance.

They moved further apart; the room went silent.

'You will sell the leg.' My paternal's voice echoes from my memories as I watch the goods reluctantly separate.

'Must it be my left? That is my strong one.

He nods. 'The Dome will pay more for the dominant leg; it has more muscle fibers.

The first wight I sold was a man. He stepped onto the platform, and it displayed his goods number and vitals. He was from Valley. A good man. A kind man. My paternal had told me the first sale would be the hardest, and I soon understood why.

This man was my paternal's best friend, and I knew him well. I pushed away any warm feelings, but they did not stay away. The bell dinged, and the clock ticked down. I had two minutes to assess him.

Goods#: 1Va
Life: 45-aged
Weight: 72 stone 2 pounds
Height: 76 inches
Lean-to-fat ratio: 65% / 35%
Blood type: O+

I hoped he would cooperate. Three members of The BloodBid, clad in red, were close if he chose not to, and I was afraid of them. Afraid for him. They held controllers that, with a touch of a button, would send excruciating pain through him. If he still refused, they would get physical. Broken bones only meant it was easier to access his marrow, and cracked skulls simplified the Bone-Harvester's paperwork.

I went through the checklist in my head. My paternal's voice helped me through.

Age. Middling. The man was in grand shape. Still agile despite his immense weight. Must have a strong heart and bones. Magnificent. Heart tastes better when it has lived a fighter. Good. +6,000 units.

Birth city. Valley. Polite. He had always been of a joyful disposition. Good for him, but that fact will not help his number. -3,000 units.

Teeth. The man opened his mouth and allowed me to check for any good ones Urban could use for their necklaces. I tapped them. A few were missing, but many were salvageable. Good. +300 units.

Skin Strength. I flipped his arm over and ran a finger up the inner skin. It was sweaty but had no oil. His skin was soft and healthy. Thin but did not break open and spill sickness when I rubbed it. He shivered while I poked different areas of his body. No cold spots on his skin and very few green splotches. I poked one green spot on his skin; it held firm and did not spill The Blaze's sickness. He would make excellent fried wight rinds. Or dermer. Good. +15,000 units.

Veins. They were a normal size and flexible, not hardened or large because of a buildup of contaminants. He truly took fantastic care of himself. But I knew that already. Good. +3,000 units.

Skin Complexion. His coloring was even, not darker or lighter in places. The trio of The BloodBid lift his belly. I note the coloring and size of his penis—mottled in places and large—and added 2,000 units to his number. A delicacy nearly everywhere, his penis would sell well with others of a similar size in the market's genitalia section. I checked the skin of his barcodes—darker than his natural color—and, after that, the skin where his birth parts used to be. Soft and smooth. Good. +8,000 units.

Smell.

The final test: how did he smell?

I asked for his arm, and this was when he broke down.

"You know me, you know me, I did nothing wrong," he said. "Please do not auction me." His face was destroyed in so many places I hesitated when the bell dinged again. Thirty more seconds.

I glanced at the back of the room. The lecturer's face was tight with disappointment. I would not be demoted. Could not. My family needed the units. *Begin*, I prompted myself and took a breath. Ignored the headache that pounded. This was the last test of my first, and it was the only test that truly mattered.

"It will be all right." I offered him a comforting smile, taught to me just an hour ago, but he continued shaking his head. "Your arm, please." Despite the shaking of his head, he moved closer. I put two fingers to his wrist. His pulse beat a rapid pace. I leaned down to smell. He was very bitter—only the adrenaline from his fear sweetened his blood—but I held my face in a non-judgmental smile.

"What market will I go to? Can you tell me this, please? What of my family?" he whispered.

"We will send 10% of your price and 10% of your wight to your immediate family, but that does not include your identical twin, as autodevouring is illegal."

"But I did nothing wrong."

"Thank you for nourishing our world."

"You know me. I am Odion!" His eyes were wide, and his spittle fell on my face. "You know me! I did nothing wrong."

He screamed my name.

And he screamed my name.

And he screamed my name.

EIGHTEEN

IT WAS TIME to auction.

My insides grinded against themselves, but I knew my paternal's best friend had done something. The BloodBid did not send citizens to auction if they had not committed a crime. The few goods from Urban had gone through a rigorous judgment process. They were guilty. All had committed crimes so terrible that they were auctioned here, in Valley.

Odio—he was a liar and deserved to be auctioned. I knew that. That is what my paternal told me. My maternal. That is what the lecturer said. It had to be true. It had to be true.

It had to be true, so I smoothed everything from my face and called out the first bid—an eighth of what I assessed. Low to signal his bitterness and, when cooked, sourness.

Many participated, but, finally, two remained: A six-dot Anomaly man from our Urban and a Common woman from First Africa. The beauty of her stunned me.

One side of her clothing was red, the other gold. Glittery lines sewed the pieces together and created triangles and graffita symbols in her three-foot train. Every inch of her outfit glowed a faint gold. Tiny bamboo sticks laced through her threaded braids; they were connected into a pyramid at the top of her head and puffy at the ends, like a volcano erupting. A tall, fanned collar stood straight, framing the back of her head. It highlighted the gossamer fabric, showing her perfect brown skin under most of her barcodes.

They were not sweating but comfortable behind the invisible barrier. Even more so because the man's Keepers arched behind him, fanning both of them.

As they fought bitterly, the waiting goods bowed as far as they could. Some citizens adored the taste of sour wight, and I raised his price by immense amounts with every lobby.

They combined their devices into one hologram and dissected him. Played an ancient game called Chess with his parts. Spoke quickly. The man was easy to understand, but I had to listen closely whenever the woman hurled a demand at me. Often, her speech was so relaxed it ran together into a mumble.

"You must study First citizen's speech, my dear daughter." My maternal. I had not listened. Never believed I would actually meet a First citizen or hear their accent.

I should have listened.

They added and subtracted numbers almost as fast as a Calculator and created rules at a speed I could not follow. His parts glided across the board.

The woman shook her head. "Pona ya somo."

"Nah, best choice I've made." He smiled. "You'll see." The red glow of his suit mingled with the gold of hers. I did not know their worths, but I knew any Anomaly's was immensely more than a Common's. They kept on, strategizing how to get the most units from my paternal's friend.

Eventually, he sold for far more than he was worth, and I was happy for it. 80% of his price would go to The Dome and 10% to fees, so I made a compromise. Even though these goods had committed a crime, it was more than likely a small one, so I would always get the highest bid for them. For their families.

"Sold to the gray markets of First Africa," I announced after the woman used five premium units and ended the battle. I would not forget how hard she fought. Or that a Common had won against an Anomaly.

The lecturer smiled, and I fell into a rhythm: call the goods number, assess, answer three questions, auction, pretend all was well.

—+—

"But we do not need the reward from my leg," I tell my paternal. I am five-aged, and I know so little. "I do not want to sell it, Patty. I do not want to sell it. I want to keep it. We are doing well."

"Yes, we are. But in Valley, you never do well for long."

I swipe the back of my hand across my nose, wipe snot across my cheek. More drips to my lip.

Where is she?

I crane my neck, sure the door will open soon.

"Verify. Where would you like the amputation?" The Wight-Harvester turns to my paternal. She holds a marker in her gloved hand, poised over my healthy, bare leg. Mine.

"At the pelvis." My paternal signs next to my maternal's signature, while the woman puts a red dotted line along the side of my stomach. He smiles at me. "You will get used to the new one. I promise this."

"But I want to keep it. It is mine, miss." The Wight-Harvester's face is flat. Unlike the mask covering my mouth and nose and muffling my words.

Where is she?

I turn to my paternal. "I did not mean to break the paintbrush; it was an accident. Ask Matty. Ask Matty. She will tell you." I look around for her. Back at him. "I apologize. I will not do anything wrong aga—"

My paternal shushes me. "None of us did anything wrong, my angel. We are wrong. Still, we must survive."

I lie back, exhausted suddenly. My eyes are heavy and shut of their own accord. He kisses my forehead. "There is a better life, but we cannot have it."

I force my eyes open. The Wight-Harvester is blurry, swaying side to side in my fatigue. She holds a thin device in the air.

I drift off to the sound of the laser startling from a silent sleep.

—+—

After fifteen hours and sixty goods sold, I went home in the early morn and answered my parents' questions.

When they could not think of any more, I fell into bed. I had eight hours to rest my nine-aged mind, but sleep eluded me as I held the two vials tightly. They were not worth the awfulness that weighed down my thoughts. Or the dreams that had turned into nightmares.

Over the next couple of months, we went through second and third trainings. The lecturer stood at the front of the room, staring at each of us for a long time.

"Can ya auction without empathy? Yes. Should ya? No."

I knew what was to come.

"This week, you'll be auctioned."

I stood naked on the stage, fattened up and oiled down. At nine-aged, my body was flat. A line of children stood to the side, chained together and sweating. Some clutched infants; many cried.

She pulls the bands tighter around my seven-aged body. Tighter until I am in pain, as rigid as the pole I am strapped to. 'Your head may bow, but your spirit cannot. Remember this, my dear daughter.'

The lecturer sat at the back, ready to place his bid. His and the other lecturers' aloof gazes were the only intimidating part of this training. Many *ding*s sounded in my head as I looked at them.

I stood straight. Head high. The pole against my back was not there, but it felt as if it was.

The bell dinged, and a boy—who had rarely talked to or looked at me during these months—assessed me, calling out my checklist numbers as he went. *Ding.* 85,000 units. An okay number. His voice was strong and clear, and he was more efficient than I was.

I opened my mouth, and he checked my teeth. Tapped on a few gently with his finger. Smelled my breath, which was not part of the assessment. He rubbed the skin of my inner arm and caressed away the sweat in my barcode a few times. I fought my urge to slam my fingers into his trachea.

I stood still as he poked a few of my green spots. They were firm. He ran his finger down my veins and called out an accurate number before checking my complexion. Even all over. Dark brown and darker still at my vulva. I stood there, proudly, as he looked—a little too long, but not obscenely. The clock was ticking.

And finally, my smell. He held my inner wrist to his nose.

His assessment was much higher than it should be.

When the final bell dinged, and he had auctioned me off, he whispered, "I like you. All of you. Beautiful."

The lecturer approached, and the boy took a step back. He narrowed his eyes at the boy, put my wrist to his nose, and smelled deeply. The lecturer stared at the boy, and he collapsed when the zap tore through his body. He screamed and writhed and spasmed until the lecturer released the button.

As he lay there, breathing hard, crying, the lecturer yanked him up and held him close to his face. "Empathy in care. Objectivity in numbers. Never auction with ya emotions." He dropped him to the ground and, a second later, slashed a savage mark in the air, on the boy's file. "Switch."

I dressed, and the boy undressed, stepping out of his wet pants. His eyes filled with tears, but he stood still. He had been demoted. Stupid boy. The lecturer already knew our worths. What was he thinking?

I stood in front of him as the lecturers gathered in a circle to enter his final numbers. A stream of snot ran from his nose. Before it reached his lip, I wiped it from his face and onto my dress. Brushed the tears from his eyes. Later, I'd hit him and rob him of his air, but not now.

I mirrored the detached stare of the lecturer and assessed him objectively. Our worths were similar. When my assessment's final bell dinged, I whispered, "Meet me before our lecture tomorrow."

I awaken in a clean room. Five-aged, alone. Everything feels the same. I flutter both feet. The sheet presses against the tips of my big toes. Perhaps Patty changed his mind.

I nearly tripped as someone shoved me from behind, but I caught my balance, as did the children roped in front and behind me. Our heads and bodies were bald. We were packed closely together and herded into the empty wing of a farm.

Dings. Millions of units.

A girl in front of me stumbled and received a quick zap. She cried out and bit her lip but was not bid. The autodevouring laws were laxer during third training,

which was designed to cement our empathy. Someone hit her. Yanked her up. Pushed her along.

We were shoved again, and the entire line pitched forward. Cries echoed from every direction. Lecturers shouted at us, cursed us, hit us, and zapped us. The farm was boiling, and the lights were at their brightest.

Earlier children screamed as they hung from their wrists. Some coughed and gasped as they went into a clear chamber. Their lungs filled with hints of a gas that would stick to their wight—and end their lives. Pink circle. Smoky flavor.

The girl in front of me fell into a white circle on the floor. She was missing her forearm and hand, but that was not an issue. The far edges of our barcodes contained all the information needed. She ran to the side and crashed into an invisible barrier. Banged on it.

The circle turned blue, and she screamed.

My breaths were short, overlapping gasps as my turn came. A machine cut my rope from the other children, and I stumbled into the circle, looking from left to right. On both sides of me, six circles fanned out. Red lasers scanned my barcodes. All parts, present and gone, accounted for. My circle turned orange, and I fell to my knee with my head down, tucking my wrists against my stomach.

The sorting machine's metal rings whipped down from above, adjusted, wrapped around my arms, and pulled them free. Slices sheared into my biceps. The rings wrapped around my wrists and wrenched me up. I screamed as the pain exploded through my body, and my blood splattered on my face. I was going to perish here.

The conveyor belt moved at a quick clip.

Orange circle. Farm-to-plate.

I watched as those in front of me, drenched in oil and seasonings, got closer to the flames. They kicked and screamed and shrieked louder as they disappeared into them.

"No, please, no! I did nothing wrong!"

I will perish here.

Oil, thick and consuming, crashed onto my head and ran down my body. I gasped for air—there was none as the grease filled my nose and mouth. Lemon seasoning detonated in my mind, but the flame was my focus. It was so hot, and I was going to fry. My heart thudded in my chest, faster than I thought it could beat.

I shook my head, spat out the oil, and looked through my clouded vision. A calm came over me, burst, and I screeched as I went through the flames.

My skin melted—and I came out the other side. Unburned.

I had survived third training. There were fewer of us when we gathered again.

In the tiny bed, I slide my hand down my chest, my belly button, and pause at my waist. My hand trembles. I take a breath and move lower. There is nothing but gauze and air to greet me. I lie there, thinking only one angry, desperate thought:

I will have that better life. No matter the cost.

NINETEEN

THREE WEEKS LATER, I visit my parents on the Anniversary of Anomalies. Parades, laughter, decorations, and food surround me. Most are happy to celebrate the Anomalies and take the day off without paying for it. It is even grander because First America paused their audit for this day.

I am close to my travel request quota for the year, but I use another to go to the Terrain line, a mile from my maternal's childhood home in Upper Valley 1.

I stand at the barrier, my hand up, millimeters from it. A girl sprints through, no hesitation, red light, and joins the other children laughing and running through Terrain's market.

They pull self-cleansing straws from the walls and drink clear, cold water.

I do hesitate. Move my hand forward. Touch it.

Green. *No.*

Press my hand harder into the barrier.

Green. *Not you.*

The barrier pulses from my palm. A handprint ripples out, larger and larger still.

I push more.

Green. *Not worthy.*

I am. I am worthy. I lean all my weight into it.

The barrier shivers, and I yank my hand away as the zap tears through my arm, pushing my heartbeat into overdrive.

I shake my hand. Massage the spasms out. Kick that stupid thing and turn around.

James of the Pillars sent more than the usual amount of units and food, so I have brought dried vegetables with me. And the infant. Their home smells of roasted wight buns, seasoned wax beans, and Catamor stew. Oh, my favorites. I kneel on the floor with my head bowed until my maternal acknowledges me.

"My dear daughter, welcome! A grand anniversary to you." I stand. My maternal hugs me before lifting the infant from his carrier. At nearly two months old, he is small and light.

She nuzzles his neck, and he rewards her with the serious look that rarely leaves him. She holds him close to her chest and makes a silly face, sticking her tongue out at him. He squints, snuggles into her, and giggles gently. "Oh, he is quite darling. Serious but darling. He looks like James of the Pillars. Cuter though… he has your smile."

This woman.

I put the vegetables in their cupboard. Their neighbors have given them much, as my parents are far old enough to be Past-Knowers, but I would never dishonor them by coming empty-handed.

I stare at their food. Run my finger down the packages. But it is a fantasy. I cannot remove any from their home. This food is registered to them, and I will not risk one of the punishments The Dome will met out.

The news talks of problems in Valley and Terrain. Always this. I ignore it as I peek into the pot of stew and take a quick taste. Pop a wight bun in my mouth. Bite into the ball of crispy, fried skin, tender wight, and fluffy sourdough bread in the middle. *Mm.*

"Delicious."

I have had many of these, but none better than the ones I will eat here. Next, I check their water stores. A quarter gallon is left for this week. Finally, their Kuru Acid.

"Stop that. We are well." I turn around and smile as my maternal stares at me, love pouring from her.

I have her wide, squared nose. Deeply bowed full lips. Smooth dark-brown skin. Forty years older than me, she is 70-aged and grayest at her temples. Beautiful. "Have you two decided on his name? You have"—she puts her thick monocle over her eye and leans toward the infant— "a week remaining?"

"Yes, near that. James of the Pillars can name him whatever he likes. It does not matter to me, I—"

"Is that my grandson and youngest daughter?" My paternal walks into the kitchen, and I kneel to him. His prostheses are flexible, and his shoes beep when he approaches the table. "My angel, welcome! Are you enjoying the holiday? Have you two already signed for his name?"

"Yes, it is great fun." I stand. Their home is decorated in red, gold, and brown banners and knickknacks for the holiday. It is like mine in size but modern, clean, and freshly painted. My maternal and paternal kiss as they hug the infant between them. *Ding.* 20,000 units each. "No, we have not signed. His name does not matter to me."

My parents are severely green-tinged scarred from their childhoods. Large, dark-green spots cover most of the brown skin that has not been replaced with synthSkin. When they were young, the filtering laws were much stricter, and they struggled to afford them.

Three gaping holes dominate my paternal's face. His eyes and nose were sold when he was a boy, but still, he tips his head to my maternal. They exchange a "look" before handing the infant to me.

"We know you pretty well, our dear daughter. Let us help with his name." My maternal touches her fingertip to the dimple on the infant's cheek.

"He is property," I whisper.

"Living property. He should have a good name. You named every limb of your pull-apart teddy, did you not?" My paternal laughs, and I do, too. "Even sewed in the names so I could read them."

"She did. Such focus." My maternal bends, holding her stomach. Talking through sputtering laughter. "As I recall, you renamed the parts when you put it back together. For the arms—Carmin and her twin Armino. Remember?"

209

My stupidity as a child will never be forgotten. I see that now.

My paternal side hugs my maternal, resting his chestnut brown hair, like mine, in her black, intricate hairdo. She pecks his lips, and both of them put a hand out for the list. Their prostheses are getting older, but they are still in good condition. Terrain-made. Both have twenty charms dangling from their wrists—four fewer than the maximum we can have.

My paternal smirks. "And if we know your husband, he has made a long list of names. Let us see."

I smile and shake my head. Hand them the list. My maternal unrolls it, and my paternal bends to catch it. He touches the ground, pretending it is so long it stretches across the floor, even though it did not thump against their gleaming tiles. His exaggeration is not far off, though. The note unrolls only a few inches from the floor.

"I will get anijsmelk. Creamy or chunky?" He pauses.

"Chunky, please," we answer.

We go into the living area and sit on the couch. My maternal hands me the list as she grabs a cover.

"Why did you not stay in Terrain after the shortage improved?" They could have stayed there. "It is better there."

"Better?" She laughs. An aged sound that is still strong. "This is our home. Our city. We will always return."

In the kitchen, my paternal's shoes beep when he nears objects, but the warnings provide him no benefit here. He knows the layout of their home better than my maternal.

He returns with three wight buns and three steaming mugs of aniseed milk, chunky with small cubes of caramelized wight dyed in holiday colors of red, gold, and brown. Sits beside me. Hands a cup to my maternal.

I am in the middle, and they press their shoulders against mine. I give my paternal the rest of the cover so we can all enjoy its warmth. Every few seconds, they reach over and touch the sleeping infant in my arms.

My paternal hands me all the tender, meaty buns, and when I am done eating them, he passes me the milk. I look into the mug.

Peek at my maternal. Do you ever feel as I do about auctioning? Does it frighten your sleep awake?

Glance at my paternal. Do you still feel like nothing? Does deciding someone's worth ever rob you of yours?

I smell the drink deeply, lost in thought, until my maternal shifts on the couch.

"What does this one say?" She sips a cube through the fat straw while pointing to a name written in sloppy letters.

"And these ones." My paternal runs his hand down the entire list.

They wait. I take the list from them and read it:

"Armino."

TWENTY

IT IS 2 morn, and James of the Pillars and I are on a screen call. Visiting with my parents three weeks ago helped to lift my spirits. I do not bring up the missed donations. All calls are recorded, and that is our business. His room is empty except for the floor-to-ceiling bookshelves built into most walls. I put my palm to the screen, and he does the same.

Urban has done his body much good. Over these last six months, he has filled out and put on much muscle. His skin— cold milk chocolate frosting before—is a warm, sweet river now. His hair, no more patches, only thick, shiny curls.

"You were handsome before, but now." I fan myself, and his exhausted, guarded expression crumbles into a shy smile.

He runs his fingers through his hair and shrugs. Much of the weariness leaves his face when I hold up the infant.

"My Trinity." He presses his fingertips to the screen. His nails are no longer thin or broken, but his voice drags. Adoration pours from his bloodshot eyes and smooths the stress lines from his face. He looks at me, a full-toothed grin crinkling the corner of his eyes. "You chose a grand name. Will you, uh... Will you bring him closer?"

I move the infant—Trinity—nearer to the screen. He is ticklish at his shoulder blades and so laughs. James of the Pillars moves closer, too, and vibrates his lips. Trinity only cocks his head at the gesture.

"He has your gorgeous smile, my love." James of the Pillars swipes a hand across Trinity's hair, and I move his rich black curls, following the arc of my husband's hand. "Luckily for him, that is all."

"Oh, oh, okay. You know what?"

"I do not. What?"

"Your DNA has made a disaster of him. Look at him." And we do. He is ours. A product of my husband and me. Soft, warm... and new. I am Common, and I have made something new.

"I am looking. You are right. He is a dud."

This man.

It has been a long time; I have missed his jokes. His voice. He exhales softly, staring at both of us. "I am most excited to meet our son. What of you, my love?" I glance at my arm. Smile widely at him. His speech is slow, and he keeps wiping his mouth. Vomiting from the stress must be regular.

"I am well."

He narrows his eyes. "Uh-huh. I do not believe one word. You have not been sleeping well."

"No, but when you return, that will improve."

"Yes, I will hold—"

The Anomaly woman walks into the room, her hair and clothes redder than before. The glow from them brighter. We bow to her.

"Farewell, my husband. Many loves." I make a silly face and put out my palm a second before the woman flicks her hand and ends the call.

James of the Pillars comes into our room a month after our screen call. He smells of sweat and dirt. Smears of the earth are on his cheeks and forehead. Now that I am not pregnant, our quota is distributed more equally, and he will remain healthier. I bow to him.

A chunk of me has missed the bowing; a growing sliver of me has not.

He pulls the shirt from his body. I watch him do it.

"How is my Trinity?" He kisses me before moving to the tiny bed.

"Sleeping as infants do."

My husband does not move. He only stares at the three-month-old—Trinity—with so much tenderness I am certain he must feel the warmth in his sleep.

"May we, my love?"

I give him the same response. "Perhaps."

He looks at me, his face sagging, so worn for his twenty-six years. "'Perhaps' is not an answer, but here is mine: I will not sign this time."

"Sometimes we must when we are in need."

He fiddles with his charms. "All are in need. They find a way."

"Yes, they do, but we have already found ours. If you took your Vow, we would not be in need."

"Again and again, this."

"Yes, again, this. How easy for you to say, 'Find a way.' You are an Anomaly. A six-dot. Given freedoms others do not have."

I sigh. I do not want to fight. It has been seven months since he left, and we could use the relaxation. Use each other. I could use him.

He swipes his forehead, all of him tense. "Those freedoms are small and closed on both ends." He taps a lump on his side of the bed. "I apologize I was not here when…"

The empty refrigerator, my panic, comes back. Ripped dresses, suits, Urban notes. I run a finger along the identiPro. Press my finger into its wrist, then higher to my palm. They feel the same. When I am not reminded to pay for the arm, I forget I was not born with it.

"I am okay. I was not here when those thieves stole from us."

"Thank the Inventor. I found out who they were. Three Valley teens. They have been sent back to their parents. Well, two of them. The eldest did not receive the same fate." His face flips through emotions quickly, so fast I cannot tease them apart.

"A moment." He leaves and returns with a mattress. We put the damaged one outside to be recycled. I lean against the headboard. This mattress is grander than our ruined one.

"I received a bonus for our successful project, my love. There is a new fridge, security system, and the replacements for our other belongings will be delivered in a week. The network was helpful?"

"Yes, it was."

He holds up a finger, goes into the kitchen. Questions ping through my mind.

Why did the donations stop for so long?

What happened to the security system?

When is the best time to bring this up?

Not now. I am too tired. Sweat cools on my chest. The night has been long.

I sprinkle sand on our bed before sitting near its edge. He makes something in the kitchen, humming a Common song. James of the Pillars returns with a cup of hot strawberry juice and cumin, blowing it.

I take a sip. The heat of the juice relaxes me. "Many thanks."

He sits on the foot's edge of our bed. "We have much to talk about." Yes, we do. "I'm sorry, my love. There were many checks for it. Many." He looks at me, choosing his words carefully. "I do not know what happened." Massages his ear harder. A sign he is lying. The wind chimes of guilt rattling across his face confirm it.

So many apologies.

So many failures.

So many things he cannot tell me.

Will not.

I hide my face in the mug. The steam fills my nose.

The most frustrating part of our marriage is how much we cannot say. How much we leave in silence that should be spoken.

I tire of it all, and I do not know what to do with the tiredness. At these times, I wish for a Common husband. It would be easier. So much easier. But I would never get to Urban with that man. Never get to love this man.

I drink more. "I want to ask questions, but not now. Let us start over."

We schedule the conversation in our devices.

"Hello, wife. I have missed you. How have you been?"

"Much better after seeing my parents. They helped with his name."

"I am sure you did much of the work."

"True. They were useless." We laugh. I have missed him immensely. "Now, tell me what happened in Urban."

"You and your demands." He smiles and stands. "We could not get one contaminated strand to stop mutating." Paces. "We cannot catch The Blaze. Cannot predict how it will change." He whips around, walks a few steps, whips around. "We replaced an entire body's blood, and still, it became contaminated once more. The Dome may stop funding the research to repair our blood. 'Long overdue,' they said."

All this was on the news.

"The citizens. The trials—" His face falls.

I shush him. "It will be okay." I pat the bed, covered in rose-scented antibacterial sand.

James of the Pillars continues pacing. I pat the bed again. He stops and looks at me blankly, lost in thought. I have seen this look before, on a younger face than his, but I cannot recall where. He musses his hair and sits on the mattress. This is how his position leaves him whenever he must go.

I move behind him and reach for his shoulders. When I touch him, he tenses, glances at me as if I am someone else. Odd. I hold my hands an inch above his shoulders. Wait until he lowers them and leans into my stomach.

Slowly, he relaxes.

I pick up the towel and James of the Pillars's bowl from the floor. "After you cleanse, let us cheer."

He collapses onto the middle of the bed, face up, arms and legs wide. "I am too tired."

"I understand." I sprinkle the sand along his chest and stomach. He chuckles and sucks in his belly. "It will be okay. Breathe, my husband."

His sweat is strong, but it is tempered by his sweet O negative. On him, this flavor is pleasant. I sprinkle more on his arms and rub it along his body. The sand absorbs his dampness and dirt and leaves him fresh.

He closes his eyes. "Paradise."

When I get to his fingertips, I look closer. Dried blood lines his fingernails. I smell. Only some of it is his. There are many flavors—and many gaps.

He makes a fist. I pry his hand back open gently, and he turns his head from me.

"It is okay, my dear."

The sand will cleanse it all away.

The squalor of our lives disappears as I wipe the dirt from his mouth, teeth, cheeks. The sand from his body. It clumps together in large balls, and I place them in the small recycling kiosk. When he is clean and naked, I hover over him. Stare at the thick scars that are soft to the touch and lie beside him with my head on his chest.

Common females, never forget a physician's appointment as you carry Anomaly females' conceiveds. How lucky you are to be given the chance to ferry such preciousness into our world. Your favored show, Today in the Past!

He gazes at the ceiling. "In this world, you do not have to do good. You need only believe you are good— and never look back to see if the path you have walked is more broken or bright than when you came upon it."

Crater thinking.

I tap his ear to remind him he must watch his words.

"They are updating for an hour."

I rub my hand up and down his arm, stopping every once in a while to feel his pulse as he falls down, down, and down. I listen to him talk for a long while as he struggles to climb up again.

"Shh, my dear. Think less."

"Am I allowed?"

"With me, in our home, yes."

"Okay."

He pulls in shaky breaths. Pushes them out through his mouth before whispering, "The new machines wouldn't work no matter what we did. They required so much testin'."

I shudder at his words.

At the hard gulping sounds of his throat. He slips, falls back down. His body trembles as sweat gathers on his arm. "Is our world better, or has it only changed form once more? Please, tell me. Is steam not boiled water and ice but frozen steam?"

"Shh, shh. It is okay, my husband."

Wild heartbeat against my ear. I scoot up, lie on my side, leveling my head with his. He buries his face in my shoulder. Holds me tightly to him, so hard it hurts. My body convulses with his. Silent earthquakes shattered by a muffled wail that explodes through my chest.

Then no more. He regains control of himself. It is another long while before he calms. Relaxes his grip. Lies on his back and says, "There is a better world."

The tall buildings, immense trees. I smile. "Urban."

"No, this world does not exist yet. We must create it."

"Tell me of this new world."

He does, and I listen, but even as he speaks, the newness fades from my mind and leaves only—Urban.

Slowly, very slowly, I lean closer and kiss the five-inch barcodes branded onto his body, recite their numbers.

"3." His scalp; it shows where his hair will not grow. Kiss.

"8." Adam's apple. He swallows; the vertical barcode jumps. Kiss.

"1." Middle of his chest, the black edge lines touch both pecs. Kiss.

"4." The inner skin of his right elbow. Kiss.

"6." His left elbow. Part of my favored arm to wrap around me. Kiss.

"3." His ticklish spot above his belly button. Kiss.

"5." His penis, I skip. Nuzzle the hair. It twitches. "Later."

His breaths are deeper now, wavering. I peek at him. The dark edge line across his chin quivers. "Must I suffer more?" He trails his hand up and down my back. Says my name. Peace flows through my nerves. From his mouth, his voice, my name feels like love. Forgiveness. I ask him to repeat it—and he does in a whisper. I continue down. This suffering, he likes.

"9." His left kneecap. The barcode touches his calf and thigh. Kiss.

"7." His right kneecap. Knobby like its twin. Kiss.

"3." Left foot. I place my lips on the top. Kiss.

"3." Right foot. One extra toe. A stubby thing. Kiss.

"1." He must turn over for me to kiss this part; I want to see his face.

I move back up his body and lower down beside him. Our breathing is erratic.

Though James of the Pillars's pleasure will have its limits, as he must be milked later this morn, I trail my tongue along his jawline, my hand down his stomach. I have been his beloved for five years, and I know one undeniable truth: his limit is very high.

After some time, we lie there, holding one another. Only then do I remember to ask him the cost. The price to be paid. But it is too late now. His listeners have reactivated. They have not received an update in all our time together, so I relax and enjoy our paradise.

We switch positions. He hovers over me with two pins in his hand—one for me, one for him.

"May I?"

"No." I giggle.

"Oh, your answer is no?" He leans down, whispers into my ear. "Are you sure?"

His breath tickles my nerves, and I wriggle under him. Hold two fingers to his wrist. His pulse is rapid like mine. "Yes, you may."

He pokes the pin into the side of my neck, drawing a pinprick of blood. Slowly licks it away. "Are you sweet?"

I smell my blood on his breath. "No, savory. Take your time with me."

I bite my cheek. A dot of blood drips onto my tongue. It is impossible to avoid biting your inner mouth. I take advantage of this loophole. He kisses me, and our saliva mixes. Dangerous. Thrilling.

I grab his hair hard, as he likes. Harder when he asks, as his pain tolerance is high. I pull him from our kiss. A deep hum comes from his throat. I rise and smell him. "You are sweet. May I taste?"

"Yes."

We enjoy each other for a few hours.

James of the Pillars may have a limit, but I do not.

TWENTY-ONE

I STARE AT my leg. The new one finally arrived a few days ago, and it is magnificent. It matches my skin tone decently. The color differences are subtler in this version.

I sit in the kitchen, rubbing my fingers against the leg. Poking it. Pulling its synthSkin. Flexing it. Rubbing my forearm on it. The identiPro registers touch and sends it to my brain.

As I recently emptied my Gold Week's last collection bag into my filtering machine, I received a premium unit—20,000 units more—to pay for the identiPro this month. How grand. And yet, the missed donations will not leave my mind.

What happened in Urban? Why were so many not sent? I must discuss with James of the Pillars when he returns.

But first, I will thank him for innovating this beautiful leg.

The weather is warm once more, and Marguerite is doing much better. She and Aniyah sit in our living area, crunching on the baked pickles with breadcrumbs and red sauce I made for them. I prepare breakfast without them, as I am enjoying walking from the back of the room to the front. And from outdoors to in.

With the bonus and help from her paternal, we ordered medication for her. She has improved physically but still cries every day, missing him.

'What did you auction him for?' her voice was soft, raspy that day a few months ago.

'He was not assigned to me.'

'But you know. How much was he worth?'

10,000 units. Two bottles of Urban wine.

'More than I will be?'

Far less than you.

Marguerite would think he wasted himself if her worth was lower. She lay there, her gaze drifting from the video call's camera. Hollowed cheeks. Tints of gray settling in her brown skin, like James of the Pillars's eyes. Slightly surprised at each new breath.

'He was worth enough for you to continue your constant chatter, little one. It was his choice to be auctioned early. There is no more you need to know, so stop asking.'

She closed her eyes. 'Okay.'

They laugh loudly. I peek in. Marguerite and Aniyah sit on the sofa, playing a game with Trinity. The bottoms of Aniyah's legs are near me, leaning against the door. I study James of the Pillars's design. Mine. Hers. And after, line her knees with one another and wipe the SynthSkin clean.

She kicks her thighs while passing Trinity to Marguerite, who tickles him and makes silly faces. Hot Potato. An ancient game. They pass him back and forth, trying to see which of them can make him smile the most.

Soon after the Distribution War, many children were snatched from the streets and illegally bid. But do not worry. We track wight more carefully now. Your favored show, Today in the Past!

It is unclear who is winning, so I watch them a long while. From what I can tell, both of them have low points.

I turn away as James of the Pillars walks into the kitchen, dropping a few items. His arms are full of books, food, cleansers, and more. I skip to him, take some bags, and empty them one by one. Lining up matching items as I go. Turning cans and boxes the same way.

Peace inside me.

He dumps the remaining bags on the countertop, organizing by seeing everything laid out.

I exhale slowly. So messy.

Ignore, ignore.

"You have done a most excellent job on this leg. Many thanks."

He smiles with all his teeth and hands me a can of Jitla beans. "I am glad to hear that, my love. This version lessens skin irritation, and the knee joint is far more responsive." He speaks faster, creating pictures in the air with his hands. "We adjusted the Naxus rotator 2.6 degrees, so there is no delay when going up and down stairs."

I listen as he talks and points to my leg.

"Look at this." He walks closer and pushes a finger hard into a middle section of my thigh; it bounces back out. "It is a Hydracoil. It eases swimming."

"Because there is more resistance in the water?"

He nods. "I have not gotten the patent yet, but I will after changing its name to Trindracoil."

That name sounds like a most unpleasant type of hernia, but I keep that to myself.

My husband links our devices to share images of the tiny, silently whirring parts so my brain can retain the newness.

It is fascinating, especially the way he explains it and lights up at all the details.

"Would you recommend I read *The Musculature of a Coil*, husband?"

He stills, shock plain on his face. "You have read that?" No, I have gotten lost up to page 15. "I can show you a most grand adventure on page 569." He smiles hard as he goes to our toilet room and brings out the massive book, flipping through it quickly.

I stare at page 569. It stares back at me. I gulp.

What torture have I admitted I have some knowledge of? There are letters where numbers should be. Squiggles, dots, symbols I am sure the Anomalies made up for fun.

Still, I remember another thing. "Water reduces muscle fatigue."

"It does, it does, my love." He hands me the book, pushing his finger hard into the complicated pictures as he rambles on and fills the shelves.

I nod when he looks at me.

I do not know what he is talking about, and he knows this. Still, I laugh when he does. His enthusiasm is catching.

Marguerite and Aniyah come from the living area with Trinity in hand, each supporting half his body. Grunting a bit at his weight. He wiggles his nose. I think Marguerite's stench bothers him, but Aniyah does not remember long enough for it to affect her much.

James of the Pillars quiets, slows himself.

"Thank you, sirn and miss. My maternal would like me to come home soon because..." Aniyah taps her head. The thick scar on the side of her head extends two inches down her forehead.

"You have to study for your courses," Marguerite finishes for her.

"Yes, that is right."

A bubbling fever fills me as I watch Aniyah's confusion. The way she drops her head in shame. But there is resignation in my rage. She was birthed with an immense memory. It was taken from her and implanted in an Anomaly. Our world needed her memory, I know this, but did it have to leave so little of her behind?

"I am ready. Come on." Marguerite waits. A miracle if I have ever seen one.

"It was my turn to say that." Aniyah hands Trinity to James of the Pillars, and he gives her a sack with enough food for both of them. They go to the door.

"I wish I had an infant brother." Aniyah turns back and wiggles her fingers at him.

Marguerite looks at us, that deep sadness wafting from her. "You do."

Aniyah blinks, and they leave our home.

James of the Pillars puts the sleeping infant in our room, and we continue filling the cupboards with books and food after he returns. I open a bag and hand him a thick guide, thinking of the thieves. They had left his stolen books on the porch one night with a message. Even young thieves can leave a message.

"What happened with the donations? You have never missed so many." I pass him another book.

"The project went horribly. They reduced everyone's donations." He massages his ear.

Lie. Many Commons work on those projects, and none of our neighbors told me they had many missed donations.

"Always this. I know you are not telling the truth. What happened?"

A hot, angry flush whips through my stomach.

He avoids eye contact. "I made a mistake, and The Dome cut my donations."

"For a month?"

"Yes. I am remorseful."

I slam a book on the counter, the geyser erupting faster than I can catch it. "Why did you not send a message?"

"I did. I sent many."

Lie. So many lies.

I will have to return the forearm. What will I be able to reach with a hand attached to a bicep?

I touch the arm that feels so much like my own, but is not, and turn from him. "You are useless to me. You want to know why?"

"No, I do no—"

"You are, supposedly, one of the Grand Anomalies, and yet you contribute minimal units to our home and cannot sell any birth parts. And, worse still, you hardly ever make Anomaly children."

"No one does."

I cannot think. All I see is myself returning the arm. Perfectly made for me. Forever wanting it back. My fingers clench around a thin book; it flexes under my grasp. I turn and look at him. "I would be better off with a Common man. He could offer more to me."

"Do I get credit for nothing?" He motions to my leg. "Inventor above, I could serve you Uranus on a red platter, and you will only ask if I am hiding Neptune behind my back. Is anything I ever do good enough for you?" He drops his arm; it hits his thigh hard. "You do not understand. Anomaly law—"

"Anomaly law this, that. I tire of hearing that excuse!"

"Well, you must, and it is not an excuse." James of the Pillars stares at me. "I am an Anomaly. You knew this, and still, you chose me. You would rather be with a useless Anomaly for the prestige than a useful Common for the survival. Do not blame me for your choice."

"I assumed that—"

"You assumed wrong." He closes the fridge. The vials inside rattle. "I am useless to you?" He laughs, shaking his head. "Your mind and three billion others are useless to me. Completely useless. Only a few are even good enough to eat."

TWENTY-TWO

I AM ON one side of our home; James of the Pillars is on the other. His bonus and my three premium units from my Gold Weeks—60,000 units total—have eased much of the stress of the shortage, yet we have been like this for a week. And I tire of it. Him.

Milling about like he does. Sneaking around. Hiding things from me.

I get up, search through our room. Flip through a few pages of the massive broken-spined tome on his nightstand. He keeps it next to him every night, but it does not have a crumb in it.

Where would he put more food?

Somewhere in plain sight.

I pull out the light switches. Nothing. Too obvious, anyway.

Stomp around the room, looking for loose boards.

Nothing.

Nothing.

Too much nothing.

I open the security hatch. Feel around. Something is taped there. Flat. I pull it out.

A protein bar.

Why does he hide food? What is wrong with him?

I open the wrapper. A bit of synthHoney wafts from the dried stick of wight. A positive.

I pull the stick out. Bend it. Break it in half. Stuff the two parts into the wrapper and zip it closed.

With two hands. Two forearms I will not be able to keep. I go to our kitchen. He comes out of the toilet room at the same time. Digested brain, now vomit, wafts from behind him.

He wipes his mouth—back of his hand, from cheek to ear. It feels familiar. He feels like a stranger. I do not want him to.

I bow to him, my muscles tight, my heart insubordinate.

"Why do you do this?" I point to the heating coils. Hold up the bar. Lob it underhanded across the room.

It wobbles in the air and falls on the floor in front of him. He did not even try to catch it. Of course not. He would not have been able to catch it anyway.

He stares at the bar. Holds a hand over his forehead, shielding his face from me. A while passes until he looks up. "Why do you ask me for things you know I cannot do, my love? If I could, I would."

"I ask for simple things: a message, the truth, some comfort. That is not a lot to ask of someone who claims to love you."

"Claims?" He picks up the bar. Shakes it. The pieces rumble in the packaging. "I have told you as many truths as I can. Sent you as many messages as I am allowed. Gave you as much comfort as any husband would, but I am not Common."

"Yes, I—"

He squeezes the bar tight and holds his arm to his side. "And I will never be. You know this." He drops the bar. It hits his foot before the floor. "If I were, you would not have married me."

His hand is trembling. His gaze blazing poles through my eyes. Anger. Disbelief. Pain. Exhaustion. Tiny grenades.

"I love you."

"Yes, obviously, but would you have married me?"

No, I would have loved you and married another. This is not what I tell him. Instead, "No. I need you."

He snoozes an Innova request. A red welt rises on his forehead after.

"Ya don't need me. Ya need an Anomaly. Don't matter which one." I look at him harder. My husband. The tiny scar on the back of his jawline, only visible when I can feel the heat from his skin. His love for ancient comedies. They are awful. *This man.* It matters so much. "I won't give ya what ya want. Ya don't understand what ya askin' for."

I shrink at his high-class accent, feel my shame at wanting more, but the hidden page reminds me of what I can be. What I can create.

James of the Pillars has already given me the choice.

He may be content with this life because he can leave whenever he wants, divorce me and go, but I will do anything for a better life.

I grab a rag and wipe the counter. Try and shove the word away.

That word. Divorce.

It is a horrid word—to divide our force.

I do not want to divide us. I do not want anyone else. I do not want to lose my choice.

I scrub harder.

If he chooses to divide us, the page would mean nothing.

I watch him through the fridge's glossy surface.

He picks up the bar once more. Stays bent for a long time, smoothing it flat. "This is not about a protein bar, my love."

"Is anything ever about a protein bar?"

He sighs as he unbends slowly. Closes his eyes a moment. "Ya said I was enough. An Anomaly was enough for ya. There's nothin' else I can be—even if I wanted." He whispers the last part, winces, then winces harder. "I have an Innova to attend."

"I can see that."

That is not what I meant to say, but I cannot think of a better answer, so I wipe the clean counter cleaner. Scrub harder. It does not help.

This disappointment. This aloneness. This chasm.

Is there a bridge long enough for us?

The unease clouds my vision, my thoughts. I put my weight into the rag, rubbing the same tiny area.

It will be perfect. It must.

He opens the wrapper and takes out half. Closes it and sets the other half on the table. "You are lucky in ways you cannot see, my love." He grabs his forehead. "No one expects you to create miracles where there are none."

He goes to his office.

The kitchen exhales. How many years has it been holding its breath?

To eat.

These words are written on my face. My body. I am standing, staring in the mirror at his script all over me. Large, ill-formed letters on my eyelids. Thinner strokes slicing through my pupils, the brown of my irises. And yet my sight is clear.

Further down. Blood. A negative. My chest is open, a Y-shaped cut spreading from my collarbones to my sternum and down to my waist. My heart covered with the same words.

To eat.

Beating fast. Ribs sticking out from the immense flaps of my skin, hanging to either side.

James of the Pillars is coming. I feel him. Hear him. A clumsy shuffle. He is here. Behind me. Not a stranger anymore. His shy smile at odds with his vibrant, magnificent clothing. He removes his suit's jacket and wraps its train around my chest loosely, covering my heart. Red seeps through the soft, blue fabric.

He closes it at my back. Hugs me. Tight, intimate. Kisses the side of my neck. Kisses my brain. Blood is on his lips. The glint of a spoon is on his fingertips. A knife is in his other hand, trembling as he focuses. My brain thuds at the same rate as my heart, only stuttering when he slices into it, scoops a piece out. Throws it onto the hot pan atop a scale.

Ding. 1 oz. 20 units.

Scrambles me. Cooks me well done.

"There's nothing worth siphoning, my love. But that's not the point, is it?"

Corn shells and wight and onions float to him. He bites into the taco.

A sharp pain bursts behind my eyes.

"Are you okay? Another nightmare?"

I have become sweat. James of the Pillars moves closer to me in our bed. Nuzzles the back of my hair. "I can make you strawberry juice." His words are slurred with sleep. He grips my stomach gently, pulling me into him further. Hums my song. Imperfectly. Misses a few notes.

None of him helps right now. Has not for the last few days. His presence only makes my nightmares worse. I set his arm next to him and get out of bed.

Look down at him.

To eat.

Is that all we are to Anomalies?

Silence is not what this is.

James of the Pillars and I are in two bubbles, prying them open only long enough to slip the infant back and forth.

It is early morn, and we have barely spoken for six days, ten hours, fifteen minutes, and seventeen, eighteen, nineteen seconds.

James of the Pillars holds him, bounces him in his arms. Paces around the kitchen's table. The infant is crying. Loud squeals. Tears slide down his obese cheeks. He has been crying far more than usual. It is annoying. It is comforting.

Sound. Any sound is comforting.

My husband sits at his table in the corner, with his back to me, focusing all his energy on changing the infant's clothes. I ignore him in return. No less angry and confused than I was.

I glare at his back. Urban trash. Turn from him.

Six bottles are lined up on the counter. I carefully pour my breast milk to the eighth line. This glutton infant has an appetite befitting a grown man.

I bend and stare at each bottle, making sure the milk does not slosh around. When it reaches the line, just so, a calm spreads over me. Fades. I measure another and another. Put them in the fridge and close it.

When he is old enough to not need my milk, I will pump for a few months more and send it to the Donation Facility, as required.

Hmm… that does not even make sense. If it is required, how can it be a donation?

James of the Pillars glances at me, angry too.

Fifty years ago, to this day, our world has had the lowest record of fome bugs. There has not been another global infection in all that time. Make sure your local market and gardens have the latest sensors. Your favored show, Today in the Past!

I shake the last bottle. Set it next to James of the Pillars.

"Many thanks." He takes it.

"Varsågod." I leave.

We are never so polite to each other. Rude wretches. That is our way.

—✚—

Three more days have passed. James of the Pillars and I sit on our couch, not talking. As far apart as we can be.

"I am correct, you know," we say in unison.

The infant coos, and it sounds like "no."

We look at him.

"My love, admit it, Trinity is smarter than us both." James of the Pillars nuzzles his tiny forehead as he puts the bottle back in his mouth.

"I admit that. While his looks are pathetic"—he adjusts the bottle and laughs—"his intellect is immense."

"Do you think that is why he smiles so little?"

I shrug. "I do not know much about infants. My parents said I smiled little as well."

"Ah, he got it from you. Your smile and your reluctance to show it."

"Hmm. James of the Pillars, tell me truly, what happened in Urban? What happened to the donations?" Though I have tried all these days, I cannot get them off my mind.

"I made a mistake." He massages his ear. Still lying.

I do not press any further as his body shivers involuntarily. "One day, tell me, but not today."

The gnawing thoughts will not quiet, but I push them away and slide down the couch. Lean against his shoulder as I did that night at Ancient Dreams so many months ago.

—✟—

"I'd like the final bottle of Manoir de Sang. Non-alcoholic." I slur the words together and smile because of it. Laugh lightly. Mouth to my husband, "Ya Keeper looks dry."

James of the Pillars looks behind him, at the man standing against the wall. Turns back to me, confused. "I watered him before we left."

"Don't worry, sirn. I'll gladly handle anotha waterin'. No need tuh stress yaself."

My husband waves off the happy-maker and takes a glass of water to the man. His hand shakes as he focuses on lifting the glass to let his Keeper drink. Some of the water spills onto the man's cream-colored shirt, but he only smiles.

Other Anomalies watch James of the Pillars.

"Must've slipped mah mind" and "How could ya forget tuh water mah Keeper?" ring through the room.

A flurry of snapping fingers ring through the room. Most of them send a happy-maker with a glass of water behind them.

Not the seventeen-year-old birth day boy. He does not send his Keeper a cup. The woman stands against the wall, grinning as others get water.

James of the Pillars wipes the man's mouth and clothes with his sleeve and sits back down. Says loudly, "Water the rest."

The woman's big smile slips. Into a small one. Into a real one.

—✟—

239

I forgot this part of that night. I snuggle deeper into my husband's warmth. Into our peace. He is a good man.

The infant spits up, my breast milk spewing from his nose and onto James of the Pillars's shirt. He pats his back while I wipe his wet, smelly mouth with a small rag. Hand it to James of the Pillars.

It did not take long for peace to run away. Cowardly thing.

He wipes the spit-up from his shirt.

"Yes, he is certainly your boy." I kiss my husband's shoulder. Leave my lips there a moment. "I apologize, my dear. I know you are doing your best, and I have been ungrateful of your efforts." I take the rag from him.

"Me too. I apologize for my words. I should not have said what I said. You are far more than I ever deserved. If you were not my beloved, I would most certainly eat your brain. It would be my grandest honor."

It would? Immense flattery.

Would it? Milder offense.

The feelings war inside me a moment until I laugh. "Of course, it would be your most prestigious honor." I glance at his listeners. Look at him out of the corner of my eye. Whisper this last part, "But you could only have a little."

James of the Pillars arches an eyebrow high. Anomalies choose how much of our brains they want. Not us.

He clears his throat and wipes a finger across his forehead, careening down to push his eyebrow back to its usual place. Smooth away what we both know: I have far overstepped my place, and he does not like it.

"That... would be more than I could ever need, my love."

The infant burps. A loud sound out his quiet body.
We exhale out this week.

I close my eyes, smiling.

'IdentiPro: 49 days remaining.'

TWENTY-THREE

TWO WEEKS LATER, and the sunlight streams in. The heat feels grand, and so do I. Not only am I close to having enough to make the identiPro's first payment in a month, but the shortage has finally ended.

After seven and a half long months, our food supplies are back to normal.

We stand in the kitchen, my husband and I. Small pots filled with fake flowers brighten the room. A pinecone sits next to the largest flowers.

Trinity smiles in James of the Pillars's arms, and he cannot take his eyes from the five-month-old. He makes silly faces and coos at his son before lifting and lowering him until his arms wobble. He has been granted the aft off and has been enjoying his son during the time.

Feeding. Burping. Playing. A half-hour passes. He lifts the infant once more, well above his head. "My love, I feel excellent today."

"It is because you ate less dirt." This is true, and it is a lie.

James of the Pillars's complexion has warmed immensely as the extra blood circulates through his body. He focuses on the infant so intently that he does not notice these changes.

Trinity giggles more than usual and flails about as he drools on my husband's shirt. The tips of James of the Pillars's large, flat fingernails are pink with blood, though I feel no different. For me, the extra blood must be delayed.

My husband takes one relaxed breath, then many quick, unrelaxed ones. His face fills with terror, and he looks at me.

"What have you done?"

TWENTY-FOUR

AROUND AND AROUND he paces, mumbling to himself. Every three circuits around the table, he shakes his head and slaps his hand hard on the beautiful pine. Trinity sleeps in our room, able to doze through anything.

Finally, my husband stops pacing. "Do you know what you've done? How could you do this? How?"

"I did it for us, my dear, so we could be well off." Some of his anxiety fills me, but I push it away.

We will have that better life.

Would you like a synthGato? Cute, fluffy, never hungry. The animal meows. Place your order in ten minutes. Your favored show, Today in the Past!

He pulls at his hair. "We? There will be—"

Three slow, strong, confident knocks at our door startle me. And breed fear. James of the Pillars hesitates, takes a deep breath, and answers the door. His back is as straight as a pole.

Bright red light streams in from the outdoors, reflecting off their uniforms, and icy daggers, stabbing and spreading, seize my insides. My husband shakes his head as two of the three bow to him.

"James of the Pillars, we've received ya submission. Let us in?"

"You—" He closes his mouth as his face twists in much… hatred. I have never seen hatred carve jagged lines through his features.

She leans forward. "Let us in."

A moment passes before James of the Pillars nods and moves aside. Three people walk in. Why are they here?

Why are they here?

Before the door closes, our neighbors peek out from their homes. That is as far as any of them will venture.

The door locks.

The BloodBid stands with unbreakable, rigid posture in a triangle, with the woman at the peak. The leader of all BloodBids stands in front of me. In our home.

Their barcodes glow red. I have never seen a BloodBid made of Anomalies.

Three *dings*. Static in my head. A light headache forms as my brain calculates. Near sixty billion units combined. In my kitchen.

That much. Here, in Valley.

James of the Pillars is to my left. He and the woman are locked into a stare, neither moving an inch.

Nausea rises in my chest as I drop to my knees and bow. The pressure on my stomach worsens my desire to hurl. I clamp my mouth shut. Bend until my forehead touches our floor and put my palms face up in front of me.

Oceans of fright churn inside me and harden. Freeze me in this position.

James of the Pillars's shadow moves across our floor as he bows to the woman. Unbends.

Seconds, tiny eternities, tick by. I stare at her shoes, bright red. They—are they moving closer to me? Every part of me tracks her shoes. Yes, they are.

Little by little. Closer to my hands.

I exhale every couple of seconds, the muscles in my arms jumping from wanting to pull away. Out of her sight and into my stomach.

Her shoes stop at my fingertips. Press against them. Hot bile lurches up from my stomach. Acid on my tongue. I swallow it. Her shoes lift. Move forward. Come down on my fingertips.

I hold in a whimper as she leans forward, grinding her weight in. James of the Pillars's and the other Anomalies' shoes do not move. All of their shoes face her.

A tsunami of pain spreads up my arms, into my neck, and the headache explodes into a migraine.

Do not move. Do. Not. Move.

My husband clears his throat.

A long while passes before the leader says, "You may unbow." Her light voice carries through the room.

Finally, she crawls back. Blood, an excruciating tingle, rushes back into my numb, white-tipped fingers.

I unfold myself and stand. Hide half my body behind my husband, my fingers behind my back. Clasp them together so she will not hear their quaking. Inside, I wobble. The migraine is making me dizzy.

I glance at her. Away. She is still staring at James of the Pillars. Her gaze hurts, though she is not looking at me.

My thoughts ricochet in every direction, slammed around by the growing panic racing through my mind.

She studies James of the Pillars, our kitchen. Scanning me, our belongings, as if we are disgusting specimens in her lab.

Nothing of her body is hollow, missing, or lacking in the comforts of life. If I were born right, we would look similar.

Behind her, the other two have three dots on each temple. One wears black bands around their forearms. Either a softer-faced male or a harder-faced female, neutral of gender. The third is a short man with an extremely young face. The Martinet. Fear spikes through me as I watch him for any movement.

James of the Pillars's hard gaze, unmoving focus, unbreakable stillness, melts. He looks at me with so much distress I put my hand on his shoulder. He places his over mine and rubs my fingertips with his thumb. Any other time, it would be reassuring.

His gulp is audible in the quiet. "Welcome to our home. Would you like some ClearJuice?"

The woman takes in our kitchen. Grungy, cracked, and mismatched. Embarrassment fills me as she clears her throat, raises an eyebrow at him. Steps toward him. Waves of power radiate from her. "We're immeasurably happy fuh ya submission, James of the Pillars, but mind ya tone."

"I'm sorry. Where've mah manners gone?"

"Intuh the roaches' bellies, I assume." The leader flicks her hand toward me. "Introduce ya beloved."

"I didn't submit this piece. Ya know mah stance. I wouldn't."

"It's submitted. Introduce ya beloved."

I breathe as softly as possible. This is both Urban and Anomaly business, and so he ends my introduction with "Speak freely, mah love."

I will do no such thing. Cannot even if I dared. My words have gone; my body trembles with his.

"We've waited many, many years fuh ya submission, and we're most excited." The silent two behind her nod as a hint of warmth creeps into her voice.

They are excited? Okay, that is good news.

I peek at my husband. His fingers clench around mine, but why? Why does he resist the submission so much? The price was not that high.

Just one infant.

"Don't do this. I put in no submission. Tell them ya did this." He turns to me, but I shrug and feign the ignorance expected of those from Valley. "Tell 'em, mah love." When I remain silent, he drops to his knees, pulling me with him. "Please don't take 'em."

He looks up to her, transformed from 26-aged to 2-aged, and weeps from a deep part of himself that even I have never witnessed. I know our neighbors hear it.

What have I done?

She bends and grabs his face. Shakes it hard. Her fluorescent barcode flashes in my eyes as she stares into his. He quiets, and she whispers, "It's a mercy. You'll wonder about their wellbeing no more. Wonder of their happiness or misery no more. Tuh know what became of 'em, tuh think of 'em no more, is a mercy fuh all Anomalies. Our world needs ya—fully." She smiles softly.

Them?

She moves a few inches from his face, pulls a black cloth from her pocket, and puts it over his eyes and temples. It latches to his face and makes a whirring noise. He does not react, but I smell burning flesh. I squeeze his hand. What is she doing?

She pulls it away and stands. Looks down at him. "Ya Vow."

He glances at me, our room, her. His eyes do not look harmed, but six dots now sit on his temples.

My husband stands. Answers in a strong voice, "I vow tuh innovate as only an Anomaly can. I dedicate mah life tuh the evolution of our world." A long pause. "I'll love none after her."

Wait, what is happening? Have I just—

"Accepted." She scans his body, and his barcodes light up. Red is all around me. I am suffocating in it.

The leader places a hand on his shoulder. "Take us tuh ya daughter."

"She's not yet of age; she still has time." His voice is hoarse. James of the Pillars leans on me, and I use my strength to support him. "What of mah Trinity?"

"He'll be shipped tuh ya beloved in Urban."

Urban. Urban? It is all I can understand.

Finally. We are going to Urban.

My husband and I walk away from our home—to a daughter I did not know he had.

TWENTY-FIVE

JAMES OF THE Pillars has a daughter. A daughter. Too many thoughts and emotions swirl through my head. They fly in panicked directions, making the pain worse, and so a hint of surprise is all I can muster.

The leader of The BloodBid walks in front of us. The other two walk behind. Twelve Keepers in black form a wide circle around us. She flicks a hand at me. "She didn't need tuh come."

"That's mah choice, not yours." James of the Pillars's tone is no longer pleading but stone-hard.

The new dots at his temple are pink at the base. Freshly branded. I put my finger up to one. Hold it close as if there is anything I can do.

"They do not hurt, my love." His face is broken. Voice soft. For a long while, he rubs his eyes.

"What did she do to them?" I swipe my hand across his hair.

The Martinet behind us laughs. "When I took mah Vow, it wasn't so bad. I disliked mah paternal, brother, and three of mah four sisters, anyway. Glad tuh be rid of 'em."

The other person's voice is quieter. "Ya don't mean that."

"Don't tell me what I mean." The Martinet cracks his knuckles.

"Do not *tell me* you have forgotten where I was birthed." The person's laidback accent is now a painfully enunciated Abyss dialect, all gentleness gone.

Spending even a year in Abyss will harden anyone. Growing up there can turn them into concrete if they allow it. I glance back. The person motions to James of the Pillars and whispers, "Luckily fuh him, he was allowed tuh choose tuh take his Vow. I wish I could've." I peek backward again. They press their finger to each of their three dots. "I loved mah family. Mah brother, he was mah best fr—"

"Boo-hoo, they were just Commons."

I do not hear anything after this. My mouth becomes a sauna. "Wh-what is happening?"

"It is Anomaly law, mah love." James of the Pillars looks at the woman with unreserved hatred. "When an Anomaly accepts their Vow, The Dome severs outside connections." He kisses my hair. Rests his cheek against my forehead as his arm quivers around my back.

"Commons, you mean."

251

He nods. "You will receive enough time to care for our Trinity until he reaches Vow age." He gulps, and his beating heart skips. "Then you will be auctioned. And so will he if he is not an Anomaly. And so will—"

"What? No. No."

Numbers sweep through my head far too fast to stop the calculation. Nine, no eight-aged. Eight-aged. That is Anomaly's Vow age.

Seven years, seven months left.

My hair grows wet with his tears. My ear full of his hushed voice. "If they are not Anomalies—"

"It is okay." My thoughts are rambling and fuzzy, fast like his quick breaths. I grab onto the clearest one. "My husband, you have gained wealth, comfort, and fame. Urban. A better life."

"I was born wit those things. I didn't need tuh gain 'em. I never needed 'em." His high-class accent is thick now, a few words little more than a mumble. I have never heard him use it fully. I drop my head in its presence.

A tear slides down my forehead and lands in my eyelash. I wipe it away; it is brown.

Brown?

I glance up, back down. We pass a tall, flat, gray rock. No. No, this cannot be.

We turn right, down a familiar path. Street 12A.

All around me has gone silent.

He wipes his eyes. Brown streaks stain his sleeve and leave—gray. His eyes are gray.

My stomach clenches, and I take in a few deep breaths. Nothing good will come if I scream.

The world comes roaring back.

"James—"

"Perfect pitch is received through heredity, mah love."

Three hundred seventy-five years ago, all grass was green. Yes, that is awful, but it was a sign of health. Your favored show, Today in the Past!

I look around. Try and understand all that is happening. We come to her house.

A hoverLimo, red and luxurious with gold triangular designs in the paint, gold accents, and gold-tinted windows, floats fifteen feet above us. Nothing like the white, four-wheeled groundVan whirring behind it.

The BloodBid knock on their door with three raps as they did our own. A flurry of activity happens behind the door before it opens.

"We've come fuh ya daughter." The leader's light voice only makes her more terrifying.

Xaia hobbles out of their home and falls to her knees, half bowing, half collapsing. The door slams behind her. Though her body shakes, she is silent, waiting for permission to rise.

Tap, tap, tap…

I focus on the leader's shoes, measuring their distance from Xaia's fingers. Both of her arms are prostheses now, but they send signals to her nerves.

The leader does not move. Does not step on Marguerite's maternal.

For a minute, there is silence; it is broken by trembling breaths from Xaia. Soft nos.

The woman blinks. "Ya may unbow. Speak freely, all."

"No, no!" She looks up at James of the Pillars, still for a moment, staring at his eyes, and screams at him, "Why did you do this? Sirn, you said you never would." Her voice rings through the air, bringing out neighbors filled with morbid curiosity.

"I didn't. I swear to ya I didn't." He holds me tighter as her tears flow down her face. The Martinet moves, does not ask to come into her home, but brushes past her, knocking her over. When their door does not open, he yanks it outward, breaking it off the hinges. Small thuds sound as her children's bodies fall on the ground.

*Ding*s become a buzzing, screeching sound in my head. Her children scramble out of their heap and bow as their maternal had. Sniffles slip from them.

High-pitched yelling and cuss words come from inside. Smashing sounds. Soon after, the Martinet exits their home with Marguerite. Holds her like you would a plank, pinning her arms and legs still. Her breaths are loud, sucking sounds, and her hair is half-braided. She twitches once. Slackens. Exhausted.

A small scratch is on his angry face.

"She is an Anomaly, marm!" Her maternal stares at Marguerite. Moves her gaze to the leader. "Please listen. Her pitch is perfect. James of the Pillars has told me this." She continues, shouting Marguerite's virtues.

"Stand and stop crying. Now." The leader's nose scrunches as Xaia struggles to stand. "Inventor above, bless me with patience."

When she is standing in front of the woman, Xaia sucks in a large breath, taller but bent down, hanging from the other woman's words.

The leader turns to the Anomalies behind her. "Empty-headed. Of course." She shakes her head. "Ya must explain everything tuh these… citizens."

Both of them laugh softly. Nod. There is fear in the sound.

James of the Pillars's body vibrates rage.

She grabs Marguerite's maternal by the back of her head and pulls her face close. "Can ya understand me?"

Xaia nods with quivering lips.

"The mark of an Anomaly ain't their ability tuh echo a grand idea or song. Her pitch don't mean nothin'." The woman grabs her hair harder, and she winces. James of the Pillars steps forward; I pull him back. He squeezes my hand until it is numb.

"Leave her alone." Marguerite gasps after screaming these words. The Martinet twists her wrist and covers her mouth with his hand.

The woman continues, "Anomalies possess a nearly extinct skill: The ability tuh innovate. That means tuh imagine somethin' new." She releases Xaia and wipes her hand on her red pant leg. Tiny hairs fall from the fabric. "Can she do this?"

Her maternal stammers, looking back and forth from Marguerite to the woman. The uniformed woman turns to James of the Pillars. "Have ya witnessed this girl innovate?"

"No, but she's got a few months 'til her eighth birth day."

Chaos. Misery. My fault.

I turn away, toward the path back to our home. Aniyah is standing at the edge of Marguerite's house. Her eyes are jumping from person to person—panicked, confused marbles. She is breathing hard. Must have sprinted half a mile here. A smear of food is on her cheek, stretched as her mouth hangs open, and the dress she bought dangles from her limp arm.

One hundred twenty years ago, the wight farming process was horrid. Through much trial and error, the Anomalies innovated the pleasant process you enjoy now. Give them many thanks. Your favored show, Today in the Past!

"Please listen, marm. She writes pages. Music." Xaia gestures to Marguerite, who stands now, twisting in the Martinet's arms, a defiant look on her face.

"Well, go and get these pages." The woman's tone is patronizing.

Her maternal and siblings run into their home and come back with many, many pages. The leader snatches a couple and hands them to the person with the black bands behind her. They skim them and shake their head.

James of the Pillars steps forward again. I reach for him, but he moves his arm away from me. "May I?" His voice rings with authority, though the whites of his eyes are pink.

The person glances at their leader and hands the pages to him.

My husband hides it well, but I see his dismay. "She's still got a few months."

The person with the band's face softens, and they nod.

"At four-aged, ya wrote ya first composition." The uniformed woman's face takes on an infatuated look. All theirs do. But still, no matter who they are speaking to, they will do as their position dictates. "Our monitorin'

tells us it's highly unlikely she'll become an Anomaly, but yeah, The Search'll verify."

She turns to Xaia. "Do ya love that man?"

"No, I do not, marm."

The leader whips around to James of the Pillars, her red eyes trained on him. "Do ya love that woman as well?"

"No. She was mah previous beloved who left me and married anotha. I got no feelings fuh her." His voice is icy.

A few feet in front of us, Xaia stares into her children's eyes. Each of them. When she reaches Marguerite, her thread snaps, and her resolve shatters. She points at me.

"James of the Pillars, this is your fault!" My husband's body shakes hard as she glares at him. "That woman. She caused this." Her finger wobbles. "You caused this. She is wicked. Eight charms. Eight." Xaia is inconsolable. "I let my Margee visit because you promised you would keep her safe. And for years, I have worried this day would come. Years." She looks at him with nothing but hatred and screams, "Is she safe?"

The uniformed woman surveys everything, a smirk on her face.

Despite the instructions given to her, Xaia collapses to the ground again, rocking back and forth, holding her grieving children.

The leader flicks her wrist toward the hoverLimo, prodding James of the Pillars to get in. There is suffering all before him, and he does not move. Only stands there with a blank, horrified face.

"Get in, or I'll bid all but the defective one."

He blinks. Hugs me. Every part of my husband shakes, but his voice is strong. "I will always love you."

He glances at Marguerite and steps away from me.

The long vehicle lowers and opens its door. It does not demean itself by touching the concrete. He walks to it, holds up a trembling palm, and gets in. The door sighs closed.

"He lies about despising the maternal. Handle this."

She goes to the hoverLimo. The door shuts again, and the vehicle lifts with no sound and disappears.

"Who will care for my children?" Xaia screams. "They have no paternal; they will perish."

No one answers or gives her children a second look. The BloodBid moves quickly, and Marguerite, her maternal, and I are taken.

TWENTY-SIX

BEFORE HE CLOSES the doors, the Martinet throws the dress onto the floor in front of Marguerite. Dust coats its fabric.

"Here. That dirty-faced girl wouldn't shut up about it." Aniyah's shriek confirms his words. He slams the door, and their screams stop.

We are scanned. The groundVan pulls off, heading to the northernmost tip of Urban, sixty miles south of Fourth Canada's border. It glides along the unbroken concrete. The smoothest ride I have ever had on land.

Xaia hobbles to the window and puts her hand to it.

Her children grow smaller. She wipes her face. Takes deep breaths before turning to Marguerite, leaning against the back door, whispering, "I do not understand. I do not understand. I do not understand."

She sits across from me, sets Marguerite on her lap. "Let me help you put on your new dress. It is beautifully made." I sit a few feet away from them, near the front. Their backs are to me, but I watch them in the long strip of mirror painted above the door.

No tears will fall. My insides are frozen.

What have I done?

Marguerite coughs. "What is happening? Why is… James of the Pillars—" She coughs again. Gasps. Looks at me. "Maternal, why, where are we goin—" A coughing fit doubles her over. Xaia holds her as her wheezing, gasping breaths get louder. As sweat covers her forehead and dots her dress.

I look away as the minutes pass. When the attack finally ends, Marguerite rests her head against her maternal's shoulder. She dabs the sweat from her daughter's forehead. Her stench has been washed away, and the groundVan fills with her immensely sweet flavor, stronger because of her adrenaline. My mouth waters against my will.

"There is much you do not know, my little one. Long ago, I made a mista—"

Marguerite whimpers. Xaia quiets.

She buries her face into her maternal's shoulder.

"What is going to happen to them?"

"I do not know." Xaia presses her lips together to stop the trembling. "Maybe someone will help them."

A long while passes. The groundVan is near silent.

It is broken by a laugh from behind me.

Xaia smooths the wrinkles from her daughter's freshly sown pleated dress with a light purple hemline and nuzzles her cheek. "Oh my, little Margee Pargee, your hair needs more love." Her voice is hoarse, her collapse close to the surface.

She undoes what remains of Marguerite's braid and smooths down the hair.

"Will you help me braid it?"

It takes a few tries for Marguerite to take the hair her maternal offers her. Even more for them to begin rebraiding it. She passes one strand and then another to Marguerite, who gives each back to her. The process takes a long time as their arms shiver.

Common chefs, always work closely with your Anomaly supervisor while attempting new recipes. They must verify the originality of your creations. Your favored show, Today in the Past!

When they are done, she kisses her daughter's head. Marguerite sobs and holds her maternal around the neck. Her freshly-done braid whips from side to side as she shakes her head.

"Listen closely. My last lesson is about your heart." Xaia kisses Marguerite's cheek and wipes her face dry with the other dress.

"If you meet an Anomaly woman, do not fall in love with her. Learn from my mistake; keep your heart closed to them. I would have done the same if I had known, but I did not." She hugs her even tighter. "He told me this law after two years had passed. I swear to you. I swear it." A wobbly breath. "Anomalies are dangerous. Their promises are lies."

She pauses and takes the braid apart as Marguerite leans into her chest. With a light touch, she combs her fingers through her curls and lets her hair flow free. "But, if you are an Anomaly, do not inflict your existence on a Common. You will only cause her suffering and shadows." Her voice goes hard. "And if you should meet a woman, wicked as *that one*, run from her. Do not look back." She clips a black barrette near Marguerite's hairline as she stares down at her.

Marguerite looks at her. Her face contorts, ages well beyond her seven years. "But, what about—"

"Leave her in Valley. Please. Do her that favor."

They sit there, her maternal squeezing her muscles so Marguerite will not become stiff.

"Terrain" hangs in the air as we approach the largest city in our region, and a red light passes the windows as we cross the invisible barrier separating Valley from Terrain.

It is quiet for a long time.

Xaia looks at me as she rubs Marguerite's back—her eye pink and glossy. Her gaze a hard, broken rage.

She raises an open hand. Metal under a layer of SynthSkin. Deep, shaky, violent breaths pour from her.

Forever. It passes. I cannot look away.

She swallows and closes her eyes. Lowers her hand and rubs her daughter's back once more. When she opens them, a sliver of pity is in her fury.

"He would have never let you go. Anomalies like to hoard their toys." She points out the window and wipes me from her memory. "Look out there, my little one. It is a beautiful day. And tomorrow will be even more beautiful."

Xaia talks of buildings and plants and explains how the water system works in Terrain. She tickles her daughter and kisses her cheek. Holds her without speaking.

The groundVan stops. She hugs her so tightly that her fingers dig into her small arms.

"Margee, you are my grandest gift."

The doors open. A trio of The BloodBid forces Marguerite and her maternal apart before shoving Xaia into another vehicle. Windowless.

Both doors slam, and we continue to Urban. I shake my head, trying to clear it of all that is happening, but I cannot. Out of the chaos, one thought surfaces, certain where the others are not—progress cannot be made without sacrifices.

Marguerite bangs on the doors. Coughing. Gasping. "Maternal! Maternal!" I move toward her. "No!"

She backs into a corner. Terrified. Of me. Her breaths come in long, deep gasps until, finally, she does not have enough energy to scream. Her body slackens, and dust springs from the van's floor when she crumples against the door. Lies down. Quiet.

What have I done?

"Marguerite, I am—"

She covers her eyes with the other dress.

A half hour. Maybe longer. I wait until she moves a fraction, all of her stiff now. She whimpers as she uncovers her eyes. Sits up. Picks up her barrette from the floor and tries to put it back in her hair. Her hand shakes; the barrette slips from her fingers and falls into her lap. One time. Two. Marguerite comes over to me. Overlapping streaks of tears have dried on her face. She stares at me. Her lip poked out. Her eyes glossy.

"Will you help me?"

I nod and clip it into her hair. Straight. Perfect.

She looks all around. Back at me. Her face crumples, and she grabs me. Holds me to her.

This was not suppos… I did not mean…

I tune back into everything else only when the buildings grow taller, and Marguerite pulls away. Sits next to me. Looks at me.

"How will my maternal find me when she comes back?"

She counts the charms dangling from my wrist gently before throwing each to the side as she recounts. Short whispers of grief. Eventually, she yanks them, jerking my wrist harder the more rounds she completes.

Pain erupts under my bracelet. Disappears. Flares stronger when she finally stops.

"Is all this your doing?"

"… Yes, it is. I am remorseful."

"Why? Did you hate my maternal that much? Do you hate me?"

"No, I love you."

Marguerite's head jerks up, emotions flitting onto her face. Confusion reigns. "Did you know the consequences?"

"No."

"You should have. That is what you said!" She drops the charms. Wheezes hard. "That is what you said." A whisper.

She moves as far away as possible and looks down at her lap. Smooths out the wrinkles and wipes most of the dust from her hair and dress. Marguerite stares ahead. Sits straighter. Proud and strong like her maternal.

I look out the window, away from all I have caused.

Forty-five years ago, ya devices were updated to get our broadcast. Took long enough, but still, how lucky fuh you. Your favored show, Today in the Past!

We enter Upper Terrain and slow down because the streets are full. *Ding*s everywhere. There are so many Terrain citizens that they work in shifts. The low houses, barren land, and unbroken concrete of Valley are gone. We crawl past the boxy, tall homes, small trees, and thin bike roads of Terrain.

Many citizens get clean water from black marble fountains placed every 150 feet. A calming stream of smoke drifts down the fountain's ornate petal-shaped steps and transforms into liquid in the basin. Each fountain glows—a small, blue world drizzled into an onyx mirror.

Circular tables surround these centerpieces. The Terrainese eat, talk with one another, and trail their hands along hanging plants. The weather outside does not matter, as invisible barriers encase them in climate-controlled bubbles.

The youngest children wave at us, not knowing we are rogues going to the auction cells. No, not we. I. I am a rogue.

An hour and a half passes. Marguerite has not spoken a word. She only stares ahead, her expression blank, horrified.

What could I possibly say to her? 'I am remorseful' will never be enough. For her. For any of them.

Red light covers my view as we cross the invisible barrier and enter Horizon.

Four hundred ninety years ago, Horizon was barren land, swamps, and dragonflies. Hard tuh believe, we know. Always recycle and stay relaxed. What's life but a fun interlude from a beautiful sleep? Ya favored show, Today in the Past!

Long, flat buildings with horizontal windows cut off the immense expanses of neat, multicolored grass in front of them. Gleaming, modern designs. The line between the two is precise to mimic the horizon. Each building is three-quarters covered in graffita, and the designs dominate my senses. Real squirrels and birds, bred to be various colors, sixty-foot trees, and well-fed citizens dot the city. Each person worth large amounts.

Marguerite does not look out but rubs her fingers along the dress, clenching and unclenching her muscles. Her chatter runs through my mind: 'Why are there rail tracks in front of the buildings?' 'Oh, do you see that? The little carts are delivering them water. Delivering!' 'That girl has to use the toilet. Where do you think—'

I stare out, unblinking. Horizon grows blurry.

I did not know she could be silent. Now, I see she never had a good enough reason to be. I glance at her.

You did not deserve this.

I gaze out the window again. Horizon is beautiful. I have never been here, only saw hints of it when our hoverCar to Ancient Dreams flew over. The citizens peep at the van. Disgust overtakes their faces. I turn, avoiding them. Turn again. Avoiding Marguerite.

Red light covers the windows once more, and when it clears, expansive lawns, immense trees, and carefree citizens sprawl as far as I can see.

Glass sneakers—every color but green—hang from power lines by wire laces. The sunlight shines through the glass, projecting the letters etched into the shoes on the ground. Names. Small memorials of the first-discovered Anomalies. These shoes are all over Urban, and they will light up in the night, as they did when we went to Ancient Dreams.

Welcome tuh Urban. Follow the rules, and you'll have a grand time. Don't and ya won't. Never forget tuh take care of our city...

Okay, sorry, that's all they'd allow us tuh say. Ya favored show, Today in the Past!

The Urban dialect fills my device as healthy, laughing, comfortable citizens bike along the streets. Walk on the transparent concrete with water running underneath—the long trains of their clothes flowing behind them.

Glittering flowers and massive, radiant leaves sit atop giant trees connected by multicolored bridges. The trees are interspersed between the buildings, which are covered in murals of leaders of the Republic of the United First Regions, and citizens turn and disappear into rooms from the bridges.

Oh, I am here. I cannot believe I am actually here.

Children and adults pull large Brazilli grapes from the trees' bark as they ride transparent platforms up and down. A one-dot boy with a glowing barcode across the top of his head reaches for a grape almost as large as his palm and laughs when it disappears into the tree.

Ding. 10,100,000,000 units. Whoa.

At the bottom, jam flows through massive, elaborately designed tubes that spell "Urban" and drips into jars hovering and rotating around the base.

A four-dot Anomaly woman—with large and small braids fashioned into an intricate upright triangle at the top of her head, yellow thread weaved through it, and wrapped in a stunning yellow robe vibrant against her mid-brown skin—grabs a large jar as she leaves. She moves so quickly she drops it. Gray jam and glass cover the ground. After flicking her train out of the way, she keeps walking.

Ding. 19,300,000,000 units.

A man wearing a green uniform runs to give her another jar and clean the mess. He is bent over. Tired. Seared with dark barcodes like mine. A worth like mine. 125,000 units.

A thin, floating circle opens and tightens around the crook of the woman's elbow. It fills with red and deposits her blood into The Dome's underground system. She never stops walking. Or smiling.

Will I smile like that someday? I look in the distance. The Dome's silver facilities only exist on the farthest edges of the city, and The BloodBid are tiny specks in the rest of the colors. Forgettable.

Urban.

Oh, I am in Urban.

"Look, Mar—" I turn to her. Away.

Press my forehead against the warm glass.

We go through the most magnificently designed trees, bushes, and flowers I have ever seen. Each one has an overlay that shifts the colors, changes the messages. The trees have glowing graffita images and words written down their trunks.

The groundVan stops. The same Martinet opens the doors, yanks us from the back, and sets a walker on the ground gently. We bow to him.

A dozen white groundVans are perfectly lined up next to ours. Each has many more citizens in them than ours. Marguerite grabs my hand and leans into me. I wrap my arm around her shoulder.

A man from another groundVan sprints to the trees. When he reaches the edge, the barrier lights green and buzzes. He screams and falls onto his back.

The Martinet laughs loudly. "Every time. The beauty of the trees must confuse ya intuh thinkin' ya not goods." He looks at me. "This is the back of Urban, where our garbage goes."

"We are not garbage." Marguerite scowls at him.

He steps closer. Bends down. I move her back. "Mah lil sistah was like ya. Stubborn. Stupid. A worthless Common." He stares at her before tapping her nose with his finger. Laughs as she scrunches her face. Sticks her tongue out at him.

A fraction of his smirk falls. Grief. Guilt. Both age the Martinet. Quiet his voice as he looks into Marguerite's eyes. "I didn't have a choice." He unbends. A more sinister smile replaces the broken smirk. It is forced. "Only six-dots get one."

He swipes a finger across his forehead and turns away. Jerks the disoriented man to his feet and walks through the barrier, leaving him with us.

Under the shadow of a 200-foot redwood, they assemble us into a crowd, shoving slow-moving people. And there are many. Most are in some stage of shock, and a few are dragged across the ground as they are unable to move.

A spectrum of clothing make up our group: most wear the perished-gray colors of Abyss; a third are from Valley and Terrain; a few Commons wear Urban's stunning colors and speckles of unparalleled beauty cloak Anomalies, who are wrapped in tight bonds.

*Ding*s. Near a billion units.

"I didn't do nothin'," Those from Urban and Horizon scream at the trios of BloodBids weaving between us— Common like us.

Fear screeches through my stomach, louder still at the sight of the red-tinged person smiling down at us from a platform.

Tall. One dot on each side of their head. Light brown skin the color of Aniyah's. Their red hair is shaved in triangles, creating a never-ending optical illusion.

Most bow.

"Welcome tuh the auction cells. Each building's split intuh wings, and you'll be sorted by crime committed. Please, go ahead, resist. You'll be freed sooner than ya think." The Urban citizens and Anomaly rebels shout louder, but everyone else pauses. "Because we'll cut ya remaining time tuh zero."

All go silent but one Anomaly woman. She screams through her muzzle; it distorts her words and makes them unintelligible.

Each Anomalies' muzzle creates a different distortion. The auction cells will not risk them banding together and innovating an escape. It has happened a few times before.

The woman fights against the bonds around her arms and legs. Falls over. Three guards grab her. She kicks and yells, and any other bold Anomalies go mute.

The person above us chuckles. It travels through the air. They pull their index finger down the middle of their forehead a moment before walking away.

Everything moves quickly. Too fast for Marguerite. She falls, and I snatch her up as a guard shoves me from behind. An image of the Anomaly woman pops into my device. Stamped across her face reads *Relocation: The Fields*.

The Martinets bark short orders before going through the barrier and leaving. We are herded into single-file lines, packed close to one another. Marguerite is in a line to my left, and guards in simple, dark gold uniforms surround us. The Dome's crest on their chest and back. Under it, "West Auction Cells."

A tense calm is what remains of the chaos.

I look around; all of me vibrates with fear and excitement. Seven years, seven months.

I get Urban for seven years and seven months.

Marguerite pulls at my hand. Holds it tight. I look down, blink a few times. Smile at her. "I know you are scared, little one."

She stares at me, her puffy, panicked eyes squinted in concentration. Let's go of my hand.

"I see you now. My maternal was right."

TWENTY-SEVEN

DING. 400,000 UNITS.

"Sirn, where are you taking her?"

A man grabs Marguerite's other hand, lifts her, and carries her to a groundVan filled with children.

"Focus on where we're taking ya." A woman turns me around, directing me toward a long line of citizens following another guard. *Ding.* 470,000 units. The line shuffles toward an immense tree.

Wh-What? I am going to a tree?

Back of the line. I crane my neck, trying to find Marguerite, but she is gone, into one of the groundVans.

Only a few remain.

As we get closer, a tall building appears—in the hollowed-out middle of the tree. She pushes me forward when I pause, staring at the hidden building. Hundreds of arched windows line the building's face, which is painted to blend in with the tree's bark, and massive leaves grow up the sides.

"Where are they taking her, marm? Please tell me." I ask again.

"Tuh the section where the orphan midpotential children go. Now, shut up and walk."

Red benches, lounge chairs, and lunch tables are scattered throughout the neatly trimmed gold grass. The air is temperature-controlled and subtly changes scents. And Marguerite is somewhere I cannot visit.

The guard pushes my shoulder forward—I resist the urge to glare at her—as the door lights red and allows us through.

Green.

It is all I see.

Horrid, sickly green everywhere.

A deep moan comes from the others. The same groan is inside of me. We have never seen so much of this color.

"You've chosen tuh destroy. Now we'll force ya tuh rebuild." The guard's voice is loud, easily reaching me far in the back. She floats on an invisible platform, guiding us forward from high above. She is thin, under five feet tall, and terrifying. "Be silent."

We walk down a long, hot hallway and turn right, into another scalding hallway. Hotter than the first, I am sure.

In front of me, sweat darkens the man's beautiful white suit. Perhaps it rarely rains in Horizon, as it does not seem waterproof at all. *Ding.* 830,000 units. He is a sour A pos—I am not sure. There are dozens of flavors around me, made stronger by the heat.

Clogging together in this tiny, green tunnel.

Letters, numbers, and shapes are painted on the hallways' top borders. I do not know what they mean.

Many of those ahead of me look around. I am thinking the same thing—where are we going? what will happen to us after we get there?—but I do not look around. Only ahead.

A thrumming excitement overtakes my fear.

These walls are in Urban. I am in these walls. *I* am in Urban.

The guard points to these walls, where lighter green sentences glow. Rules. Thousands of rules. Each numbered.

She does not explain one of them.

The third hallway goes on forever. My back is soaked, and I must keep wiping my eyes.

"It's so hot in here. I ain't never sweated so much," a woman in the middle of the line whispers.

She collapses to the ground. The man behind her trips and falls. The one behind him tumbles, too.

None after those three. We adjust and maneuver around the small pile like ants marching past a pebble.

A few people peek around. Big eyes. Rigid backs. Shoulders high.

No explanation. We sweat quieter.

The men get up and rejoin the line. I pass the woman. Glance at her. She is crumpled in the fetal position; her saree is crumpled with her. Unconscious? I watch her chest. Stale, hard sourness comes from her. Overpowering in this small space.

She is perished, but from what?

I glance around the space now, too, holding in the terrified, stampeding breaths welling up from inside me. Too loud. Much too loud.

Something is in the air.

My device fills with the woman's face, a message over it—*Auction Immediately*.

960,000 units collected immediately.

I crush my lips together. Not one sound will come from me. I am in Urban, and I will have my seven years and seven months. Each and every day.

On ya Gold Week, empty ya collection bags and send ya Gold every morn. You'll receive one premium unit converted to ya local currency. The Dome rewards dutiful citizens. Ya favored show, Today in the Past!

Dark, locked doorways break up the disgusting green every few feet. Plants I have never seen before sit in the corners. One has blue flowers and reaches up near seven feet. Others crawl up the walls.

Rogues in green uniforms crouch in corners, watering and feeding the plants. Their clothes' fabric is matte, and it is of immensely high quality. They do not look up but pour all their energy and attention into the plants.

I have lost count of how many hallways we have turned into; they are nearly identical except for the markings at the top of each. I stop trying to count. Vague has never been soothing to me.

A third guard approaches us, holding a clipboard. He walks three-quarters down the line and stops a few people in front of me.

"Goods behind me, turn around."

They do, and he steps away. The line makes a U-turn and follows him. Disappears into another sickly hall. There are only about fifteen of us left. Maybe we are about to be auctioned. Maybe I will not get my seven years and seven months.

No, no, that cannot be. Please do not let that be.

The hallway continues, ending in stairs. My clothes are drenched, and now these. The front guard slowly glides up the stairs. We follow. My legs are burning, and my chest is an infinite inferno.

I count the stairs. 46, 47, 48, 49. Hold onto the rail, though it is wet with someone else's sweat. Disgusting.

Ahead of me, the most bitter flavor I have ever smelled is wafting back. I am suffocating in a boiling green gourd. I grasp the railing with one hand, trying not to slip, and hold my nose closed with the other.

The man in front of me pauses at the tenth landing, bent, holding his chest. His magnificent white suit is now a dull, soggy, wrinkled brown plastered to his skin. I smell. Yes, A positive.

He is young, 19-aged maybe, somewhere near a Martinet's age, and looks fit, but he has probably never climbed a stair in his life. The man lowers to sit, breathing hard. One glance into the air—and he rethinks his impulse.

We do not know Urban's rules. Whether we make it matters to no one but us. I pass him. Nod for him to continue.

He looks up at me, smiles wide with hopeful eyes, peace flowing from his Horizon veins, and nods back. Peels his jacket to the side and shows me his chest.

What the… I have a husband.

I pause, my foot suspended in the air, thinking on this. Horizonites are relaxed and free with their marriages. They enjoy small marems, harems, and ambiems. This must be custom.

A long, faint scar runs down the middle of his chest. Over his heart is a photo tattoo of a handsome man near his age. Brown skin, light blue eyes. No hair. The barcodes on his scalp and neck are bright red, and he has a mischievous look on his impish face.

The man takes a deep breath, stands straight, and peeks into the air. Mouths to me, "This was an accident."

He flattens his right hand, palm down, fingers tight together. Kisses his thumb, and holds it to his heart, an unyielding awning over his beloved.

Eighty-three years ago, we installed the first movin' bridge. Too much work tuh be carryin' boxes up and down. No citizens allowed. Ya favored show, Today in the Past!

I continue up. I do not know how many more stairs there are, and I will not waste energy on anyone else lagging.

By the fifteenth landing, my legs are disappearing. At the twentieth, I cannot feel them anymore. I keep tripping up the stairs and remain at the back of the line, trying not to slip on the slick steps. It has been three eternities, I swear it.

Grow ya hair as long as ya want. Never cover ya neck's branding. One warning. That's all we give. Ya favored show, Today in the Past!

I think there was more to this message, but I do not hear it. On the thirtieth landing, I do not know anything. My thoughts have stopped thinking. They only repeat:

One. More. Step.

Someone collapses a few stairs ahead of me. A human lollipop drowning in a Valley gray smock. Their eyes dart into the air, searching it as they wheeze loudly. Get back up.

I ignore them. Their labored gasps. I will not risk my seven years and seven months again.

One.
More.
Step.

One.
More.
Step.

One.
More.
Step.

Eventually, the words meld into sounds. I hold onto those sounds and keep going.

"We're here." The guard turns to us, stoic and dry on the fiftieth floor's landing.

I cannot believe I made it.

An intense, stale sourness blows from in front of me. I keep rising until I reach the others. 1,089 stairs.

The man in the white suit has a relaxed smile on his face. Eyes open. He is slumped against the railing, his arm in his lap, under his heart. One breath in. Out.

His face in my device, laughing while his picture was taken.

Auction Immediately.

We walk out of a door and onto a long, narrow, metal-roped bridge. It is eve now. Hard to see as the sun is setting quickly. The Dome's crest is painted on the bridge; its fluorescent glow casts a helpful light. There is no wind. A barrier surrounds us.

My body is aching, every inch of it, but I do not pause. As we cross, the bridge glides to the side. Another rises next to it, filled with boxes and supplies. Oh, wow.

Dorsica Urbanisara. Urban's national plant's bloomin' after two years. Get ya tickets tuh see this purplish-black beauty. Ya favored show, Today in the Past!

We enter the building on the other side and stop in our wing. A short hallway with dark doorways.

"Walk to ya number." The guard shoos us forward.

We do not walk. We hobble and wince like injured baby deer. The others fall through the openings. Confusion stops me from doing the same.

Etched into the wall outside of my door is "DI#431855*." I stare at it. The guard pushes me through.

"I—"

"Inventor, forgive mah bothered thoughts. G'head, ask."

Her dark gold uniform matches her eyes and the small, triangular decorations weaved through the tight bun at the nape of her neck. Stitched on her uniform is "J12."

I swallow and glance at the hallway. "Marm, I am not sure why I am here. What is my crime?"

She moves closer and yanks me down. Stares into my face. "The most horrid of 'em. Disruption of Innovation."

Oh. "The asterisk?"

"Disruptin' the innovation of a six-dot."

"But I did not—"

She holds up a hand. "Keep ya lies tuh yourself. Ain't ya damaged our world enough?" She pushes me back and steps away. The doorway turns black. Locked.

I wipe my sweaty palms on my dress—they become more wet—and take a few breaths. Turn around.

Green. Everywhere.

The room is large, covered in intricate graffita wallpaper, and furnished with a two-person bed on the right and a small infant bed on the left. A comforter and pillow rest on each, both with The Dome's crest sewed in with neon thread.

Diagonal from me is a bookcase built into the wall. To its right, the toilet room. A mirror. I avoid it. Dig my toe in the soft, thick carpet. Wince when a loud beep blares through my device.

At its tone, a small, metallic table and two seats slide out of the wall next to the large bed. Sectioned plates are built into the table. Plastic tops over most of them. A white band is in one of them.

What is that for?

"Dinner. Five minutes remainin'." A countdown appears above the table.

I run over and sit quietly. Glance in the air. I do not know if we can talk in our rooms. After taking off the tops, I inhale deeply.

Two steaming slices of O negative wight sprinkled with herbs and green peppers, okra bread with butter, apple and carrot chunks in blue DiamondJar sauce, almonds, a thick strawberry shake, and a small Diane candy.

I dip my finger in the DiamondJar sauce and stick it in my mouth. *Mm.* Everything but the wight is stuffed in next. All is grand except for the shake; it is sweet and cold but has an odd aftertaste.

I will get used to it.

The countdown ends, and the table slides back in. My stomach is fuller than it has been in a long time.

I sit on my bed. A green uniform sits next to me, folded neatly. "DI#431855*" is stitched all over it. I am not ready. I stay in my smelly, soaked dress. I do not know if I will get to wear another.

A hiccup erupts from me as I wipe the juice from my mouth.

The room: *No wight eaten in a meal. Balanced meals create healthy Urban citizens. This is ya last warning.*

Last warning? I did not have Kuru Acid. How was I to eat the wight?

My questions fade as two words take over all else:

Urban citizen.

Urban citizen.

Urban citizen.

Me? An Urban citizen.

I lie down, smiling hard at the ceiling. A document pops into my device. I read the instruction manual to my new life.

My better life.

James of the Pillars hovers above, smiling down at me from above. A wide, silly smirk. A quirk of his eyebrows.

This man.

The lights turn off. He disappears. My smile with him.

He is here, in Urban, yet I will not see him again. Or Marguerite. Or my parents. I squeeze the thick cover in my fists, melt into its softness. Gaze into the darkness.

It rises. I fall up into the darker darkness.

I have a husband.

The words echo in my mind. No, had.

I will not see you again.

Smell you. Feel you. Tease you. Comfort you.

My husband, we are here together, separately.

I have lost you.

It is my fault.

TWENTY-EIGHT

THERE'S NO TIME in the cells. No clocks. No way to ask our devices. There is only beeps and instructions.

I glance at the small dot on the right side of mah hand. It's 2 and a half morn. A countdown's ticked in mah head the entire two months I've been in Urban. I ignore it and go tuh the small, near-transparent bed where Trinity sleeps.

Ding. 70,000 units.

Six months now, he's as quiet as ever. Fatter than ever. Like me. I flick the bottom of mah stomach with mah fingertips. It jiggles.

I have never had a jiggle. I like it.

I press my, mah, fingers into his green mattress; it creates an imprint that soon goes back tuh its original height. The comforter. Not a hint of scratchiness. So soft.

Urban. Will I ever believe I am truly here?

I tap his shoulder softly, harder when he does not wake. He yawns. Wide. Gummy. Wiggles around and rubs at his face. Stares at me as he often does: serious gray-brown eyes, inquisitive expression, and flat mouth.

He blinks a few times and dozes back off.

"Wake up." I shake Trinity's shoulder and lift him from his bed. I do not have all the day tuh wait fuh him.

First, his filterin'. I put mah arm through the hoop slowly.

Please work.

A familiar panic races through me as the needle descends to activate his filtering.

It lights red and works as promised.

One day, I'll trust it, but that day has not, ain't, come yet.

I go tuh the rocking chair next to the foot of his bed—real pine. I cannot believe we've got real pine here. Bend tuh smell. I adore this wood. There's excitement in it. A bubbly chatter. It is rare fuh me to be able tuh detect the emotions of trees; it takes a different nose than mine, but sometimes, yes.

This one was born with a sunshine disposition. I whisper a joke tuh it and sit. So comfortable. The chair's green cushion has molded to me after these months.

I look down. He's dozed once more. This infant'll sleep his life away. I smile at that. In Urban, he can do that.

A small, circular device detaches from the wall and glides through the air tuh him. I hold his arm open, so the filtering machine can latch ontuh his elbow. He does not, don't, startle when the needle pinches him. Like a mosquito, we're numbed first. All Urban citizens get this.

A thud. No scream. The black of mah room's barrier flickers. A woman's collapsed against it, her cheek pressed intuh it, shaking lightly as it zaps her.

She will not stop it. Cannot.

Her face pops up in mah device. Though I've seen her near every day, I only recognize her by the thick, dark birthmark that runs down the middle of her lips.

Auction Immediately.

Urban has so much wight it doesn't put everyone through The Fattening, and that reality keeps most people in line. The cells're calm. The air's filled with invisible, silent drones that monitor how many rules we break and decide whether we should be perished. Sometimes, the system counts wrong. Does not matter. Our name still goes on The Wall.

I'm careful in our room. Careful everywhere. I've read the manuals and walls many times.

After digging in the bag hanging from the chair, I poke the rolls in Trinity's legs and then the soft creases they make. My milk's bubbles float up the bottle lazily, complainin' at every step. He's a slow drinker. Slow in general. Always loungin' around.

This child.

I kiss the green patch of skin on his forehead before putting a small dab of brown over it. Rub the makeup in until his skin is perfection. Imperfections are only tolerated inside of our rooms.

He burrows into mah stomach, and I twirl one of his curls. With each turn, the lock wraps itself around mah finger again.

He's still a most pleasant infant. Quiet. Not too messy.

The ticking in mah head grows more insistent, and I dress him quickly, rubbing the green fabric of his clothing with mah thumb and index finger. His long shirt is immensely comfortable—and covered in "DI#431855*." Hand-stitched by rogues.

My crime. His crime.

I look away from him. Lie him back in his bed and pull the covers over his horribly protruding belly. Tuck this lazy seahorse in tight.

I ignore the pain in the bottom of my stomach; it is immense today.

A scream explodes intuh our room. A loud zap follows it. Trinity don't stir. I dress myself quicker, glancin' at the door every few seconds. Hopefully, Guard J12 won't burst in.

She's unable tuh comprehend any other way of enterin'.

Four hundred eighty years ago, researchers discovered music boosts fertility. Go enjoy compositions by our talented Anomalies. Ya favored show, Today in the Past!

I go tuh the toilet room. Sink tuh mah left. Toilet and shower tuh mah right. I wipe the sink with disinfectant. F564 Lemon. One mirror's in front of me, another tuh mah right. All's green but the mirrors' glass.

It is 3 and a half morn. I watch Trinity through the mirror. Will this reminder of all our world has lost be his favored color?

Maybe.

I pull a protractor from the large toothbrush holder and follow the instruction manual dictating how mah hair must be styled. Check it fuh correctness in both mirrors.

There're five options: I choose number three and wrap mah curls into a bun—45-degree angle, two-inch-thick pieces of hair hangin' from the middle of the bun. After braidin' the loose hair and wrapping it 'round the bun's base, I slather a hardening gel on mah edges so no strands cover my branding.

I do not look into mah eyes. There're shadows in them. Shadows in mah ears. Screaming, crying shadows I can't face. What can you do with an unending shadow but get lost in it forever?

I stare into the basin. Spit spicy toothpaste intuh the sink. Watch as it slowly goes down the drain, never tuh be seen again.

I turn on the water. Turn it off. Turn it on.

Clean, clear water, every time I want it. No metallic taste. No yellow. Only crisp. Cold, cold. Hot, hot. On, on. As much as I want.

Perfect.

I scrub and dry the marble until there's no trace I ever dirtied it.

"Breakfast. Thirty minutes remainin'."

I sit at the table and put the white band tuh mah inner elbow. It releases fast-acting Kuru Acid into mah blood, so I can eat wight whenever I like.

I did not know such an acid existed.

A green number trickles down in mah device; it did not used tuh be there. I ignore it and focus on the fried toe rolls dipped in pancake batter. *Mm.* AB negative. There is much of it in Urban, and so they even give it tuh us.

Beep!

The sound echoes in mah head.

Why? It is hard to tell. I am thirty minutes early, so there must be some small task I've forgotten. I scan the room, think on it a moment, but no longer. I try not tuh think on anything—or anyone—too long.

Time to go. I pull out mah access card. Flip it over. It is green now with white text, and The Dome's crest is engraved in the back.

An image of me—sweated out, panicked, and lookin' horrid—with mah name under it is on the front. But none of that matters. What matters is the embossed letters at the bottom:

"City: Urban."

I glide mah fingers over those five letters. Again and again and again. This is real. I am in Urban. When I have stared a while longer, I swipe the card across the doorway's scanner; the black disappears and someone speeds past me.

Someone is always rushin' around.

I step out. The Keepers will take Trinity tuh his Anomaly classes, taught tuh him in case he is not Common.

I drag mah feet as we move down the hall in single-file line. It is hot. Always so hot.

It's hot. Get a new handi-fan. Charges itself as ya walk. Always enjoys ya company. Only 15,000 units. Available now. Ya favored show, Today in the Past!

The glowing rules create columns of text on the walls, lighter green than their darker green surroundings. I have read every one many times. Committed each tuh memory.

To know what tuh do. Tuh know what tuh expect. Is comforting.

Even the drones recording our every move is comforting.

A woman winces, touches her forehead, and runs back tuh her room. Though we read the instruction manuals often, Urban has many unwritten rules.

I stare ahead, like everyone else. Their voices fade as we pass the faith center's door. I cannot see in, but still, I do not look. I am not ready for whatever is in there.

Instead, I focus all of mah attention on the man in front of me.

"They're bringin' in a new crop. Mostly Horizonites. Can ya believe that?" Sharod whispers this as he fans himself with his shirt.

Ding. 4,600,000 units. Wow. A Common with his number always amazes me.

I sniff softly as a woman across from him smiles. About a tenth of him. "Yeah, they'll resist, I know it." Her eyes're eager.

"Me too. Finally. A bit of excitement 'round here." He keeps fanning. "Who knew becomin' a rogue would be so borin'? Each new day, same old day."

His words are true. Not many risk discord. My thoughts freeze when he fans himself harder. His flavor's everywhere. I lean forward. Smell deeper. Oh. Mah body shivers.

Sharod stiffens. "I can hear ya smellin' me. Stop it."
He sighs. Whispers quieter, tuh himself, "C'aint even wait
fuh mah number tuh reach zero." He looks at the woman.
Louder now. "See? That's why I loathe Auctioneers."

"Who don't?" She laughs, and so do others. I step
back, embarrassed, and bump into the person behind me.
They push me forward, but I can hardly feel their hands
as mah senses're dulled. Sharod is everywhere.

I glance around. Other Auctioneers peek at him. Wight-
Harvesters, too. The Tasters stare openly, their tongues
pink with red dots, flicking out slowly every few minutes.

Lions waiting fuh the perfect moment tuh pounce.

Still, his shoulders relax. He has no need tuh worry. We
don't wanna perish early, and only The Dome would
benefit from the units his wight would bring. They got no
need fuh his millions now. They're paid far more the longer
he stays in the cells.

He continues their conversation. "It's scaldin'."

More fanning. Mah mouth fills with spittle. I
swallow it.

The woman nods. "I've never been so miserable."

"I have. Once, the water was shut off fuh two days.
We had tuh use sand. It was horrid. How do they live like
that? I couldn't. I really couldn't."

What a tragedy. Do Urbanians ever stop complainin'?
I look around. "We," "they."

Though we're in near identical green uniforms, we're
still different.

*Sixty years ago, the Past-Knowers gathered their knowledge
intuh The Wisdom Library. Ya can access it through ya device.*

Anomalies, half of it's mandatory reading. Ya favored show, Today in the Past!

Dots of sweat litter our clothes, and the back of Sharod's shirt has a long, dark waterfall where it plastered tuh his back.

He fans himself again. "Did ya hear about the guard who reported her wife tuh The BloodBid but was stopped by their Third?"

"What, how did *a Third* get that much power?"

"Well, he applied fuh a—"

I'm curious about the guard, but their voices fade. His immensely sweet AB negative is everywhere. Candy I cannot eat. Yet.

Hmm. How much time does he have remainin'? Maybe they will serve him durin' the Anomaly Gala. I have heard we will get a plate of food before it starts. I set seven reminders tuh get tuh every gala early.

A man across from me points tuh mah shirt. I look down and wipe the drool away. The large, darker green spot stays. I hope we don't have an

Inspection, the wall announces.

TWENTY-NINE

IN ONE IDENTICAL move, we turn toward the walls, put our foreheads against it, and hold our arms rigidly against our sides. Palms open and facin' outward.

Not today. I must go tuh The Wall.

Three guards walk down the space, efficient, scannin' our hair and clothes. *Ding*s. A few million units.

I do not focus on that, but on the green scanner beaming from the ceiling, checkin' the front of our bodies.

Why did I have tuh drool on mah shirt? Why?

Beside me, Sharod's large Adam's apple drops low, jumps high when he swallows.

His hair is correct. Clothes proper.

Fear makes his blood sweeter. I don't even know how that is possible, but liquid heaven pumps through his veins. More drool pools in mah mouth. I hold mah lips tight.

Shiver with him. I know what he is afraid of. I am afraid of it too.

There are no seconds here.

I am laid down in a bed of green. A most comfortable bed. Darkness is around me. A patch of light is next to me. This room is massive, and I am face up in the shadows between the lights.

I wiggle my shoulders. A weight presses harder when I move them. Another weight on my sides. On my legs. On my feet. On my chest. On my stomach. On my head. I panic.

My breath shakes.

Stay calm. Slow. Breathe.

I do, but it is hard to keep myself peaceful. For no reason at all, the weights lift, and I can move. The bed cocoons me perfectly, cradles my body, warms to the temperature of a well-drawn bath. I relax.

Cold. Hot. Weights. Stuck. Panic. Relax. Panic.

My mind does not know which I am—free or not.

I swallow my scream. I will not be able to hear it; it will be gobbled up and sent away.

I take a deep breath, close my lips tight, and push out the smallest stream of air I can.

"Lemme out!" Their pleas layer, colliding and mixing in my ears. It is from those all around me. It is from Sharod. "Please, lemme out. I ain't do nothin' wrong. I've been in here more days than I was sposed tuh."

His vocal cords are fresh, at the beginning of their song.

He will scream until they reach their raspy, tormented end.

They all will, and their croaks will be a relief.

Sometimes, when I am put here, I do not even have their screams. Only silence and weight and comfort.

There is nothing to grasp onto here. No time. No change. That is what makes it feel like forever. Like I have stopped existing.

My eyes blink close. I do not blink them. They are blinked for me.

I want to close them.

The thought whispers in my mind before traveling down behind my eyes, grows louder as it passes my nose and turns into a wail at my mouth.

No. No. Do not.

If I scream once, I will scream twice, and on until I can no more.

A pressure presses against my eyelids. I am growing tired. Maybe it is time to sleep.

I stare up into the darkness. I am not alone up there. I am not alone in here. My thoughts are with me. Them and their shadows.

The light in front of me beeps.

A guard turns me and pulls me in front of her. "What's on ya shirt?"

I don't say a word. They don't hear answers.

I hold mah breath as she holds the scanner to my neck, tuh send me there. Her finger hovers ova the trigger, stops when a shout comes from ahead of us.

"It ain't mine. She put it in mah pocket. It ain't mine!" A metal tube is at the man's feet. He struggles. His eyes bulge out, and spittle rockets from his mouth. Blood turns his cauliflower-colored skin hot pink. *Ding.* 360,000 units. "Please."

The guard twists me back around, and I release a tremblin' breath. Oh, that was close. I close my eyes, but it doesn't stop the video in my mind.

I hear it. One zap. So loud. A strong current. The man screeches and drops tuh the floor. His body spasms a few times. Another guard puts a white patch on his forehead. His eyes roll back.

When they are finished with him, they do the same tuh the woman next to him. I smell urine. See the thighs of her uniform darkening as the liquid spreads down them. *Ding.* 420,000 units.

Their faces show in my device, "interrogation" stamped over them.

I open my eyes.

"Forward." One guard motions fuh us to keep movin' before floatin' above us on a platform. We trudge ahead in two lines, one next tuh the other.

Finally, I reach the hallway's door and step onto a bridge connectin' my building tuh another. I hurry to meet the woman, shakin' off the inspection.

Ding. 160,000 units.

She is from Valley too. Her crime is not mine, but we're kindred—both wantin' more.

Each day, she faces the rest of Urban and touches the clear wall. Green light. She looks down. We are so high.

"Urban's magnificent, ain't it?" The dialect is awkward on mah tongue, but I savor every word.

Anomalies, *static* Census Zoo. Ya favored show, Today in the Past!

A Census Zoo? What could that be? I don't know, so I push it from my mind. Stare out at the wide, transparent street. Sparklin' vibrant blue water movin' slowly under it. People in stunning dresses and suits right in front of me. I do not draw them anymore, only go to the bridge when I can.

But there is something that even eclipses their clothing: the thirty-foot statues of the first-discovered Anomalies. Their seven statues are to my left. They stand in a wide arch, holdin' pieces of our world out tuh one another. Their names are etched into their foreheads.

Sacred. Forbidden to be used as namesakes.

A ring of Corsage Orchids lie at their feet, small red lights twinklin' within them. In the night, the red lights turn gold and the seven statues glow bright red, their names an equally bright gold.

Nzingha.

Lucia.

Mohammed.

Alexander.

Aki.

Nioka.

Jupiter.

The first tuh dedicate their lives to our evolution.

But the beauty of Urban ain't all I'm looking for. I scan the streets for a gangly walk, black curls cropped at the back, gray eyes. He is here. He will be able tuh see the trees. Hear them. But not see or hear me. That does not matter. Even though I won't be able to hear him, I can see him.

*Ding*s. Millions of units. I watch every adult who passes. Not many. Not him.

A group of Anomaly children runs and plays as they pass the cells, their shimmerin' trains flowing behind their layered pants and dress suits. Oh, each day, they are more stunning.

Most of them are yellin'.

Their Keepers are in a circle around all of them, simple clothes matchin' the color of their Anomaly child.

There is one six-dot among them. *Ding.* 30,700,000,000 units all by herself. Her number plus theirs: so very many billions.

Urban has so much.

She looks tuh be the oldest, 14-aged, maybe. She is the most exhausted and wildest of the bunch. Careenin' from child tuh child, whisperin' in their ears and poking them. Cacklin' loudly when they push her gently. None will risk hurtin' her.

The five- and four-dots are more serious; they slip out of their labor tuh smile a little. Throw out a joke. And the lowest dots are heathens, doin' cartwheels and sprayin' water on their Keepers.

They weave in and out of the trees, play with their reflections in the arched windows of the skyscrapers. Leave their fingerprints on the windows after bitin' into immense pieces of DiamondJar steaks I have heard are excellent.

In every Urban, there're many Anomalies tuh carry the weight of our world's evolution, but still, all the children have dark-rimmed eyes.

Once in a while, the six-dot girl's body spasms. One of her Keepers runs tuh set down a chair—before her body slackens and she disappears into an urgent Innova.

When they come upon the statues, the children still. Their Keepers cluster in sets of matchin' threes, turn away, and kneel. All other Commons do the same. This private moment happens every day.

Each child twists a foot on the ground and rises tuh the statues' foreheads. They touch their palms to the marble, close their eyes, and press their foreheads into the backs of their hands.

When they open them again, they look tuh the six-dot girl. She trails her fingers along one statute's name before nodding tuh the others.

They glide down.

And turn back into wild beasts.

"It's grand tuh see more of them're happy." It has been months now, and I'm surprised every time I use the laidback accent without reprimand.

I'm a citizen of Urban. Worthy.

I drag mah eyes from all the beauty around me. Back tuh her. She does not answer but presses her hand flat against the barrier. Green light.

Knock. Green light. Knock. Green light.

I don't know what it means.

She looks at me as she wipes her sweaty hairline. The bridge is even hotter than the hallways. When there is no more to share, we walk in opposite directions.

I glance down. *Ding*s. Near half a billion units. A guard puts their hand out tuh a barrier—red light—and joins a circle of others loungin' lightly, eating rapidly, and talkin' quietly. Outside of the space, their colleagues prepare. More white groundVans will arrive soon.

Ants. Storin' food for the snowflake season.

I tap mah foot as the long, quiet line tuh wing six slows on the 30-foot bridge.

Commons, three more months until the Siphoning Parade. Are ya excited? Ready tuh present ya brains? Of course ya are. What an honor. Ya favored show, Today in the Past!

The countdown continues tickin' in mah head as I stride forward. When I'm close, I stop fuh a moment and stare out at Urban again. Smile.

I'm one of them.

I enter the lecture room, early but later than others. Scan the room quickly. Tons of millions of units in the small area.

"I'm sorry."

Foot-to-ceiling bookshelves are on every wall, and three long tables face the lecturer, one in front of the other. The books are the only things that aren't green.

Everything is bolted into place. The manuals dictate the room's layout. I sit at the second table. A woman and a man, on either side of me, stare ahead. Leanin' their chins on their palms. Bored until the lecturer announces, "It's time fuh second breakfast."

The lecturer is cheerful at this early hour. It is too early tuh be so happy. We line up by months remaining and grab trays from the front of the room.

"I adore mashed potatoes. What do you think of the pickled spleen?" The man behind me rubs his palms together, balancin' his tray on his arms.

"It is all delicious." Another laughs.

Those with the most time left fill their plates first. Some have just gotten here, and they're morbidly thin. Livin' skeletons. Crepey complexions with light fur on their arms and legs. Thick makeup tuh cover their green-scarred skin underneath. They move slowly, not much energy tuh them.

Valley is here; it will not stay where I left it. I look away.

Today, scrambled cow with baked beans in a sweet, green sauce. Apple slices. A glass of water and one thick shake. Strawberry. No candy today.

Cow is good, but wight is grand. There're so many more flavors of it, and its smell has many different stories. Cow is just cow.

I reach the front of the line, and mah weight is taken. 9 stone 7 pounds. I'm on track. Those in the back waddle forward, flabs of fat pushing against their uniforms. Second chin meltin' into their chests. Tiny feet holdin' their masses.

When they reach the scales, their portions are increased if their number is too low.

They're given four shakes. Every day, they eat slower. Take smaller sips.

When we have all sat, a clock ticks from the wall. Thirty minutes. No more.

I don't delay. The apple is first. The fruit's always first. It is crisp and sweet. I smell its life. Wifts of sweet buzzin'. Next, the cow. Soft. It merges perfectly with the beans. There's a hint of disgust in me at eating this spicy, green sauce, but I push it away. I don't have time tuh think on that.

And last, the shake.

"What flavors are yours?" A new person turns around, talkin' to the man next tuh me. He has three, and each day, he finishes those first.

"Strawberry, Peach, Lime." He shows each shake. "In half a year, I'll have four." He looks at a woman twice his size.

She raises one of her shakes tuh him and nods. "Grand. Blueberry's the most grand. They put somethin' special in this one."

She sips slowly, savoring the flavor. Closes her eyes and cocks her head to listen to the conversation. There is a slight bounce to her leg.

In half a year, someone else will be where she is not.

The breakfast countdown reaches zero. We place our trays in the wall, and they ride down the assembly line.

When I sit once more, the lecturer places a thick book in front of me: *How tuh Select a Husband the Right Way.*

In Urban, there're classes—and instructions—for everything. I already know how to select a husband, know I have four months tuh choose him, and know I have two months remainin', but it requires teaching in Urban. Still, I enjoy learnin'. I open the book and take notes.

'All shall be memorialized.' This was signed into law in 2343, a mere 150 years ago. Many thanks tuh The Republic of United First Regions. The only smart thing they've ever done. Ya favored show, Today in the Past!

Some laugh. Only this show can publicly make such jokes about the First regions.

I browse the people like unmarked boxes on a shelf. I don't know their names. Don't remember their voices or faces. It is better this way.

I only see what I have known.

The woman next tuh me has horrid handwriting like James of the Pillars. The person across the room walks like him, and the nervous man across from me taps his finger like Marguerite.

I watch his tappin'.

Oh, Marguerite.

What happened to you?

THIRTY

BEEP!

THE LOUD *sound screeches, and the farm in my dreams shift, growing ever more blood-soaked. Marguerite's walker drops from the ceiling. Its metal wraps around my wrists and carries me forward.*

James of the Pillars is on my right. We are moving at the same pace. He stares at me, smiling. His blue conveyor belt speeds up, and I watch as the machine dunks half of his body into the boiling water. He comes back up, smiling still. His bottom half drips like a lit candle.

This time, he does not look at me but at the person to my left. I do not look over but up. One of my hands is sown around a lever, and I am pulling it down, picking up another Marguerite or her maternal or my husband or. Or. Or.

Soft music pipes through the bright, metallic warehouse. It wakes me. I stop the scream from leavin' mah mouth when I smell the air. It is different. Mah chest heaves, each breath crowdin' the next. I hold mah hand tuh mah chest, still unused tuh the lightness of mah wrist. I miss the comfort of mah bracelet's weight. It's been a year and a half since I last saw mah charm bracelet. Locked it away. I'll need it again.

Breathe.

Her voice soothes me in the early morn. I close mah eyes, let mah thrashin' heartbeat calm itself, and relax on the bed.

Bein' the beloved, even the doomed beloved, of an Anomaly allows me tuh want fuh nothin'. I ain't never been in so much comfort.

Mah husband lies behind me, his hand restin' on mah immense belly. "I think she'll be beautiful and smart like our son."

Andre kisses me, his stubble brushin' the back of mah neck. Unfamiliar but pleasant. I move closer tuh him and soak in his warmth. Open mah eyes.

James—no, Trinity—stands in front of me.

Ding. 200,000 units.

He's a quiet, intelligent child who looks so much like James of the Pillars it makes me ache. Cry in the night, go numb durin' the day. He's serious where James of the Pillars was silly, patient where he was impatient, and calm where he was anxious. Even at two-aged, his personality shines handsomely. An ache in my stomach. I shake mah head to clear it.

304

Trinity's not him, shouldn't be compared tuh him. He's himself. I want nothin' more fuh him than tuh be himself. New and wonderful.

He holds out a groundCar. "Play wit me."

Wide gray eyes with brown flecks behind thick glasses. Dimple on the left cheek, but not on the right. Squared nose. I close mah eyes and swallow hard. Open them and take the groundCar from him.

He steps back a few feet and lowers tuh the floor slowly. Trinity's soft, black curls are pushed tuh one side, though he sleeps little durin' the night. Instead, he watches actors and actresses in his device. Listens tuh the music funneling into our room all day.

Angry, happy songs from Antoine of the Glades.

Despairin' compositions from James of the Pillars.

I look away from Trinity and around the room instead.

Checkin' it fuh imperfections.

His small bed's neat, the comforter tucked in tightly. The small toy chest under the heavy, smooth metal is crooked. I will adjust it later.

His desk's nearer the door, tuh the left of his headboard, and it faces us. Bolted down like everything else.

I stare down at him as he pushes a groundTruck along the plush, green carpet and directs a hoverCar through the air. He turns tuh me and smiles. Tiny teeth showin'. Rare fuh him. Above his eyebrow is that swipe of green skin.

I loathe that green mark, the shadows it refuses tuh let me forget. But he does not enjoy wearing the makeup.

Three hundred thirty years ago, the Spotless Routines were added tuh the manuals. On ya auction day, clean ya room thoroughly. Urban citizens're considerate. Ya favored show, Today in the Past!

Andre helps me up. Kisses the back of mah head before jumpin' out of bed. He's always filled with energy, like a groundTrain goin' off course. Red permapaint dots surround his lips and coat his tongue. *Ding.* 1,300,000 units.

Wow. These numbers are commonplace here, but I've yet tuh become used tuh them.

Born in Urban, he's never known hunger or water or blood pangs, but stress mars his features as he obsesses ova the time. He grabs a groundCar from the floor and zooms it intuh the toilet room. Watches the screen there while he readies himself fuh his position as a Taster.

When a beep comes from the wall, he dries his hands and steps out. Leaves the water runnin'.

'Update tuh morn routine. Turn tuh page 685.' The voice is as calm as ever.

He goes tuh the bookcase and pulls out a thin notebook. Thick, pristine manuals fill most of the other shelves. Though the books have pages, the text is digital. A nostalgic reason, I imagine. One page would've worked.

"Wake up time's ten minutes early. Confirm ya understand." He signs the book before bringin' it tuh me. After I sign, he takes it tuh Trinity, who's holdin' out his thumb. Andre presses his thumb intuh an empty square. The page lights red.

'Thank ya fuh committin' tuh the well-bein' of Urban.'

I watch the water. Stare as it drains down the sink, clear and good and clean. Mah heart thumps in mah chest as I drift back tuh the ledger on the cracked walls of our home in Valley. Feel mah fingers holdin' the marker as I slice slashes intuh the boxes of our remainin' water stores. The boxes disappeared so fast.

Turn it off. Turn it off. We'll run out.

Aren't ya keepin' track?

No, he's not. He doesn't count water. I've reminded him many times tuh not leave it runnin', but he only laughs and says, 'There's more.'

I take deep breaths, starin' at the water. Yeah. In Urban, there's always more.

As I like it.

Andre wipes the outside of the book free of his fingerprints and puts it back. Continues gettin' ready.

"1…" He counts from the toilet room, waitin' fuh Trinity tuh whisper the next number. Andre must've played this game with his own son. Many years ago, of course. The boy's ten-aged now.

'Your child is not here with you?' I ask him this as I unpack Trinity from his box. It took a month for him to arrive.

'Nah, I'm Urban-born. The consequences fuh Disruption of Innovation're different.' Oh.

He coos at Trinity, uses a wet rag to wipe the marker off his fat cheek. Numbers and letters showing where he should be shipped. 'When they came tuh collect us, I found out mah previous beloved had two options: send us tuh auction immediately or send us tuh da cells fuh ten years.' He smiles and bounces the bed a little. No reaction from the infant. 'We were given mercy. Me here, mah boy servin' the orphan midpotential children.'

"And your beloved taking their Vow did not anger you?"

"It did. I was mad fuh mah boy. Didn't even get tuh say goodbye." His bouncing pauses. "But I was grateful fuh da ten years."

"You would have had more time with him."

He shrugs. "Maybe. I don't know what I would've had. Still don't." He lifts Trinity from the bed and hugs him. "I do know I ain't gonna waste it bein' mad. Wouldn't be a good paternal if I did."

—✛—

Trinity watches him brush his teeth with that inquisitive look on his face.

Since I got an hour until mah position begins, I get down on the carpet. Trinity drives the groundCars as you should. Hoverin' back and forth, speedin' up, slowin' down. Never upside down or zigzag. He obeys the traffic lights he's set up.

How odd.

"Car tuh Mat-Mat." The hoverCar moves away from him and whirs near me as he pushes the groundTruck along the carpet. He doesn't care too much fuh hoverCars; groundVans are what he sees most in the auction cells. Bringin' in citizens, takin' citizens away.

While playin', he makes a few rumblin' sounds of the groundVans, but mostly, he screams. That's what he hears when they're near.

I tell the hoverCar tuh fly upside down—Trinity frowns at me—before pushin' another along the carpet with him. He runs the groundTruck along mah left leg. An identiPro like mah forearm, it's identical tuh mah birth leg. Mah maternal...

My maternal...

My maternal had taken scans before the sale. It was in the system, and Urban aged up my leg before purchasing its replica. It is magnificent. As I make far more units here, I will pay off the arm in two more years and the leg in four more.

When Trinity carefully places the groundCar on the carpet, I tickle his chubby cheek. He pulls away. "No. Car time. No tickle."

"Okay, lil one. It's ya choice. Later?"

"Mm-hmm."

"It's always tickle time." Andre runs back into the room, lifts Trinity, turns him over, and blows on his stomach.

My son's high-pitched squeal rings through the room, but not fuh long. "No tickle now." His voice is frustrated, and his face is stoic, so mah husband sets him back down and sits on the floor with his ankles crossed.

Calm. The opposite of Andre's nature.

Trinity settles into his lap and pulls his own knees tuh his chest. He positions my husband's dark brown arms around the tops of his legs. When he's cocooned, he runs the groundCar across Andre's arms and his own knees.

My husband kisses the top of his head while I drive the groundCars up and down their bodies. Trinity smiles as we use random sounds fuh the toys. Crash them. Give them the voices and personalities we heard durin' an Anomaly children's show.

Some weeks, we're not let out of our rooms, so we make our fun.

One hundred years ago, our ancestors tried printin' water. They did it wrong, and many perished. Be smart, Urban citizens, not curious. Ya favored show, Today in the Past!

Soon, we're flyin' the hoverCars in every direction, mah husband and I. Trinity laughs loudly. He's more adventurous in smaller spaces. We exaggerate the voices, as he adores them. After a while, Andre hands Trinity tuh me and kisses me farewell.

He tickles mah cheek before runnin' out of the door, smilin'. He runs everywhere tuh avoid the loud, painful beep that'll blare years after mine.

I play some more, doing the creaky voice Trinity cackles over before dressing fuh mah position. When I finish, I dress him fuh the day. Horrid green pants and a shirt made of soft fabric and well-made graffita designs. But the sickly green's always a reminder of where we are.

Standin' near the door, I watch him play. No crashes. No tipped ova bikes. Any rules he knows, he obeys. He's a borin' toddler. I didn't know they could be made that way.

"I'll be back later."

Trinity strolls ova and hugs me. I bury mah nose in his neck. Smell deeply. His O negative sweetens as he ages. I didn't know that happened with children. It's grand tuh know.

He's a chubby one. He's whole here. I hold him fuh a long time, as he'd gladly be held forever.

"Many loves, Mat-Mat." He pinches my cheek and walks back tuh his play, singin' the theme song of his favorite show, *Puddles.* The Keepers'll take him tuh his courses.

"Many loves, mah son."

I close the door on his singin'.

Off-pitch and beautiful.

THIRTY-ONE

LETHARGY. THE AUCTION cells are infested with it. No days. No minutes. Few windows. Without time, existence becomes a questionable thing.

The dot on mah hand. I stare at it tuh get a sense of the time. Did I rewrite it yesterday eve or this morn?

Not sure. I'll ask someone else fuh their reality.

Hour break. Eat lunch.

My device tells me this, and a timer ticks down. I go on break after Botany. Urban's got thousands of plants, and I'm interested in none of 'em.

'The perfect representation of evolution.'

Urban's obsessed with them.

After eatin' quickly, I go where I always do: The Wall. Stop at the guard desk before leavin' our building.

Ding. 1,950,000 units. "Where ya goin'?" Guard T845 asks me this every day. So annoyin'.

"The Wall, marm. What day's it?"

She shrugs. "Don't know." She does. "I used tuh go there a lot too. Don't have no reason tuh now. G'head." She smiles, scans mah access card, and waves me out.

Okay. I continue on. I don't know if it's good or bad that she has no reason to. You never know with The Wall.

The barrier lights red, and I walk out of the West Auction Cells. White groundVans greet me. Screams. Panic. Zaps. I put mah head down and walk past it all.

A pebbled path leads me tuh the center of the auction cells—the auction wing. I spend much of mah day there. Don't have any desire tuh spend anymore.

South, West, East, and North cells fan out from here like a cog. Each hidden by magnificent trees and inaccessible by the others.

The air's rose-and-apple scented today. I smell it deeply.

Hints of takti oil and preserver are in it.

It's still day. I can see the name I'm lookin' for. I hope I don't see the name I'm lookin' for.

Marguerite Kiana.

I've been goin' tuh The Wall most days since she reached Vow age. I walk, already there in mah mind.

Readin' the names of those before me. Their auction years. The small shape after the year signalin' their birth city. Valley's is a hexagon.

Anomalies, Commons. I have sent thousands of them tuh The Wall. How many were like Marguerite? How many did nothin' wrong?

I push away the vague numbers pilin' in mah mind, review what I know:

In 2234, there was a Marguerite. 2332, another. It's an antique name. Not many people use it. Even fewer use a middle name anymore. Wasteful.

Xaia, she did whatever she pleased. Middle name. No name.

Twenty-five minutes left of break. Mah device reminds me.

"Marm, I'm back from break ear*ly*." An extremely old man in a miserable green suit like mine wheels a carrier behind him. It's got bottles, a bucket, rags, and a duster in it.

Glistenin' red permapaint two inches wide surrounds his wrists. *Ding.* 3,110,000 units. He holds his palm tuh me. I bow before returnin' the greetin'.

"Ya ain't gotta bow. Always hat*ed* all that bowin'. And don't call me no Past-Knower. I *bare*ly know what I just ate." The Polisher wipes crumbs from his lips. Smacks them. "Somethin' good, it was. What can I help ya with?"

In the cells, Past-Knowers are mined fuh their wisdom, treated kindly, but they're not revered.

"Sirn, I'm lookin' fuh a child. She was put in the orphan midpotential area."

The Polisher squirts a thick liquid on a rag and rubs the fabric between his fingers. "Those kids ain't written here." Oh. "They written on The Wall there."

"Where's there?"

He reaches on his tiptoes, pointing. West. Far, far west. I look over there. When I turn back, he's pointing far East. Far North. Far South.

314

"A joke, marm." Yes, I got that. "Not ma*ny* dare tuh talk tuh a decrepit rogue. All they got is silly questions." He laughs, a breathy cackle. "Yours is a betta one. The Anomaly and midpotential cells're *hid*den. Rebel Anomalies, especially, are moved around all da time." He pours a liquid into the bucket. Stops at some invisible line he knows. "They cain't do no harm, and no harm can come tuh 'em."

Moved around. They do not stay in one place. My mind pauses, stutters, and shatters.

"D'ya hear me?"

May not be here.

"Marm?"

I blink. "Yes, I heard. And the six-dots?"

"Same. Rebel or not, they don't stay in one Urban." He shrugs. "I've heard there's *hid*den places fuh 'em outside da regions." He cups his hands around his mouth. "Ya wouldn't keep all of ya most precious eggs in da same bas*ket* and tell da world where it is, would ya?"

James of the Pillars is not here. There are hundreds of Urbans all over our world. And if not there, some random place.

He could be anywhere. I did not even think to ask this until now, and I regret knowing it. The man hums lightly.

I hold back my glare; he is still a Past-Knower. "Sirn, I could've done without the snark."

"Most people can. Ya wel*come*, marm."

I turn away and roll my eyes. Stupid man. It is no wonder he has no friends.

My break is near over.

I have eaten, but I am emptier than when I left for it.

THIRTY-TWO

"HIGHER." TRINITY LAUGHS.

I push the swing higher, stayin' far away so it won't disturb mah conceived. Another rowdy boy who kicks and punches inside me all day long as his older brother did.

"More higher."

I push harder. At four-aged, he's small and light compared tuh the other children. The higher he goes, the louder he laughs. I push as hard as I can.

There's *ding*ing all around me. A couple billion units.

"Exercise begins in fifty minutes." A guard yawns in the megaphone, fresh from his nap break below us.

The parent section of the auction cells is filled with many play structures fuh the children. Trinity'll use only two of 'em. The lowest, most borin' one and the swings.

Fresh, green grass covers the park, built high in the trees. Fresh air comes from the decorative bars atop the green, nearly translucent walls surroundin' the play area. Children climb the trees and water the flowers.

On both sides of us, the other children pump their legs, propellin' themselves higher.

"Soon, ya must push yaself." He kicks his legs and laughs again, reachin' one hand up tuh the sky. "Make a wish."

I push him more. At the peak of the swing's arc, Trinity launches off. His back arches as he flies through the air, arms out, legs bicyclin', and lands gracefully before lookin' at me with that intense stare. "How come?"

I exhale. Everything with this child is how come. "Because... wishes help."

"Mah paternal won't lemme." A boy whines while other children jump from their swings.

"Do it anyway!" They laugh as they land. Mah knee aches just watchin' their impacts.

I hold out my hand. He takes it, and we walk tuh a bench facin' the bars. Stand in front of it.

In ancient times, there were millions of cells all ova our world. People'd live behind bars fuh decades. What a waste of wight. Luckily fuh us, the lower regions're filled with The BloodBid and sortin' machines. Ya favored show, Today in the Past!

"Show yaself," a guard mumbles, and we turn toward the wall, foreheads restin' on the warm barrier, arms tight against our sides. Palms out. The guard scans us before walkin' off without another word. I'm sure they do this because they're bored. It'd be excellent if they learned tuh entertain themselves some other way.

317

How annoyin'.

Trinity laughs. Fuh some reason, he finds inspection stance funny.

I stare far below us, at the guards. The people pourin' out of the white groundVans. *Ding*s. Millions of units. Screams come from below, and the groundVan rumbles away. Trinity does not react. None of the children do.

I sit next tuh him. He kicks his feet. Holds his hands in his lap. Looks up at me.

"Make me… not me, Mat-Mat. I don't wanna go."

His face is still; his words are crisp.

"I can't do that, lil one."

"Oh. Who can?" He's starin' harder at me now. That face has been starin' at me years more than his age. I look away.

"No one."

"Why wish, then." He slides off the bench and walks across the park, past a woman bein' dragged away, cursin' and screamin'.

He sits at one of the knowledge stations—a table, books, paper—and rifles through the selection. Picks an Anomaly manual. His reading has improved immensely over these last two years. Behind him is a large space of concrete and a wall where the children can write and draw as they study.

Soon after he begins, the whiny boy runs over and points at the book. "Show us, Trin."

Most of the children come from the swings and play structures and gather around him. The playground is near silent now.

318

"Yay, please, we're ready." Their voices ring through the air.

Trinity nods. Calm. And gets up. Moves in front of the wall. The children turn toward him, a few of them push the whiny boy back.

"Hey, that was *mah* spot." The boy's bottom lip pushes out, and his eyes grow glossy. "I was here first." They ignore him, and more pile in front, shushing him.

Not surprising. He is most annoying.

Trinity steps forward. Waits for them to let him through. He stands in front of the boy for a second, staring at him with that intense gaze before pulling his arm forward.

"He was here." He lets go of the boy when he has positioned him in front of the other children. "He stays here."

Trinity smiles at the boy.

This child.

"Woo-hoo!" An older boy takes off his jacket and hands it to him as he strolls back to the wall. In his four years of life, I have seen Trinity run fewer than twenty times.

He does not rush. Anywhere. To do anything. For anyone.

The others settle down next to one another, some standing, a few sitting on the grass. They give Trinity room, but he asks a few, including the whiny boy, to come closer. He enjoys smaller spaces.

All of them leave a path to the knowledge station's table for him to walk through. Some are as young as him, others much older.

Their eyes turn black so they can see the background he has chosen behind him. He reads the manual from his device, one of his gray-brown irises overlaid with black now, and adds emphasis and suspense. His flat expression animates as he mimics the actors he has watched so many times.

"Urban citizens, ya bed must be made… before sunrise." He sounds like the girl from *Puffy Pigtails*. A silly show. Popular. He mimes the girl, giving ominous news to her friend. Opens his eyes wide and trembles his lip.

The children laugh. One, "I adore this episode."

"Ah!" Trinity yells and waves the jacket at the front-row children. They jump back. Ten minutes in, he creeps to the table, hops on it. Drama, chaos. Slashing, loud whoops.

The children are excited to learn about how to stay focused for a long time now. The children are very strange. What have we done?

"Get rid of distractions." He kicks hard into the air.

No guards stop him from this. They do not care as long as the children learn their lessons. Some of them sit and enjoy his performance.

He turns in a tight, fast twist and pulls the jacket over his face. Lowers it. Smiles. Bows. And gets down from the table with two dramatic steps.

"More, more, Trin!" They clap and cheer him on.

He does one more voice, one more lesson, one more massive smile before pointing to his ears and sitting. It is a universal sign in the cells. In Urban. Time to study. His eyes cloud as he watches Anomaly artists.

A few seconds pass.

One girl pouts. Loudly says, "He didn't even shake our hands." She crosses her arms over her uniform. Same wing as Trinity. Her crime, his crime. Louder now. "His shows ain't usually that short. I wanted more."

"Maybe he's sick today." The whiny boy.

Most of them sigh, nod, and drift back to the swings and play structures they came from.

A few who were already at the knowledge stations glance at him. Leave him sweets and write him show requests before going back to their learning.

Eventually, his eyes uncloud. He grips a pencil tightly and makes a deep line in the paper, focusing hard. His hand shakes, and when he is done, he folds the paper into four perfect squares.

THIRTY-THREE

I WALK INTO our room an hour early for my position. A white fungus is growing in the shadows, haunting my days. I look at it. Over this half year, a small stack of pages has multiplied in the far-right corner. Trinity's. I walk over to it and leaf through a few.

Show requests. Notes. Many sheets are blank. Others have drawings of artists' works—Basquiat, Joshua of the Tiles, Monet, Ann of the Roads, Muholi, Denise of the Pines, Banksy, Ali of the Lords, Kusama, Lewis. And more. He has left no artist uncopied.

None are good imitations. He has much learning to do, so he studies the Anomalies for hours, especially in the early morn.

He studies many subjects whenever his time is not consumed with practicing for performances and those 'waste of life classes.'

How lucky he is to only have these concerns.

A large book is on the top of his desk. Dozens are on the floor.

'Matty, a grand actor needs tuh be well traveled in knowledge."

Later, he will study more.

He is always studying.

I straighten the pile until it is perfect. I hope he grows out of this phase soon. Our room will not become an orphanage for misfit pages.

Still, I smile. There were sketches of pinecones, too.

I sit on our bed. It is quiet now. Completely. That is rare here. I enjoy the space between noise. Close my eyes and feel the silence, a warm, soft nothingness. The walls of my body melt away, and I expand and become all else.

BEEP!

I crash back into myself. Get up and dress.

On my way to the auction wing, I stop at the faith center's door. It is tall, closed, and I cannot see in. Have never dared to see in. But it is time. I will not avoid this room any longer.

Words are etched into the door: *Faith's fuh everyone. Come believe with us.*

Most Urban citizens are of the Inventor faith, but the religion used to only be for Anomalies.

"As I get closer to my name going on The Wall, I have grown fonder of the idea of the Inventor." A tall, immensely fat man greets me, grabs my hand. Breathes loudly. Stares ahead like me. "Someone, something, anything to welcome me back where I am from. Promise they have been waiting. Swear they have missed me while I was away."

Ding. 80,000 units.

Unlike me, he can see above the dark section of the door, but he does not look in. He is still, staring at the green number in his device that lowers every day.

"I—" He swallows. "I was a good husband, marm. I was a *good husband.*" He squeezes my fingers gently. "This wait. This knowing. My previous beloved was not worth this agony. Anomalies are…"

Dangerous.

Xaia's voice echoes in my mind. As clear as it was five years ago.

My fingers shiver. The man is gone.

I enter the room. The top is triangular, painted in pastel colors. The high ceiling towers over emptiness. No furniture, signs, or people. I head for the farthest corner and stand there, facing it. The present. But it is the past that calls to me. I glance at it and suck in a deep breath.

No, the present. Only the present.

I tilt my head, squint until only the thin line between the two times exists. James of the Pillars, Marguerite, and so many more hover in my peripheral vision. Their voices bubble up, talking, screaming, laughing, humming. Smiles, frowns, sobs bombarding my left side.

I peek to the right.

Trinity is there. Folds of fat cover his body, and jowls hang from his cheeks. Solid, blurry, appearing, disappearing, holding his arms out for a hug.

The voices pile on top of one another.

No, no. I shake my head. Close my eyes. No. No more.

Someone touches my shoulder, and I whirl around.

"Excuse me, miss, are ya good?"

I look around, disoriented. *Ding.* 15,300,000,000 units.

The three-dot Anomaly woman's face is angular and patient. Her hair has been shorn off, and her brown scalp is beautifully polished. An empty red triangle is on her simple, black gown, resting over her heart. The leader of this faith group. I bow to her. "Yes, marm, I'm good."

"Okay. I saw ya standin' here, and I thought ya might need tuh talk."

"Why? I'm worshipping like ya do, marm."

She looks at the wall a moment. "Facin' the corner?"

"Yeah. That's how ya pray, right?"

"No, not usually. Well, ya can pray whatever way ya want, of course, but it's not our usual position. Who told ya that?"

"I don't remember, marm."

She stares at me. "Well, if ya wanna talk about this person ya don't remember…"

"He was no one."

THIRTY-FOUR

THE CANDLES FLICKER on our table as I draw from memory. Dark shadows on the inner side of each of the pinecone's rachis. Light shading on the outer edges.

Little crevices where you would think there would be smoothness. Around and around. So much sameness that is all different.

I follow each line with my pencil, fixing any imperfections by adding more shadows. I relax into the page. Time disappears.

I am in paradise.

"Pinecones? They are your favorite. Why?" My husband whispers this as he leans over my shoulder. A few of his letters slip into one another, though he is trying hard to keep them separate.

"They are simple when you walk by, complex when you sit with them."

It has only been a few months since we married, but already we are twined close. I cannot believe I am his beloved. Me? A Common from Valley. Him, a six-dot Anomaly.

Six. Dots.

James of the Pillars hums the song he wrote for me last week. The stunning notes caress my bones.

I pull him nearer my ear. Smell. O negative. A strong buzz rumbles deep in my chest. He rests his chin in my shoulder. We fit together perfectly.

As I like it.

He wears an unfamiliar fragrance—citrus, cinnamon, and a few others potent and beautifully blended. I would expect no less from Urban. I would expect no less for an Anomaly.

He holds his fingers over the pinecone, quiet for a long time. "Bless the Inventor, it looks real, like it is in the room with us. You are a most magnificent artist. What a grand illusion."

"I know."

Trinity has not slept in two weeks, only napped. Andre and I are in our bed, and we have slept almost as little. My son is standing in front of his bed, across from ours.

"And then there was a loud *clack* and a silent boom."

"And then there *was a* loud clack and a silent boom."

"And then there *was a* loud clack and a *silent boom.*"

He has been reciting this line for fifteen minutes now. Every once in a while, trilling his lips and shaking his arms. Trying on different facial expressions.

It is… I do not know, too early o'clock, and the night has been a rageful ghost. I am much too tired to strangle a chubby five-year-old. In an hour, we shall see.

"Mah son, go tuh sleep." Andre yawns loudly behind me.

"C'aint. I'm tastin' the feelin's, Paternal." He keeps the voice and mannerisms of the actors and actresses. Moving from one to another. He rarely speaks in his own voice now.

I do not know who told him that or what it means, but I hate them immensely.

"Trinity, I'm a Taster. Ya gotta rest ya tongue tuh know the grandest flavor."

"No, ya gotta. Mah tongue's strong."

There is no bite to his words, only fact.

We laugh. Me, because he delivered the remark in his own voice. Calm. Andre, to hide he does not have an answer. Though he has a quick intelligence, his comebacks are terribly slow. Maybe he does not study enough.

Soft velvet whispers in my ear. Clearer than that day.

My love, admit it, Trinity is smarter than us both.

I smile. His words are still true.

I prop myself on my elbow. "Ya nervous for ya show tomorrow?"

He nods, trills his lips again, and answers in the girl's voice from *Puffy Pigtails*, "I wanna do grand in front of the Anomalies. I wanna be the best. I don't have time fuh sleep."

One of his eyelids twitches. He rubs it. It has been twitching for a month now.

"I understand ya nervous tuh perform at the Anomaly Gala tomorrow, what with so many comin' fuh the fifth one, but ya eyelid says differently. Sleep so you'll be rested."

"I wanna be the best, Maternal." He stares at me, his mouth set in a rigid line, his voice gruff like the lead from his second-most favorite play, *The Diamond and the Wind*.

"In ya quest tuh be more, mah son, it's easy tuh become less. You're enough as ya are."

"Enough is forgettable." He whips around to face the wall. Dramatic is his way. "*And then* there was a loud clack and a silent boom."

Exhaustion grips me. I lie back down.

Behind me, Andre gets up.

He goes into the toilet room, sprays Freshest Breath™ into his mouth, and fills a cup with water. Drinks it, cleans it, fills it again.

Andre yawns once more, goes to the bookcase, and grabs a thin manual.

"First, ya attitude—nah." He turns Trinity back around.

Brownish-gray eyes look at me a long while. Calm, detached voice. His true one. "Sorry, Matty." It does not match those eyes, narrowed with a hard gaze.

"Betta. I got no problem bannin' ya from the gala. Ya listenin'?"

Trinity nods.

"Okay then. Second, here mah boy, drink dis. If ya lose ya voice, ya won't be able tuh perform." Trinity hugs him and gulps down the water. A minute later, both of his eyes go black as he focuses completely on his performance.

"Husband, we should not set this precedence. Sleep is good for him." In my anger, I slip into my natural accent.

He shrugs. "He ain't gonna sleep anyway. If he wanna be da best, we should help him."

"Tomorrow night, we gotta make sure he sleeps."

Andre nods. One of his braids is sticking up, and his uniform is rumpled. Messy. His right eye goes black. He recites the line after the one Trinity keeps repeating.

I close my eyes. I am not getting up.

Why can he not pretend to be a child who sleeps?

That would be perfect.

As I like it.

When I open them again, Trinity's curls move to the side as Andre fans him.

"This story don't work without the wind."

That is the first line of the script. My son is starting from the top.

THIRTY-FIVE

"AND THERE'S BEAUTY in good. Strength, unbreakable strength. In all walls. You're a wall, so there must be beauty in ya." Trinity rasps his favorite lines on the stage at the Anomaly Gala.

Around him, there is luxury. A massive stage and thick, red curtains tied open, held to the sides. 3D trees' paint shimmers in the light, bright and metallic. As he walks downstage, closer to the Anomalies, the trail under him shifts and takes him in different directions. He stops when a wall crashes in front of him.

Tears gather in his eyes as his character, Michelle, pleads for mercy. The lights go down. When they come back up, he is standing at the edge of the stage, alone, staring up at them.

Three beats pass.

Trinity smiles and steps back. He bows with his forehead on the ground and his palms up.

Claps from the sea of Anomalies rain down on him. The lower-ranked ones enjoy a few hours in the cells, watching musicals, concerts, and a play where a boy is the only human character.

It was a grand performance and led to Trinity booking many more. He repeats the lines now, sounding much older than his six years.

He sits on his bed, a luxurious couch now, crunching sour A negative liver brittle. Playing back his performance. Rewind. Listen. Rewind.

He has mastered the actors' inflections and gives the most life to all the characters, especially Michelle, the heroine in Angelina of the Mills's famous tales of talking walls and hidden worlds.

I sit next to him, knitting. Watching him.

Crumbs all over his lap. Some on the floor. Unease grows in me as the carpet is replaced with organ mess.

I breathe deeply through the jitteriness under my skin and focus on my knitting. His costume requires an intricate pattern I have never done. I watch the person in my device, but I still have been unable to do it correctly.

Three hundred fifty years ago, scientists discovered a heart rate of 250 sweetened the wight immensely, and so the harvesting farms' methods changed fuh the betta. Ya favored show, Today in the Past!

"Maternal, when I grow up, I'll be the best actor Urban has ever saw."

The gurgling of Andre's throat pauses, one second, two, three, before continuing. He spits the mouthwash in the sink and appears in the bathroom's doorway, wiping his stubble with a towel. Glances at me. "Of course ya will, mah boy. Ya gettin' the best roles for ya age, and they'll be beggin' ya fuh older children's parts."

"I'll always get betta." Trinity rewinds it again before switching to interviews. He leaves notes in his device as he listens to Anomaly actresses and actors.

Studies every piece of them.

It is mid-morn, and he practices whenever he has spare time from his classes. Bursts out in random shows with random children. All. The. Time.

This child.

I smile at him. "That's true."

He leans forward and pinches my cheek. "When I'm old like ya, I'll be known all over." His eyes go black.

There is a force to his words. A calm force. A certainty that quiets us both. Trinity grows more like James of the Pillars every day.

And with that thought, the pain in my stomach wrenches. The stitches over the screaming hole open and spill out the empty years we will not have together.

The man Trinity will never know—or call "Paternal."

The hole wails until it is interrupted by a flurry of knocks on the door. A high-pitched shriek.

Oh, yesterday was so long. My conceived is a troublesome thing; she has caused fatigue and nausea for the entire two months she has existed in me.

I get up slowly. Still, my knee cracks. My thirty-six years are showing themselves.

After I unlock the door: "Trin!"

Near a dozen *dings*. Near a dozen children's grins. Wide eyes. Short screeches of excitement.

Why are they here, and how glad are their parents to be rid of them?

"Marm, sirn, is Trin home? Can he show us? Please." The whiny boy.

Sigh. I thought his paternal would not let him do anything, and yet here he often is, doing things.

Andre walks out of the toilet room, scrubbing his tongue. "I'm cool wit it."

It is garbled. It is unlikely the children understood what he said. I am about to say Trinity is not here, but before I can, one of them spots him, so instead, "If he wants."

I move aside, and children of many ages flood into our room, clad in green, decorated outfits. Sequins, earrings, bangles, and makeup. They hold props of all kinds: cups, rubber knives, napkins.

The oldest boy wears pointy shoes and a tall hat. He holds up a small costume as the others quote lines to each other and strike strange poses.

"Trin, hey." The loud girl from the playground shakes him hard at the shoulder. He jolts out of his focus with a glare that quickly shifts to nothing. Himself. Calm. Flat. "Wanna play wit us?"

He looks around the room. They are everywhere. Green oddities of all shapes and sizes sitting on our bed, on his desk chair, lounging on the floor, mimicking Anomaly actors. Twisting their faces in ways faces were not made to turn.

He nods. "Not play, but practice, yeah."

"Play is practice." The oldest boy gives him the costume, and he runs into the toilet room. The door locks, goes black.

A minute passes. He rolls into the room and does a complicated twisted flip. *'I'll do mah own stunts.'*

Trinity holds a hand to his chest and stares intently at the light above. In a voice an octave lower than his, "Prince, there is a mouse where my heart should be."

"Are you sure?" The oldest boy walks to him and points to the ground. "How do you know one is missing?"

Some of the children twitch their noses and crawl on all fours around our room. Make skittering noises. Others pose like trees. And the rest lie flat, still. Perished mushrooms.

"I feel it. Listen to it in the night. A scritchety-scrat. A scritchety-scrat. Hear me."

The boy leans down and puts his ear to Trinity's chest.

Andre comes from the toilet room and sprinkles water on the unmoving children. He laughs loudly as they rise slowly, serious about their resurrections.

I hold my finger to my lips.

"Can you help me find my heart, kind marm?" Trinity's head whiplashes to me; the children's follow a second later. Their gazes are soft and focused; my son's is a penetrating, burning laser. Dozens of eyes on me.

Rest will not be mine.

I grab our cover from the bed, wrap it around me, and put on the most pretentious, highest-class accent I can. "Yay, first ya must climb dat tree."

He jumps on his bed. It was well made; it is a mess now. He holds his hand flat across his eyes, scouting for the tree. Points. "That one?"

"Nah, dat one far tuh da east of it." I point in the other direction of our room.

A hundred times. I have seen this performance a hundred times. It is a good play.

He jumps down, tiptoes past the mushrooms. The loud girl is standing in the corner, making a *creak-do, creak-do* with his every step. He looks at her, pauses a while, and laughs. Hard laughter that goes on as if he cannot control it.

What is happening?

We stare at him, silent. This has never happened before.

"You broke character," the girl shouts. A headache whispers in my mind. I swear it, she is near deaf.

Her voice does not quiet him. He laughs so long it must be painful. When he finally sobers, he looks tired. "I did. Won't happen again."

She steps out of the corner.

Creak-do, creak-do.

THIRTY-SIX

NEAT PILES OF pages are stacked in two corners of our room, each sheet carefully wrapped in plastic. Over the last two years, they have become small mountains.

Testaments of progress.

Sweat covers my body as the lingering scent of the farms fades from my conscience. Andre sleeps heavily at my front—deeply, tightly curled into the fetal position, his back pressed against my chest. I grunt and get up. I have far more than a jiggle now, and the extra weight makes my joints hurt.

It is very early morn. Trinity is awake.

"Damn it," he whispers as he balls up a page and hurls it across the room. It lands in the circular recycling bin, which shreds the paper silently.

At his desk, he has a tiny light set to the third notch, barely bright enough for him to read by. It rarely goes off when he is in the room.

Silently, he studies. Weariness radiates from him, deeply etched in over these six years. He faces me as the manuals dictate: a child's desk must be turned toward the head of their parents' bed to ensure they are studying. But how would we know if he is studying? We are sleeping.

His green suit is creased in all places suits must be creased. "DI#431855*" everywhere on it in fluorescent, blocky text. The design changed last year.

The sides of his head are shaved 3.45 inches from his ears, not one of his curls is out of place, and his posture is rigid and unwavering.

More pages are scattered on the floor. He does not see or hear me. He is zoned into a virtual lesson.

I walk into the toilet room and stand at the sink. This week, Andre has cleaned everything—the toilet, tub, sink, floors, mirrors—according to the manuals. Hints of F564 Lemon linger in the air, and no streaks are on the tiles. Everything is pristine. Perfect.

As I like it.

Anomaly children, listen closely. It's illegal tuh detach ya large birth parts. They can't be half-bid or sold. Some fingers, all toes, yes. Everything else, no. Tuh keep them is ya Inventor-given right. Enjoy. Ya favored show, Today in the Past!

It is 3 and a half morn. I watch Trinity through the mirror. Keep the toilet room door unlocked so it stays transparent.

A second chin hangs from his first, and his stomach bulges. Dark circles rim his eyes. He studies the Anomalies' works of the past, their innovations, and their interviews.

Two stacks of books are piled high on his desk—science, math, theater, drawing, theater, music, fiction, sports, theater. They are not like the manuals; they are made of unrippable paper. Unchangeable text. Encased in a protective coating.

He slows as he reads a few pages of Angelina of the Mills.

'*Do the voice, Mat-Mat. Do the voice again.*' He would badger me, and I would lower my voice. Rasp the brick wall's words to my sleepy two-year-old.

Her stories used to be his most favored. Now, he only glares at them. Studies them more.

Trinity closes the book. He sets it aside and opens another. Closes it. Opens another. And again, until the large stack of books on his right are on his left.

He does it again. Open. Read. Close. Moving them from left to right. When he has done this once more, he shoves the entire stack off the desk. The movement is so sharp that they land in a tall pile, one loud boom, then slowly tumble over.

He rubs an eye with the butt of his palm, just as he did when he was an infant, before holding the pencil above the paper. The tip is sharp. His hand quavers.

"Please stop watchin' me, Maternal." His own calm voice. "Every new day. Every morn, this." He turns to me, and so quickly away, it is as if I imagined the scathing look.

I am frozen. Cannot look away.

339

The pencil tip breaks. A spent bullet on the page. Trinity rubs the rest of the graphite in. Deep gray streaks through bits of yellow wood. When the tip is dull, he swipes the page and pencil off the desk. They fall on top of the others on the floor. I blink. Look down. Stare. Count. Nine pencils. Thirty pages. So much mess.

"Please stop." He moves the other stack of books and covers his face. Presses a tenth pencil to a page and draws magnificent lines. Stunning designs.

THIRTY-SEVEN

TRINITY HUGS ME. He is tall for his age.

The clock ticks faster than it used to. Why does that happen as you get older?

"It's okay." I hold him to my chest. These words are not mine; they are his. Calm. In his voice. "I've known a long time. I'm not mad at ya anymore, Maternal."

The clock strikes midnight, and the door to our room opens.

I kiss his forehead, the green spot above his eyebrow.

He steps away. I keep my grasp light as his arm slides through my fingers. When our fingers meet, I curl mine upwards and catch his.

Time,

do you never need to rest?

I flatten my fingers and let his slide across the top.

The door closes.

THIRTY-EIGHT

I laugh. Then scream.

Just once. Always just once.

Andre sleeps soundly behind me. The sleeping pill I gave him will wear off in the morn. I wanted to say farewell to my son alone.

"I am sorry."

I stare down at him. Pull the covers to his chin and kiss his nose. He is a good man. Kind, Common, and unloved by me.

I turn to the stacks of pages, one in each corner of the room, dated at the top. There are four years of them. I walk around the room and pick the first page from the top of each stack. Same thing, different words. Large, dark writing. Show requests from the loud girl.

This year's stack has her final show request, even though it is two years old.

I pick up more pages. Indecipherable notes, drawings,

nothing. Squint. Bring the empty pages closer to my face. They are not empty. A lightly written green number is in the middle. I dig through more. Hundreds of numbers, lower every day.

For two hours, I take his drawings from every stack and put them together. One on top of another. Just so.

Two hundred thirty years ago, our world had dozens of faiths. It's much easier only tuh have six, ain't it? Ya favored show, Today in the Past!

When I finish, I get my bracelet from its container under our bed. It digs into the scar on my wrist, heavier than I remember.

I remember... humming, the small tub of salve, minty vanilla, so warm from his back pocket. His fingertips against my belly. His scent.

His humming.

So comforting. It is loud in my head now.

After I have finished the collection, I set my device to notify me of any changes for the next hour and go to my position. No notification means The Search's three hours of testing have determined Trinity to be Common.

During a break, I trudge past the East Auction cells near fifteen minutes until the small pebbles turn into black marble. Smooth and gleaming in the sunlight.

My muscles sputter along as if they have forgotten how to work. Every once in a while, my knee buckles, and I stumble along like I am stricken with The Blaze.

There is less sun the closer I get. I come upon it.

The Wall.

Columns of names and dates etched into black 50-foot slabs of marble, only far apart enough to let two citizens through side by side. To my left and right, The Wall stretches further than I can see—eclipsing everything around it.

The Dome's crest is centered at the top of each.

In the auction cells, the rebel Anomalies' memorials are interspersed with Commons', though there are many differences.

Theirs is written in glowing red lettering, and the same color borders their slabs. When night comes, a thick stripe glows on each side, and a red beam shoots from their memorials. The Commons: white lettering. In the night, our names are invisible.

I read the names and dates. Time passes, but I do not know how much. Each of my seven years in Urban, I have come here. Read thousands of names written in the same script.

"A grand morn tuh ya, marm. Nice tuh see ya again." The Inscriber puts a palm out to me. Smiles.

Ding. 930,000 units.

His handwriting is handsome, and his face is patient. Red permapaint covers his hands, arms, and chest. He stands in front of The Wall, holding a thin device made to write legacies for all.

We will not forget the past.

I raise my palm. Stand a few feet away from him. The Wall behind him is nearly full.

Centered across the bottom—'Thank ya fuh ya contribution tuh our world'—and to its far-right—'1334A'

"A grand morn. This will be my last visit."

This is my last day.

He nods. "What's ya child called?"

"He is called Trinity."

"A good name. Did he have a unique spelling?"

"No, it is common. He is Common. I am Common."

He nods and turns on the device. It whirs as he inscribes my son's name on The Wall. Forms the letters slowly, making sure each ornate curl is perfect. He blows the dust from the inscription, gently like tickling the edges of a feather, and walks over to me, digging in the pouch sagging from his hips.

He does look kind, forgiving, so I ask, "What is your name?"

His eyes widen. "Few ask me that. They only give names." A smile. "I am Malachi. Malachi the Inscriber."

He hands me an elaborate, meticulously designed, golden "T."

I stare at it. Flip it over. '1,334A' is on the other side. I clip the charm to my bracelet as he holds up his palm. Return the gesture.

The gold "T" hangs from my wrist, glistening in the sun like the letters before it. I turn from him. Do not look back.

When I spend Trinity, my fifteenth charm will turn silver.

I walk away to enjoy his eighth birth day.

ACKNOWLEDGMENTS

FIRST, I WANT to thank my family for helping me as I worked on this novel. Your emotional support, advice, financial gifts, ideas, and more kept me going as I tweaked and tweaked.

I love all of you so much.

Margaret—my big sister, who was always patient with my weirdness and debates. She reminds me that everyone's version of success is different but the amount of work needed to reach it is the same—immense. Her rapping ability is beyond measure.

Antione—my older brother, who gave me his smile and laugh. And the vulnerability that hides behind them. For us all, I think. He put much good in my world. I should've asked to name a character after him, but I didn't.

Markia—my little sister, best friend, and the person who inspired me to write. She reads my rough rough drafts and tells me the harsh truth that can only come from someone who cares. If she gave her opinion any softer, I'd doubt her love for me. A delusion may comfort you, but it won't grow you. Truth is love. Always.

Malik—my baby brother. Ah, I love him tons. Every day, he shows me how to be resilient and to remember that hope can change your life. I haven't met another person who will go after his happiness with all he's got—and never take no for an answer to reach it. He has the fire visionaries are made of.

SECOND, my amazing alpha and beta readers. Thank you for your time, honest critiques, and ideas.

Markia ☺, **Caleb Melchior, Ally Manno, Judith Hirsch, Sloan Patton, Michele Cacano, Katie Zhou, Eric Andeen, Aislinn A., Michael Destro, A.M. Maris, Joseph C., Kyle Mifflin, Grayson A.**, **Isa Marks,** and **Tamara Foster aka Thereviewblr**

K.—special thanks to him. He didn't want to be named, but his help with the politics, science behind the science fiction, and worldbuilding was invaluable.

Rebecca Weber—she shared her pregnancy experience with me and blew my mind. So many big and small struggles I didn't know existed.

Niharikaa Sodhi—she showed me how to be spiritually and monetarily wealthy. I struggled with the monetary part. Also, she taught me that simplicity in business is key.

Ayodeji Awosika—he helped me finally let go of (much of) my perfectionism. Some perfectionism's built into my personality, so I'll keep the healthy bits. Also, he let me use a line from one of his books.

Gunner—met you on the bus. Told you I'd put you in the acknowledgments to immortalize you. Here you are.

THIRD, my book cover designer. She was absolutely fantastic.

Keylin Rivers—we went back and forth on this cover for two weeks straight, and she showed the utmost professionalism. To purchase a book cover, go to her website at <u>fantasycoverdesign.com</u>.

FOURTH, my editor.

Ellie Nalle—her advice to show the core of your characters in the first chapter was helpful. Also, she helped me understand James of the Pillars better.

FINALLY, my readers.

All of you—your passion and love for the written word inspired this weirdo writer to release the world banging to get out of her head. Many thanks forever.

ABOUT THE AUTHOR

DEON ASHLEIGH GREW up in Michigan. She grew to despise cold weather, so she left. She was born 1 pound, 7 ounces, slept under a soft rag as a baby, and loves Bran Flakes.

When she graduated with her Bachelor's, she hopped on a train from Michigan to Seattle, Washington. Alone. With no job. No housing. And no family. She was on a quest for a challenge, an adventure—and a concrete belief in herself. She wanted to test her mettle, so she did.

She's a traveler at heart. The world is big, beautiful, and vibrant. Why *not* see all that genius?

Most of her writing is of the dystopian variety. Why?

To show the strength of human love, the will to survive, and the importance of staying hopeful. If her characters, infused with her emotions, can survive their horrendous lives, then there is hope.

For us all.

If you wanna know more about Deon, get notified of her new releases, and find her when she's wandering, visit her at www.deonashleigh.com.

YOU ARE ALL LOVED

(Rest In Peace)

MARGARET ANN BONNER ♥

September 27, 1945 - 1971

MARY DENISE PORTER

HER HUSBAND, JAMES

JOSHUA JESSIE

GWENDOLYN DIANE ROUNTREE

CINNAMON ♥

June 20, 2010 - February 13, 2021

CHAT AND REVIEW

deonashleigh.com
Twitter: @deonashleigh
Goodreads: Deon Ashleigh
YouTube: The Sci-fi Space

Enjoyed *The Price of a Beating Heart?*

For updates on new releases, indie publishing tips, and behind-the-scenes goodies, become a weirdo. Join my newsletter:

deonashleigh.com/news

23cd7040-5cc9-4b71-973f-9a737deb45b7R02